NECROMANTIA

Visit us at www.boldstrokesbooks.com

By the Author

Crimson Vengeance

Burgundy Betrayal

Scarlet Revenge

Vermilion Justice

Twisted Echoes

Twisted Whispers

Necromantia

NECROMANTIA

by

Sheri Lewis Wohl

2016

NECROMANTIA

ISBN 13: 978-1-62639-611-1

THIS TRADE PAPERBACK ORIGINAL IS PUBLISHED BY
BOLD STROKES BOOKS, INC.
P.O. BOX 249
VALLEY FALLS, NY 12185

FIRST EDITION: APRIL 2016

CREDITS
EDITOR: SHELLEY THRASHER
PRODUCTION DESIGN: SUSAN RAMUNDO
COVER DESIGN BY MELODY POND
PHOTO BY SHERI LEWIS WOHL

Acknowledgments

A huge thank you goes out to Shelley Thrasher for being a fantastic editor, a wonderful writer, and a great friend. You have touched my life in more ways than you'll ever know.

Thanks also to the real Duane "Will" Willschem for all your years of keeping watch over us and making sure we were safe. For years, you asked me time and time again when I was going to put you in a book. So here you go, Will. This book is for you. Thanks for letting me have fun with your character.

Dedication

This book is dedicated to:

The women, men, and K9s
Across the country
Who dedicate untold hours of their
Time to train for deployment
As search-and-rescue volunteers.

In the middle of the journey
of our life
I came to myself within
A dark wood
Where the straight way was lost

—Dante Alighieri

PROLOGUE

No question about it. He was glad to be home. All the years away gave him a new perspective on the place where he was born. When he left, all he could think about was getting as far away as possible and leaving painful memories and those who had hurt him behind. Most important of all, he wanted to find somewhere more exciting to live his life with no history and no one watching his every move. Freedom was a drug he couldn't get enough of.

For a while the cities were glorious. New York, Chicago, Atlanta, and most fun of all, New Orleans. For a brief period, the resentment and rage that had sent him on his quest receded. Only for a while, though, and then it would ease back in like a cat slinking into the house after a night of roaming. Restlessness and discontent shadowed him no matter where he went.

But it finally hit him. Home beckoned, and only at home would he discover the inner peace he sought. Dorothy was right when she said there was no place like home.

So here he was, and peace was already beginning to settle in. The tricks he'd picked up in his years on the road helped him now. The time away had made him wiser and better equipped to deal with those around him who criticized his every move. Best, he was able to begin the work needed to create his masterpiece. All that came before was much like going away to school. With every step and every move, he'd learned and tucked each bit of knowledge away. Now he was a graduate and ready to put his education to good use.

The house was another piece of the puzzle proving his path was the correct one. When he walked inside, it seemed as if someone had designed it with him in mind. Just off the Little Spokane River and Highway 395, it sat on a piece of land that provided ample privacy. Inside, it was nice and, more important, functional and roomy. The basement proved to be the crowning piece. Unfinished, with concrete walls and floor, one end was lined with nicely built storage shelves, and on the other, a utility sink hunkered next to a washer and dryer. Nothing else cluttered the room. He couldn't have designed it better himself.

Tonight, he flipped on the light to illuminate the space and walked down the stairs. He'd already lined up his first set of jars on the shelves, and the only thing he needed to do to make all of them complete was to properly label them, which he would do just as soon as he finished tidying up. Grabbing the remote control he kept on one shelf, he pointed it toward the ceiling. There on the very top shelf lurked a state-of-the-art stereo he'd purchased at a local big-box store and installed himself, mounting speakers in each corner of the room. When the music began to play, he smiled. It was Mozart tonight. Classical and a very good choice, if he did say so.

He uncoiled the garden hose that was hooked on one end to the utility-sink faucet, and on the other end he attached a spray nozzle. With the tap turned all the way to hot, he began to spray down the walls and the concrete floor. Bloody red water flowed to the drain set in the middle of the floor. He hummed along with the music as he washed away the evidence of his evening's work, stopping only when the water finally ran clear.

Chapter One

Being able to see dead people sucked. Circe Latham didn't care how cool it looked in the movies; in real life it was just plain a pain in the ass. At least until she stumbled on a way to make it less disruptive in her life. These days it was a lot more manageable and often fascinating. And the sanity that came along with it was life altering in a way she could never explain.

Today was one of those days when she felt useful and not the freak she really was. There was a good chance someone dead would come to her and she was the only one who'd know. Sort of. Zelda would catch it too, although unlike Circe, Zelda wouldn't see them; she'd smell them. After all, that's what human-remains detection dogs did, and Zelda was an amazing one. Not that she was prejudiced, but her dog rocked.

After nearly two years of training a minimum of three to four days a week, they'd passed their certification tests and were field ready. Since certifying they'd been called out at least a dozen times, including being loaned out to several different counties. If someone was nearby, they would find them. Or rather if a body happened to be in the area, they'd locate it.

"You ready, girl?" Circe asked when she came downstairs outfitted in hiking pants, a nondescript moisture-wicking shirt, and her favorite hiking boots. Unlike a search for a missing person when she would put on a team shirt and jacket clearly identifying her as a search-and-rescue volunteer, people doing recovery searches many times tended to work under the radar. Neither she nor Zelda wore anything identifiable. For a lot of reasons, it was better that way.

Zelda was already wound up and she hadn't said a word to her yet. Every time Circe pulled on a pair of hiking pants, Zelda knew exactly what was going to happen next and started pacing in anticipation at the garage door. Living with a working dog was an adventure hard to explain to people who'd never spent any time with one. She couldn't slide anything by her because she was as smart as they came and always up for a search anywhere, anytime, including right now. Nothing made Zelda happier than to be out in the field working.

From the counter Circe grabbed two full-sized water bottles, one for her and one for Zelda. Searches were no different from any endurance event, and the motto "hydrate, hydrate, hydrate" was an unwritten law for both the handler and the dog.

Zelda's intense black eyes watched her as she slipped the full bottles into her waist pack. She smiled and nodded toward the door. "Let's go then." As Circe held the door to the garage open, Zelda raced through.

Inside the back of her SUV, Circe slipped a harness on Zelda and then hooked it to the safety belt that would keep her secure in case of an accident. Some handlers let their dogs ride loose in the back of their vehicle, and some always kept them in crates. Circe went for the middle ground and chose the seatbelt harness. That way Zelda could see out the windows and stay safe at the same time. Of course, it was also easier to talk to her during their trips, and she loved talking to Zelda. She could say anything and felt less alone. Not to mention Zelda always kept her secrets.

It took about thirty minutes to drive from their house at Long Lake to the parking area near the Sandifur Bridge just west of downtown, known for years as People's Park. Part of the city's urban-renewal effort, the bridge was a relatively new addition to an area that for decades hosted unofficial nude sunbathing. These days visitors were more likely to see runners, hikers, and dog walkers here. Nature-loving nudists were forced to move along, although on a sunny day it wasn't unheard of to run into someone sunbathing sans clothing. Circe knew that one firsthand.

When today's call came in, Circe couldn't help but wonder why this particular spot. Given the high usage in the area, it seemed an odd place to be called in to search. Then again, a good portion of land west of the bridge had been left in a natural state and remained largely unused. If she was to make an educated guess, they would most likely center the search in that rough, overgrown acreage.

When she pulled into the gravel parking area, a familiar sedan already sat there and she parked next to it. "Hey, Brian," she said to the tall, good-looking sheriff's deputy.

"Thanks for coming, Circe." Brian Klym stood bent over a laptop that perched on the hood of his unmarked cruiser. "I'll have the area for you in a sec."

She nodded and reached back through the open door of her car to retrieve the GPS unit currently in one of the pockets of her harness. After she freed it from the Velcro strip securing it in the harness, she handed it off to Brian so he could download the search area into it. While she waited, she put a bright-orange collar on Zelda, a tracking device that her GPS would pick up attached to it. When they were done with the search, Brian would be able to download the data from her unit, and it would show him exactly what ground both Circe and Zelda had covered. She did so love modern technology.

Next she slipped on the chest harness that would hold her GPS once Brian was done with it, as well as a handheld radio and a compass, along with other useful items like a small notebook and pen. The chest harness made it easy to grab any of the items while out in the field without having to stop and dig through a backpack. She also took out her waist pack with two water bottles, flagging tape, latex gloves, and the most important item, Zelda's fleece-covered tug toy. Zelda worked for the toy and would do anything for the chance to play tug with Circe.

"Okay," Brian said as he walked her way. "It's not a huge area and you won't need the GPS to grid it, but we'll want to track and mark anyway."

After she became a K9 handler she learned pretty quickly that the GPS unit was a critical part of the search, even if the area was small and easily covered without walking it in tight grids. The data contained in the unit gave her all the information she needed to know what ground they'd covered and if they left any holes.

"Our area," Brian said as she tucked the GPS back into its pocket on her harness, "is the area south of the river, west of the bridge, and bordered by the roads on the north and east. Make sense?"

Circe was surveying the search area as he talked. Given the parameters he described, she was able to visualize the search. She nodded as she clipped a leash to Zelda's collar. "Got it."

"Where do you want to start?"

Brian had done enough of these searches with her to understand how she and Zelda worked. Before they even started, she needed to determine the best pattern, based on prevailing conditions. By understanding wind direction and terrain features, she could set Zelda up for the best chance of success. Of course, she would find the dead regardless of either of those elements, but she still wanted to let her dog do her job as best she could.

No one, not even the other members of her K9 team, knew of her special skill. Everyone thought Zelda did all the work, and she wanted to keep it that way. People didn't need to know the dead came to her. Some secrets were better kept as just that: secrets. Besides, Zelda was a solid HRD dog, and regardless of what Circe saw, she did the work and deserved the praise.

She turned full circle, feeling the breeze on her face, and when she determined the direction of the wind, she stopped and looked at Brian. "We'll start from there." She pointed to the southwest corner of their designated area. "We'll walk north along the west border and then do fifty-meter diagonal grids east and west."

It was a relatively small space and probably didn't need to be walked in a grid pattern. But keeping to the same routine was good for both her and Zelda.

Brian nodded. "Got it."

In large search areas she'd have a navigator along who would keep her grid lines straight and uniform, which made sure they covered all their allotted space. Her job as a handler was to keep an eye on the dog. Today was different. The area was small enough that covering it wouldn't be an issue so she could act as both K9 handler and navigator. With Brian at her side, they walked to the corner she'd pointed out as their starting point. The breeze kissed her cheeks as she leaned down and unclipped the leash from Zelda's collar. "Are you ready?" she asked Zelda, whose answer came in the form of an excited yip. She nodded and put her on the command to work with a single word that had no meaning.

Zelda took off. Brian didn't ask about the nonsense word or what it meant because he knew. It was the command for Zelda to find human remains. The work of an HRD team was delicate in the best of circumstances, and the nonsense word used for the command served two purposes. First, it had no real meaning so no one would accidently use it and confuse the dog. Second, at times, family members of the missing person would attend a search, and the last thing those family members wanted to hear was a reminder that the dog was searching for the body of their loved one.

At the sound of that single word, Zelda's head went down and her eyes became even more focused. She was in full working mode. Zelda lived for this moment, and it never got old watching her work. Circe only regretted that she hadn't discovered the world of search dogs earlier. Out in the field, side by side with this fabulous dog, not only could she do meaningful work with something she couldn't escape, but she could participate in a heartfelt partnership. She couldn't imagine her life without Zelda.

Less than three minutes in the field, she realized this search would be a short one. Circe saw the victim shortly after they began. She didn't have to alter her pattern because the young woman was standing directly in her path. At the sight of the disheveled woman, who couldn't have been more than twenty-one, her heart ached. No one should lose their life that young. She was wearing high heels, short shorts, and a snug T-shirt that had once been a pale color but was now crimson with blood from a wound in her chest. Her bleached-blond hair hung in dirty strands down to her shoulders. Clearly, she'd seen some rough times in her few decades.

"Help me," she said, her voice whispery on the light breeze.

Circe never talked back, for she'd learned as a child that while she could sometimes hear them, they never heard her. Instead she focused on Zelda, watching for the telltale change in body language. It always happened the same way. She would see them, and shortly thereafter, Zelda would scent them. This case wasn't an exception. Seconds after the woman appeared, Zelda's ears twitched and her tail went down. She had her scent.

Without saying anything, she put a hand out to stop Brian from walking any farther. She wanted to give Zelda a chance to pinpoint her find. Both of them stopped walking and simply stood still as Zelda worked the scent cone. After they stopped it took less than a minute of searching with her nose close to the ground before Zelda gave her alert. She turned her head to Circe, who simply waited, her dark eyes focused and intense, as if saying, "Here."

"Good girl," Circe said with enthusiasm at the same time she pulled the fleece toy out of her waist pack. Zelda kept her eyes on the toy, though Circe still made Zelda wait as she walked closer. Finally, as she stood very close to her, she said, "Okay." At the same time she tossed the fleece toy. Zelda sprang up and raced after the toy with joy and enthusiasm in every step.

Brian marked the spot with red flagging tape, while Circe continued to play with Zelda and her toy. His face was somber as he stared down at the piece of ground. "I was afraid we'd find something," he said. "Everything I'd managed to pull together seemed to point to this place. As much as I was hoping I was wrong, I had a really bad feeling about this one."

The bad feeling had eluded Circe until the dead woman showed herself. After that, she'd had a hard time avoiding the dread that shadowed her like a dark cloud. Too often the dead that came to her were victims of violence. That's why they lingered. They were searching for peace or perhaps a way home. It never failed to make her feel sad even when she realized she could help in some small measure.

She'd like nothing better right now than to load up and go home, except that wasn't the way she did her job. Glancing down at her GPS, she saw a fair amount of area still left open and unchecked. If she went home now, all she'd be able to think about was quitting before the job was done. "We've covered only about a quarter of the designated area," she said. "Shall we do a quick run-through of the rest?"

She'd learned early on in her search training never to walk away, even if she discovered remains quickly. Her teachers and mentors had drilled a mantra into her: always, always finish the entire area. Besides, it went against her own internal code to do only half a job.

"Yeah," Brian said as he tucked the roll of marking tape back into his pocket. "This should be it, but let's see what Zelda has to say."

She liked working with Brian so much because he respected her dog. Anyone who genuinely liked Zelda and appreciated what she could do was pretty darned fine in her book. She nodded and motioned to Zelda, who ran back and dropped the toy at Circe's feet. She picked it up and tucked it into her waist pack once more. Then she looked down at Zelda, who stood gazing at her with intensity. She leaned down and quietly said to her, "There's more."

Those two words sent Zelda off running again, with a renewed expression of deep concentration. She'd had her time to play with her toy, and now it was time to work again. She loved her job and would search for hours if Circe asked her to. In fact, Circe would wear out long before Zelda would.

Circe glanced down at her GPS to make sure she was maintaining the pattern she'd decided upon earlier. So far, so good. It wasn't a large area, and so the remaining search should go quickly.

No big deal to finish up. Or that's what she thought until ahead of her another young woman rose from the ground. When the woman was on her feet, she stilled, with her head down and her hands clasped in front of her. She was young, maybe sixteen or seventeen, with short dark hair tinted holly red and styled into spikes that stood up from her scalp. Seconds after Circe saw her, Zelda caught the scent, so Circe didn't have to alter her pattern to bring her into the scent cone. Beneath a tall pine, Zelda dropped her head low to the ground and sniffed back and forth until she was satisfied she'd located the right spot. Then Zelda alerted a second time as she looked up at Circe once more.

"Ah, Brian," she said. "We have another one."

With agonizing slowness, the young woman's head came up and her green eyes held Circe's gaze. Unlike the first woman, she made no attempt to speak to her, at least not verbally. The sadness radiating from her eyes tore at Circe's heart. She was, or had been, young, yet the pain etched on her face spoke of a life filled with very real nightmares. She hated to even consider what horrors had created those shadows.

Once Brian stood beside Zelda, Circe looked away from those sad eyes and again fished the toy from her pack. She tossed it to Zelda, who caught it easily and began to run with joy as she shook her head from side to side.

"Ah, sonofabitch," Brian muttered as he took the roll of marking tape out of his pocket and began to pull a length of it off the roll. "This, I wasn't expecting." His face was grim and his hands shook as he set about marking the spot Zelda had pinpointed for them.

While he worked, she continued to play with Zelda, tugging on the toy and tossing it for her to chase. When Brian was done she told Zelda to bring it in, her command to give the toy back. She didn't have to ask twice. Zelda trotted up next to her and dropped the toy.

The second woman was a sad surprise, particularly considering that the area they were searching wasn't large. It was bad enough that one woman had lost her life. Two was unthinkable. She'd never found remains this close together before. From all appearances, someone didn't want to be bothered with doing a good job covering up their horrid deeds. Then again, she'd been hunting for dead bodies long enough to know that when it came to murder, there were no rules.

"This is fucked up," Brian muttered as he stuffed the roll of flagging tag back into his pocket. "I need to call in the SPD investigators and crime-scene unit. This is going to be big."

Though the area they were dealing with was small, it still technically fell within the jurisdiction of the Spokane Police Department, or the

SPD, as everyone around here referred to them. Brian was working an active case that had originated in the county, though his investigation had brought him to this spot within the city limits. In order to conduct this search, he'd coordinated it with the SPD.

Now, he had to let them know the areas Zelda had alerted them on. They would approach the marked areas as potential crime scenes because only Circe knew for certain that bodies were buried there. Of course, she couldn't tell Brian that the bodies were buried beneath the pine-needle-strewn ground. He wouldn't believe her anyway. Brian, and the rest of the local enforcement community, did, however, trust Zelda's nose firmly enough for her findings to stand up in court.

Circe looked down at her GPS and sighed. Despite the two discoveries, they still hadn't covered a chunk of the land. For a small area, it sure was taking a lot to time to check it all. She was pretty confident they wouldn't find anything else, but she couldn't walk away without doing the job correctly. True, Brian had asked her to come out and search for a body, as in a single body, and as tragic as it was, they had found one. Locating two was a fluke. Despite the two finds, they wouldn't go home until they cleared every inch.

"Come on, Zelda," she said and waved her arm to her left to let her know the direction she wanted her to cover. This was another skill they'd learned as a team, directional signals. Search up, search down, search left, search right, and she communicated all those instructions with the simple wave of the hand. "There's more."

As before, Zelda took off with her nose low and her eyes focused. Circe and Brian followed her. Every so often Circe glanced down to make sure they were traversing the ground they needed to. It pleased her to see the lines on her GPS were relatively straight and that with two more passes, they'd have covered it all.

They were halfway through with the second pass when a sound floated across the wind. Slowly, Circe turned her head. She noticed two things at once: Zelda was giving her alert, and right behind her stood a woman whose soft voice was saying, "Help me."

❖

Paul Garland draped his jacket over the back of his chair and dropped heavily into it. For the hundredth time he wondered whose dumb-ass idea it had been to move in with Brenda. Oh yeah, it was his dumb-ass idea, and in fact, he'd been the one to suggest they do it in the first place. Talk about a total disaster. Six months ago he got her to leave, and he'd love to say it was over except that wasn't how it was going down. No matter what he said, she still wasn't letting go. She might be physically out of his house, but she was most certainly not out of his life.

Today was another one of *those* days. After arming the alarm system, he pulled the back door shut and had put one foot on the step when he stopped momentarily. He silently prayed he was simply hallucinating, except he wasn't that lucky. There she stood with several of his shirts and a plate of his favorite cookies, right next to his car where he'd parked it in the driveway last night. If he hadn't been too lazy to pull it into the garage, he'd have been safe, or not. The lack of a car in the driveway probably wouldn't have stopped her. Instead of waiting for him by his car, she'd have been knocking on the back door. She gave new meaning to the term undeterred.

Head up, he kept going down the steps and hoped she didn't notice that her appearance rattled him. Calm, collected, and as awful as it sounded, cold, was the only way to approach her. Right now, he didn't look at the shirts, and he sure as hell didn't take the cookies, even if, truth be told, she baked a mean cookie. From painful experience he'd learned that any tiny bit of kindness from him and she was packing her things to move back in.

Stalker was the first word that came to mind, but he didn't want to go there. Experienced police detectives did not have stalkers. He was a goddamn professional and should know better than to get involved with someone unbalanced enough to become a terrorizing factor in his life. Except that's exactly what he did, and now he couldn't seem to extricate himself from an untenable position.

At least this morning, his strategy of ignoring her had worked. When he refused to make eye contact or acknowledge her presence in any way, she hadn't tried to stop him when he got in his car and slowly backed out of the driveway. It took effort not to glance into the rearview mirror to see what she was doing. For all he knew, she was still standing there, shirts in one hand and cookies in the other, her hair perfect and her makeup flawless.

Now, he ran his hands through his hair, thinking he needed a haircut, then almost laughed. With the Brenda problem on the front burner, the last thing he really cared about was a stupid haircut. First things first: get Brenda out of his life and then a haircut. Besides, there could be an upside to letting his appearance go. Maybe if he let his hair get long and shaggy he'd look like shit and Brenda would lose interest in him. At this point he was willing to try anything.

"What's up, pretty boy?"

He smiled at the sound of his partner's voice. He sure wished Diana played on his side of the fence because she was the kind of woman a man could count on. Honest, straightforward, and beautiful, she was special and he adored her. He knew he rated high in her book too, but she'd never be interested in him. Wrong sex. Even if he wasn't, it was never a good idea to mix professional and personal. He was resigned to be content with the relationship as it stood. He'd rather have her as a partner and a friend than not have her in his life at all.

"Nothing that can't be fixed," he shot back. Man, he hoped that was true.

"Ya sure?"

Slowly he nodded. "Yeah." He was trying to convince himself as much as he was trying to convince Diana.

So much for trying. She studied him with her deep-brown eyes and obviously didn't believe him. He also knew she wouldn't press the issue further. It was one of the things that made this partnership hum. They always had an unspoken communication, and it worked better than with any other partner he'd ever worked with in the past. She knew when to push and when not to.

"Well, let me know if I can help," she said as she patted him on the shoulder and headed to her desk, which was right next to his.

"Copy that." As much as he appreciated the offer he wasn't about to take her up on it right at the moment. Maybe someday, far down the road, though he doubted he'd ever share this debacle. Even as close as they were, the situation with Brenda was too embarrassing to share. No way did he plan to tell anyone in the department what was going on with the crazy ex-girlfriend. Ultimately, he'd handle it himself without it ever needing to go public. Some things were best kept in the closet with the door bolted.

Diana's cell rang just as she dropped down into her task chair, and he listened to her side of the conversation with interest. It wasn't that he was being nosey. To the contrary, picking up on a few key phrases, he could tell it was a call-out and so he listened openly. When she put the phone back in the holder at her waist, she looked over at him and nodded toward the door.

"Three bodies down in People's Park."

"Seriously?" That place drew all sorts of people, like nudists, dope smokers, nature lovers, runners, and cyclists. Murderers weren't the typical park user. At least not in recent years. When he was a kid it was a dangerous place, but that time was decades past, and now it was as safe as any place in an urban area.

"As a heart attack."

He grabbed his jacket and followed her out the door. If nothing else, this promised to be very interesting. At least for a few hours, he wouldn't have to think about Brenda, and that appealed to him on a grand scale. Nothing like a murder or two to take his mind off his own problems.

So far at least, Brenda had kept her impromptu visits on a personal level like at his house, the gym, or the grocery store. He'd changed gyms and grocery stores, and would move except he refused to let anyone push him out of his own home. In the last six months at least she'd steered clear of his office. His mother had always taught him to be grateful for the little things.

"I'm driving," Diana said when they were outside in the parking lot.

"Oh, come on, Dale Earnhardt. I think it's my turn." To say Diana had a lead foot was being polite. She had to have been a Formula One race-car driver in a former life while he was more like the city bus driver, always looking out for the safety and comfort of his passengers.

"You drive like an old lady." She didn't even glance at him as she opened the driver's side door of the unmarked cruiser and got in. He'd be offended if her remark hadn't contained a grain of truth. "And you should have your license suspended." Another grain of truth.

She was sliding on her black, wrap-around sunglasses. "Blah, blah, blah. Just get in, buckle up, and shut up."

He shook his head. In his time with Diana, he'd also learned that it wouldn't do him a bit of good to argue. The woman possessed an impressive stubborn streak. If she wanted to drive, by God, she was going to drive, and he really couldn't do much to change the situation. The fact that he was taller, heavier, and carried a bigger gun didn't faze her. He got in, buckled up, and shut up.

CHAPTER TWO

Two words rolled through Diana's mind on the short drive from the Public Safety Building to the parking lot at People's Park: serial killer. Her dad had been part of the team that ultimately took down serial killer Robert Yates. Unfortunately, not before Yates killed thirteen women and terrorized an entire city. Even after they put him in prison for the rest of his life, her dad was convinced there were more victims. While still on the job he pushed hard for the city and county to keep searching. It didn't do any good. They couldn't afford to spend more tax dollars on a killer who'd never be free again. Retired now, her dad was still working the case, though so far he hadn't been able to prove his theory. Dad was a good detective, and ultimately if more bodies turned up, he'd solve the case. She believed he was right, and not just because he was her father.

By the time they arrived in Peaceful Valley, marked cars blocked both Riverside Avenue and Clarke Road, barring entrance to the People's Park parking area. A cruiser backed up enough to let her pass through the barricade, and she parked next to a dark-blue SUV with a National Search Dog Society sticker on the back window—the K9 handler's rig.

At the south end of the Sandifur Bridge, Brian Klym from the County Sheriff's Department was standing beside a woman holding a loose leash with a bored-looking German shepherd at the end of it. The HRD dog that discovered three bodies in the park brought back all the memories of the days when her dad worked 24/7 on the

Yates case. He was a big proponent of utilizing whatever resources were available, and that included dogs. His respect for what dogs could do was well-known, and he would approve of what this dog was able to highlight today. Dad had also taught her there was no such thing as a coincidence, and three bodies buried in one area less than five acres total was no coincidence. Something very bad had happened here.

"Come on," she said to Paul. "Let's see what Brian has for us."

"Hey, Erni, Garland, 'bout time you two got here." Brian held out a hand.

Diana took his extended hand and shook it. "Got here as quick as we could."

"Hey," Paul said as he also shook Brian's hand.

Brian and Paul had gone through the academy together, and Paul always said he was a good guy who would probably end up being sheriff someday. It was nice to know he was someone they could work with, since this would more than likely end up being a joint investigation. Most of the time the two departments worked fine together, but occasionally tension and power plays made it difficult. She didn't think this would turn out to be one of those times.

Brian inclined his head toward the woman with the dog. "This is Circe Latham and her K9, Zelda. Circe, these two are detectives Erni and Garland from the SPD."

Paul stepped forward and offered his hand to Circe. "Call me Paul."

Diana also shook Circe's hand, whose grip was firm and confident. She liked that. "Nice to meet you Ms. Latham. I'm Diana Erni."

While this wasn't the first time she'd heard of the extraordinary team of Circe Latham and Zelda, it was the first time she'd actually met them. Word in the department was that this dog was hands down the best HRD K9 in Eastern Washington and that they were the go-to team whenever there was a search for remains. Hard to see it right now, considering Zelda was currently sprawled out on the ground looking singularly uninterested in the humans around her.

"Please just call me Circe." The woman's voice was quiet and pleasant. In fact she was pretty and gentle looking, and not at all what Diana expected to see in a K9 handler who dealt exclusively in recovery searches.

Diana nodded. "Circe it is. So, tell me what you found?"

Something in Circe's body language must have alerted Zelda because she popped up from her sprawl and sat next to her, leaning into her leg. Circe's hand dropped to her dog's head and she absently began to stroke it. "Pretty much a routine search, with Zelda alerting on the first body fairly quickly. At that point I figured we'd found all we were going to, but since we'd only covered a small portion of the area, we continued to be thorough. That's when Zelda alerted two more times. A fair bit of a surprise."

Many thoughts were racing through Diana's mind as she listened to Circe. "Could she have alerted on parts from the first body?"

It was a morbid but necessary question. True, this area was on the fringe of the downtown core and rather urban. At the same time, around these parts wildlife was always hanging near the river. The city didn't seem to intimidate deer, skunks, or raccoons. Last year just a mile down the road in Riverside State Park a cougar was scaring the crap out of runners, hikers, and cyclists. Sometimes cougars or coyotes scavenged human remains, so her question had a great deal of merit.

Circe was shaking her head. "I can see where you're going with this and why. As much as I hate to say it, we've seen it happen before, and any other time I might say it's a probable theory. Not this time. I've watched Zelda enough to know the difference between a small source and a full body. This was most definitely full body. Three full bodies," she added quietly.

Diana stuck her hands in her pockets and studied Circe's face for a long minute as she bit on her upper lip. Bottom line: she believed her. Not just because of everything she'd heard about this exceptional K9 team but because her gut told her to. She put a lot of store in gut instinct. It had saved her ass more than once.

"Okay then, three bodies it is." She cut her gaze over to Paul. "Well, let's take a look at what they found."

He nodded, and she could tell he was already working through the investigation they were about to embark on. One thing about Paul, he was always thinking. He was a good guy in so many ways, she wondered for probably the hundredth time why he was still single. Though she knew he dated, he was pretty tight-lipped about his personal life, especially lately. She sensed something was up with him on the home front. Given enough time he'd let her in. For now, he needed space, which was fine. They had a lot of work in front of them and not much time for personal issues.

Zelda, as it turned out, wasn't going with them to look at the body locations. Circe walked with her back to the SUV with the stickers and motioned for her to jump in. After a quick "stay," Circe shut the back and then turned to them. "This way," she said and began to walk briskly.

"You're not bringing her?" Diana asked. She couldn't help it, she was curious.

Circe shook her head. "No. She's done her work and was rewarded. She's entitled to her rest now. I don't want to work her through a scenario she's already covered."

"Would she alert again if she came with us?"

Circe nodded. "Yes."

"Interesting," Diana said softly.

"Very."

Diana didn't miss a step as she followed Circe from the parking lot to an area defined by yellow police tape stretched between five spindly pine trees. Techs were already on task, carefully moving dirt from the first spot where Zelda alerted earlier. By the time the four of them arrived, the meticulous work of the techs had uncovered the unmistakable form of a human being. Judging by the slim build and feminine clothing, it was a woman.

At the sight, Diana's heart grew heavy. It didn't matter how many times she saw something like this; she always experienced the same wash of emotion. She hated the feeling of being too late. No one deserved to be treated like this, and what made this one even sadder was the fact that two more bodies were buried in shallow graves nearby. It was wrong on so many levels.

After studying the makeshift grave, Diana turned full circle and swept her gaze over everything, taking in the trees, the grass, the pine needles, and the streets. For at least a moment, she tried to be inside the head of a killer, to see what he saw, to understand why he decided to bring his victims here. Why this spot? It was beautiful in this place, natural and wild. Close to the high-use areas but far enough away to provide a bit of privacy. Only a little, though, and that was the element she found most disconcerting. If he wanted to be away from prying eyes, this was definitely not the place to be. The observation led her to only one conclusion: someone liked a bit of danger.

Circe touched her shoulder and inclined her head toward the west. Time to go survey the others, Diana gathered from her look, and so she nodded. It was important to study those locations as well to see what the killer saw and try to understand why the killer would come here to conceal his heinous deeds.

Dry grass crunched beneath their feet as they walked away from the first marked area, and the low murmur of voices floated on the air. Every crime scene was marked by solemnity and sorrow. This one was even more so. It was as if all of them felt the travesty of the three deaths personally. She sure knew she did and vowed to find the sonofabitch who did this.

The two makeshift graves of the other victims were mirror copies of the first. If she had any doubts the same person committed these murders, they evaporated. At each site, she went through the same motions, studying the grave itself and the surrounding area. Again she had the same sense that whoever did this liked to flirt with danger. Yes, each grave had a bit of privacy, but the risk of exposure was always present. The cover that the sprinkling of bushes and pine trees provided wasn't that deep. If a single cyclist had cruised through, everything would have been out in the open. That made her nervous, because it meant the bastard had balls of stainless and would be hard to catch.

"I hate this," she said under her breath. It was her job to investigate murders, and she'd gone into this profession willingly knowing what she'd be faced with. Despite her father's best efforts to shield his family from the work he did, Diana had always known and admired how he tried to make the world a better place by catching killers and putting them away. She wanted to follow in his footsteps.

Day in and day out she faced the dark side of the human condition, yet this shook her up. It took darkness to a level that frightened even someone conditioned to it. From firsthand experience, she knew what staring into the face of the devil could do to someone. Her father's eyes were still haunted even after he'd put a serial killer away for life. She worried that someday that same look would stare out from behind her own eyes.

Paul put a hand on her shoulder and squeezed. "Yeah, it's screwed up, that's for sure, but we'll find out who did this and why. We got this, D."

She shook her head as she let out a long sigh. "We haven't had a serial killer working here since Yates." Her hand in her pocket, she fingered the small stainless whistle on the end of her keychain. When Yates was leaving bodies around the county, her father had given her the little whistle just in case. She'd had in her pocket ever since.

"He was one messed up motherfu—"

She gave him a look. She certainly shared his assessment of the captured serial killer. Even so, probably best not to voice that sentiment in mixed company. It was the kind of thing they could say to each other inside the confines of their car but not out here.

"Yes, he was," she said and patted his hand where it still rested on her shoulder. She let her gaze travel down to the techs who worked with infinite care and respect to extricate what was now clearly the body of another woman from her earthen casket. "With Yates locked up for life, I really hoped never to use the words serial killer again."

❖

Rage broiled inside his chest volcano hot. It surprised him that those crowded outside the yellow length of police tape didn't pick up on his rage. Then again, when it came right down to it most people were clueless.

That's what made it all so easy. Stupidity was a sickening epidemic that made him weary. How people could be so dense baffled him. The world shouldn't be like this. So much potential for greatness existed if someone could clear the path of the clutter and the junk. Or perhaps more accurately, the fools and idiots. Good thing he was the man for the job.

The work was easy if one had the skills. It was a bit like manning a snowplow: put the blade down and plow forward. He had done the job and buried the trash in this meadow, leaving the ground above clean and renewed. Or it would have been if not for that woman and her dog. They were destroying all his good work. Besides, it wasn't like he hadn't rewarded these women for their contribution. On the contrary, he'd buried them with care and a prayer of thanks for their sacrifice. In life these three did nothing of value. They polluted their bodies and the world around them. In death, they joined with him to create something magnificent. How could that possibly be wrong? It was a win-win all the way around, at least until these assholes dug them up.

One by one, black body bags were removed and put into the back of the van from the medical examiner's office. He could barely resist the urge to scream "NO." Labor such as this deserved to be honored for what it was: righteous. To remove the evidence of the work he'd done to better this world wasn't just wrong; it was almost criminal. Why couldn't they leave well enough alone?

He couldn't do a thing. Once the police stepped in like this, the control rested with them. No argument to the contrary could change a thing. The mindset of law enforcement barred them from seeing the big picture or the good work of those who did it. They were only interested in the letter of the law. They failed to understand the existence of higher laws.

In some respect, the fault was probably partially his. His time away made him sloppy. When he left so long ago, the good folk of the city rarely traversed this area. Vagrants and druggies had gathered here, to be certain. The kind of people who would call cops wouldn't have been caught here in broad daylight. Clearly that had changed, so shame on him for not checking first. The assumptions he made when he chose this place were based on outdated information and ultimately turned out to be wrong. He would be more careful from here on out.

His work had to continue, and so he had to eliminate discoveries like this. He knew only one way to make sure that happened. A plan began to reveal itself, and as it did, the feelings of rage began to fade. As usual, he found a solution to the problem. There was always a solution if one was smart enough to think of it and brave enough to carry it through.

❖

By the time they made it home, Circe was exhausted. It was always this way when they found a body. It was as if the spirits of the departed drew strength from her in order to make their appearance. The fact that three of them came to her today was overwhelming. She felt like she'd been through a prize fight and lost.

Zelda was obviously tired too. Though she couldn't see the departed like Circe could, her skill at detecting the odor of the deceased took a toll on her just as it did on Circe. She firmly believed her dog felt each find as deeply as she did. Zelda hit her water bowl for a long, loud drink and then crawled up on the end of the sofa and promptly went to sleep.

Some people took exception to animals on the furniture, but not Circe. They both lived in this house, and they both had a right to enjoy the comfort of cushioned furniture. Her one concession to sharing her home with a large dog was to choose leather for the sofa and the chairs. It was an expensive route to take, but the cleanup was a hundred times easier than if she'd opted for cloth. Because she got black leather, it rarely looked like a dog had just slept there for hours. Worked for her and, judging by the dog now snoring softly on the sofa, worked for Zelda too.

In the kitchen she pulled a bottle of wine from the fridge and poured herself a glass. She just wanted to sit down, put her feet up, and enjoy the lovely dry Riesling she'd picked up from a local winery owned by an old high-school buddy. It seemed to flow through her veins and quiet the buzzing that had started when the first woman appeared to her. There were other ways to relax like yoga or mediation, and she employed those methods on occasion. Wine, on the other hand, was a quicker and more satisfying route that called loudly to her at this moment.

With the remote she picked up from the end table, she clicked on music and smiled as the strains of a blues song by Susan Tedeschi filled the room. This was what she needed to decompress after a search like the one today. Good wine, great music, and a comfortable chair. Circe closed her eyes and let her body relax.

It wasn't easy. Intellectually she understood that what she could do was important. But finding a way to work without people realizing that she, not Zelda, was the one locating the dead was a daunting challenge. Once she had discovered a way to use her special talent, it kept her sane yet at the same time wore on her because it took her to the dark side of humanity too often. To come face-to-face with that horror hurt all the way to her soul.

Today was one of those days that seemed to hurt just a little more. Every time a murder victim was discovered she wanted to break down and sob. How could a person do something like that? Why would they do something like that? Life, all life, was precious, and to steal it from someone and then toss them aside like garbage was nothing short of pure evil. Whoever did this, who took not one life but three, surely sat at the right hand of Satan.

How much she wanted to see only the bright side of humanity: the people who helped the less fortunate, mentored children, and rescued animals. She wanted to watch parades and smile, sing in choirs and dance with wild abandon. That was the world she wanted to live in and couldn't. It had been denied to her from the day of her birth.

For whatever reason, she hadn't been given the option to live in the world of her dreams. Most of the time she reconciled herself to the fate she'd been handed. She took what she couldn't escape and used it to try to do some good. Usually it was enough. Today it made her sad. Something about those three women pulled at her heart. She hoped the police would track down the monster that did this and make sure it never happened to another. Sometimes, though, the monsters slipped through the cracks, and she hoped this didn't turn out to be one of those times.

The wine was doing its job and the muscles in her shoulders relaxed. A movie might be what she needed to take relaxation to the next level. She clicked through the list of recent releases, settling on a movie featuring a favorite comedic actor who, no matter how many times she watched him, always made her laugh. She was seconds into the film when her doorbell rang.

CHAPTER THREE

Diana sat at her desk with her head in her hands. Paul was long gone, as was most everyone else in her squad. Identifying the dead from the three shallow graves hadn't taken long. Whoever killed them must not have been too concerned with identification, because beyond the fatal injuries, their bodies were unmolested. Taking their fingerprints was quick and effective. From there, it was just a matter of routine. All three were in the system, so tracking down their names and next of kin had turned out to be relatively easy.

Notifying the families wasn't quite as easy. It didn't matter if a victim came from the wealthy upper South Hill or the poverty-laced West Central area, loved ones lost at the hands of another brought pain and sadness to those left behind in equal measure. In her line of work, it was clear that tragedy came to everyone regardless of their station in life. In situations like this, it was even worse. No one deserved to be murdered and then buried in the hopes of never being found.

Together she and Paul had delivered the news as gently as possible under the circumstances. The mother of Anna Sorto, the first victim, was so high Diana wasn't certain she even grasped what they told her. Her bottle-blond hair with black roots didn't look like it had come close to shampoo in weeks, and a couple of missing teeth hinted at her drug of choice. She wanted to get pissed off at these people who threw their lives away to drugs and street life, except she never quite got there. Always in the back of her mind was the tiny question that kept anger away: why? Until she walked in their shoes she could never really know how or why they ended up at the sharp end of a needle or in a cold, dark grave. Until she did know, she wasn't about to cast the first stone. And so, she gave this mother what comfort she could, hoped it would break through the drug induced fog, and left her card on the cluttered coffee table just in case. Chances were she'd never hear from this woman, but then again, stranger things had happened.

The grandmother of Kathy Kane, the second victim, was the only family she had, and the news seemed to crush the life out of the woman, who had to have been at least eighty. The house was tiny, the furniture old and worn, yet it was clean and smelled of cinnamon as if she'd just baked an apple pie. The walls were adorned with photographs of a woman who must have been Kathy's mother and at least six more of Kathy at various ages. The face in the pictures was cute and alive with fun and laughter. What had happened to the little girl who smiled out at them from the frames of those pictures? Worried about leaving the grieving woman, Diana called social services to make sure someone could come be with her.

The third victim's family members were quite a surprise. They were far from the low-income housing of Anna's family or the small Shadle area home of Kathy's grandmother. The final house they pulled in front of was at least twice the size of Diana's own and solid ruby-red brick. The long driveway was also made of brick laid out in an intricate pattern and lined on either side with elegantly trimmed shrubs. It screamed old money.

Lana Falco's mother, petite and beautiful, had silver hair and expensive clothes. Though it certainly couldn't be an everyday occurrence in this neighborhood to open the front door and find a couple of cops standing outside, little surprise showed on Mrs. Falco's face. In fact, it was far from surprise. If Diana had been pressed to put a name to the expression, she'd have picked resignation.

Diana held up her badge and asked, "Mrs. Falco?"

Silence met her question as sad gray eyes studied their faces. Then she let out a long breath. "She's dead, isn't she?"

Keeping her shock behind a neutral expression, Diana nodded slightly. "We're very sorry," she said.

Stepping back, Mrs. Falco opened the door wider. "Please come in. I'll get my husband." She left them in the doorway to the living room, her shoulders slightly bowed as she disappeared down a hallway.

Diana leaned close to Paul and whispered, "Not what I was expecting."

"Copy that," Paul said under his breath. "Get the feeling she was expecting us?"

Diana nodded. The same thought had occurred to her. "I think she's just been waiting. If it wasn't today, it would have been tomorrow or the next day." She grew quiet as the sound of footsteps approached.

A tall man with thinning gray hair and rimless glasses preceded his wife into the room. He held out a hand. "I'm James Falco. Please, have a seat."

Diana and Paul both sat, and she delivered the awful news as gently as she could. These parents might have known that one day this visit would come, but it didn't make the reality any easier to take. Heartsick pain showed in both sets of eyes.

Though Lana's background was vastly different from that of the other two, her story wasn't. As so often was the case, drugs and poor choices had taken Lana down a path leading far from the big brick house and the parents who tried every avenue to help her. Counselors, rehab, special schools, tough love. In the end, they had to let go because they discovered, as so many did, it was impossible to help a daughter who didn't want to help herself.

After trying everything possible, they had walked away, knowing one of two things would ultimately happen. She would one day get sick and tired of the life and finally make the choice to go clean. Or, she would die.

Diana had learned quickly in her profession that drug abuse is an equal-opportunity employer. That reality was never more evident than after today's notifications. The pain and heartache that the senseless murders of three young women caused showed equally on the faces of their families, and it had nothing to do with their net worth. They all felt loss and grief.

That thought rolled over and over in her mind as she now sat at her desk staring down at the half-finished reports. It had been hard enough doing the notifications today; having to relive those moments as she put it down on paper was torture.

"You need to go home."

Her head snapped up. She hadn't heard anyone come in, yet there stood Greg Warner, wearing his trademark Carhartts and black T-shirt, gun and handcuffs on his belt. "Jesus, Greg, you just about gave me a goddamn heart attack." Sometimes the guys on the late shift were like ghosts, which is probably why they were so good at night.

Greg smiled. "Good thing my first-aid card is current. I would have gotten to rip your shirt open and give you CPR."

Diana laughed and stood. "You're a sick bastard, you know that?"

He put a hand to his chest. "Ah, Diana, you wound me."

"Yeah, well, you just want an excuse to get your hands on me."

Greg had made a run for her early on. After he found out where he stood with her, they'd been friendly ever since. The situation could have turned out ugly, but he was pretty laid-back and didn't take the rejection personally. All in all, a good guy. Too bad there weren't more like him in the world.

This time he laughed. "Guilty. But seriously, what are you doing here this late? Go the hell home. I promise we'll keep the city safe until you return in the morn." He patted the butt of his gun.

She squeezed his shoulder as she walked by. Yeah, she slept a little easier knowing guys like Greg had her back. "The city's all yours."

❖

Circe recognized the SUV in the driveway and it made her smile. She needed to get out another wineglass. When she opened the front door, Zelda's best friend, Lila, zoomed in. Sixteen months old, the German shepherd knew her way around Circe's house as well as she knew her own.

"Hey," she said to Vickie, who followed Lila through the door, although she opted to walk in rather than zoom.

Vickie didn't say a word, just enveloped her in a hug that was warm and tight. She didn't realize until that second how much she needed that hug. Tense muscles suddenly relaxed and her shoulders felt lighter. Her heart felt lighter too.

"What's this for?"

"Oh, please," Vickie said as she let her go. "You know exactly what that was for. Go sit your ass down. I'm getting my own glass of wine and will join you in a sec."

"Well, you are older and wiser so I guess I have to do what you say."

"And you're a little bitch," she said with laughter in her voice. "Now go sit before you collapse."

People became best friends for a reason and stayed best friends for even more reasons. She and Vickie had been tight since the day they met. Sometimes she wondered if they were perhaps friends in another life too. Made sense on so many levels, at least in her mind. Before Vickie returned from the kitchen she grabbed the comfy corner spot on the sofa left vacant when Zelda headed through the dog door and out to the backyard with Lila. It would do Zelda some good to run and play for a little while.

Vickie was back in minutes, carrying a wineglass in one hand and the bottle of wine in the other. She grinned and told Circe, "Figured I'd save time by just bringing the bottle with me." She filled her glass and, after putting the bottle on the low table in front of the sofa, took a seat on the opposite end. She kicked off her shoes and pulled her legs up onto the cushions.

Circe smiled both at the wine and at the way Vickie settled in. "Good plan." It was going to be that kind of night.

"Uhm, good," Vickie said after a sip. "Now, tell me what happened today."

"We got called out."

Vickie tilted the wineglass in her direction. "I know *that*, girlfriend. I saw your bright shining little face on the six o'clock news. I want to know the rest of the story."

Emotion rolled up, washing away the momentary sense of calm brought on by Vickie's impromptu visit, and for a minute she couldn't say a word. Vickie simply waited her out, which was one of the benefits of having a friend who really understood. She trusted only one person in her life enough to share the truth. Even with Vickie it had taken years before she'd finally summoned the courage to tell her. At the time she'd figured Vickie would react like her family had done when she was a child. She was a licensed professional, after all, and while crazy wasn't in her vocabulary—at least not professionally—that's undoubtedly what she was sure to believe Circe to be. When she realized Vickie actually believed her, she'd broken down and sobbed. Every bottled-up emotion from a lifetime of pretending poured out, and still Vickie stayed her friend. There wasn't enough money in the world to buy that kind of loyalty and friendship.

Holding her wineglass between both of her hands, she stared at the wine and started to speak. "When I saw the first woman I thought, great, we're done here, but you know how it is. You go out to do a job, you want to do it right. So Zelda and I kept walking our grid intending to cover the whole area. We should have blasted through it in half an hour, tops. Then a second woman appears and then a third! Three women, Vic. Three murdered women. What kind of sick sonofabitch does something like that?"

Vickie reached over and covered her hand with one of hers. "Oh, kiddo, I'm sorry. That is so messed up. You've got to feel like your ass has been kicked."

She nodded. Oh, she felt like she'd been kicked all right, and not just in the ass. Her head and her whole body as well. "I've never experienced anything like this, and I hope to God I never do again. It was so wrong."

When she was a child, the dead usually came to her one at a time. Before she was old enough to grasp what it all meant, she'd thought of them as friends. Odd friends with not a lot to say, and sometimes hurt and bloody, but friends nonetheless. She knew even back then they didn't mean her any harm. It was the only world she knew, and so she was comfortable there even if no one else understood.

But she truly had never experienced anything like today. It went beyond the multiple victims who'd come to her. Today it all felt different and not in a good way, and not because the women were murder victims. They certainly weren't her first. As a K9 handler she was in on a number of finds where the victims lost their lives through foul play. It was all part of what she and Zelda had signed up for. They trained for it and they were prepared.

What made today different was the whispered plea, "Help me." Those who came to her seemed to know their fate, and what she typically heard, if she heard anything at all, was, "Thank you." They wanted to be found and seemed to know that because of her they were going home at last. They would no longer be cold, lost, and alone. So why today did two of these women ask her for help?

Vickie leaned forward, picked up the bottle of wine, and topped off her nearly empty glass. Her eyes studied the dark liquid as though it was something new. Then her gaze shifted and her eyes met Circe's. "You know, I'd really like to be all cheerful and comforting and tell you this is the last time you'll feel like this, but I'm not going to lie just to make you feel better. I'm not *that* friend."

Circe smiled despite the less-than-comforting words. In an odd way they actually were a form of comfort rooted in Vickie's never-wavering dependability. She wasn't the kind of friend who told her whatever she thought would make it all okay. No, she always told her the truth even if it was painful and ugly. Her honesty was one reason they stayed close. She loved Vickie's attitude about life, along with her way of seeing things for what they were and then dealing with them. Despite all the ugliness she encountered in her own day-to-day work, she found a way to keep the light in her world. It was a gift she freely shared with her friends, and Circe, for one, was grateful she was one of those friends.

"Given what you're doing and given what you can do, this won't be the last time something like this will happen. You just have to find a way to deal with it and work through it. You have the guts, girlfriend. You just have to use them."

Good advice. Not so easy to follow. Today made her uneasy on so many levels. Usually bringing someone home left her feeling complete and like she and Zelda had done a good job. But right now it felt as though a loose end was hanging out there, and a sense of urgency was pressing her to pick it up. Whatever it was, she needed to discover it and tie it up before she would find peace.

As if that wasn't enough to leave her with a sense of uneasiness, a niggling feeling at the back of her mind said this wasn't a simple case of murder, or serial murder, given the multiple victims. Calling serial murder simple was a bit of an oxymoron. Something far darker and more sinister lay at the heart of the murder of those three women, and she wouldn't be able to rest until she knew what it was. They asked her for help and she intended to give it to them.

Circe held up her wineglass and stared at it for a long moment, almost seeing the young women and hearing their pleas for help. The mild scent of the wine tickled her senses as she tipped the glass back and forth. It wasn't a crystal ball and the answers were definitely not there, no matter how much she wished they were. She brought the glass to her lips, closed her eyes, and savored the wine's sweet taste. Opening her eyes once again, she picked up the bottle.

Vickie had the right idea when she'd brought the bottle out here. It was going to be the kind of night that called for the whole thing. Trying to push through to an answer wouldn't work. Instead, she poured a healthy amount of wine into her glass and smiled. Sometimes finding the answer meant letting go. She tapped her glass against Vickie's. "Bottoms up."

Chapter Four

The book was open on the workbench and he studied the words carefully. Latin was such a bitch. Hated it in school and hated it now. It was funny how the world worked. He would never admit it to the priests and nuns who beat it into him as a child, but damned if the detested Latin didn't come in quite useful now. Never would have guessed that back in the day.

Of course back then how was he to know that reading the stuff would change his life? Or that his penchant for purchasing rare books was his ticket to glory? Yet here he was putting all that expensive education to good use. Wouldn't Mother be pleased? Probably not, considering that nothing he ever did seemed to make the old bitch happy. Of course, after trudging through the Latin, one thing became very clear: it took guts to get to the glory, and he definitely had those.

His attic office was as functional as his basement work space, except here golden light flowed in through the big picture window. Darkness was his comfort zone, and he worked exceptionally well when most of the world slept. At the same time, daylight worked very nicely, and it was a good thing he didn't need much sleep.

Most of the time, he came here to work, just as he was doing right now. The light through the windows made the room bright, and it was easy to concentrate. At other times he simply needed to get away to somewhere quiet and unwind. Too often for his tastes, she left messes around the house and he had to clean up after her.

Her lack of respect for their home appalled him and went against everything he was taught. When everything was in its place, he was most comfortable. She thrived in chaos, and he spent an inordinate amount of time cleaning up after her. At those times he craved solitude, and so he came here. He could relax in the warmth of the sun and read his first editions of Edgar Allan Poe and forget she ever existed.

Today he wasn't reading Poe. As much as he loved the Gothic stories and poetry of the man he admired, this book was in a completely different dimension. Simply holding it in his hands was incredible. Some would call it luck, but not him. He saw it more as destiny. The original *De Nigromancia* text, translated and subsequently attributed to Roger Bacon, lay open on the desk in front of him. As he labored through the Latin he began to understand what had compelled Bacon to do the famous translation. It was no mystery to him how Bacon had ended up known as a wise possessor of forbidden knowledge because this beauty told it all.

In his opinion, Bacon had held back in the English translation he presented to the world. This astonishing text illuminated the world with a range of possibilities he'd never before considered. Until now his life had gone along fine. Well, it had gone along fine after he'd been able to strike out on his own anyway. He played his games, did his work, and kept them all pleasantly in the dark. The world he'd carved out for himself was a good one.

Now, everything was about to change. All he'd managed to accomplish before today, all the skills he'd worked on and refined foretold what he was soon to create. He could use this beautiful, magical text as he wished, and within its delicate pages lay the keys to greatness.

Soon what had begun as a hobby would elevate him to a position of unparalleled power. The world would literally be his. He could envision the money, taste the spoils, feel the touch of beautiful people as they crowded close just to be near him. No one would ever be able to control his life again or take away the freedom he cherished above all else. This book, this beautiful book, made him promises he could hardly wait to collect.

Slowly, he closed the cover and placed it back into its silk-lined, climate-controlled box. Nothing was too good for this treasure, and he planned to keep it as safe as humanly possible. He wasn't sure why he went to such measures, considering nothing in ten centuries had managed to destroy even a single page. The book, it seemed, was impervious to damage, and just as the book was immune to destruction, so too was he.

He was smiling as he descended the stairs, though he frowned when he kicked a high heel left carelessly out on the landing below. God, he hated it when she did that. It didn't matter what it was, she dropped it wherever she took it off. Blouse, skirt, designer heels. Regardless of the cost, and she spent plenty on her things, she discarded everything as though it were trash. He would find clothing, shoes, or purses in the kitchen, the entryway, the bathroom, or like now, the middle of the second-floor landing. With the toe of his shoe he sent it flying through an open bedroom door. Maybe if he was lucky the expensive heel would break off when it hit the wall.

At the back door, he plucked his keys off the counter and went into the garage. As he passed the small wall-mounted rectangular box with the glowing orange button, he punched the button to engage the automatic garage-door opener. Earlier he'd put his supplies in the trunk of the sleek automobile, so he didn't need to check now. Everything he required for the next few hours was tucked nice and tidy in the plastic container with the bright-blue lid.

❖

"What's up with you?"

"Huh?" Paul stopped and looked over at Diana. He sort of heard her question, but his mind was elsewhere. Not really good. He needed to be present and to leave his personal problems at home.

"I said," she began slowly, "what's up with you? You've been off since you got in this morning."

He couldn't really refute her observation. The problem was, it had happened again. One step out the door and there she stood: Brenda, with her long blond hair, perfect makeup, and slim body.

Any guy at first glance would find her beautiful and, under normal circumstances, pleased to find such a vision waiting outside the door. Once he did too. Not now. Behind the pretty façade lay something dark and frightening. Given what he did for a living and all the shit he'd seen through the years, if what he glimpsed freaked him out, then she was one scary bitch.

Today the excuse that brought her to his door was mail. Smiling and dressed in a designer suit guaranteed to bring out all her best features, Brenda met Paul at the garage door before he could even get close to his car. Last night he'd been vigilant and parked inside the garage. No getting lazy again. He'd patted himself on the back for being proactive and figured he'd avoid another encounter that way. Of course, he was wrong.

His mail for some strange reason had showed up at her house. Considering he'd rarely been at her house, either before or after the split, the probability his mail would end up there was about a million to one, not that the reality of it stopped her from claiming exactly that. She smiled and fluttered her long lashes, undoubtedly thinking she looked irresistible. She was always certain she was the center of attention. He'd been around a lot of narcissists in his career and should have been able to spot the defect in her. She probably banked on the rush of testosterone to blind men to the truth, and at least in his case, it had worked. At first.

Without even looking at the envelopes she handed him, he'd grabbed them and left Brenda standing at the edge of the driveway with her neon smile still at full power. His behavior was flat-out rude, and all he thought at the time was "so what!" He couldn't get away from his house and to the safety of his office fast enough.

Nothing he said or did seemed to make a damn bit of difference, and he was running out of ideas about what to do next. He'd been sitting here at his desk for an hour fuming and running through a list of what-if scenarios. There had to be a way to make this stop.

"Sorry," he muttered to Diana. "I've got a lot on my mind right now."

"Don't we all? Like three murdered women buried down by the river."

He ran both hands through his hair and again thought about the haircut. "Yeah, but believe it or not, they're the easy part of the equation." Murder he could deal with. Former girlfriends who turned into stalkers was a whole other ballgame.

Diana's eyes narrowed and he knew he was out of time. Even her legendary patience had limits. "Seriously, Paul, what in the hell is going on?" she asked. "Everything points to a serial killer, the kind of case you usually obsess about, yet I can't get you to focus for more than about three minutes. If I didn't know you better I'd suspect drugs or alcohol. You going off the deep end, partner?"

Maybe she was done giving him time to work out his problems, but he wasn't quite ready to fess up. "Diana, I'm sorry." It was as far as he planned to go.

"Brenda."

The name fell like a hot rock and left him speechless. Considering he was never at a loss for words, it was a pretty good feat on her part. Also made him wonder how transparent he was being about the whole Brenda thing. He thought he was keeping it on the down-low. By the look on her face, he wasn't so sure he was keeping anything down or low.

Diana rolled her eyes. "Look, you dumb-ass, we've worked together how long now? You don't think I can figure out when you're neck deep in crap? You're a good guy, Paul, and you don't typically do stupid things, but I gotta tell you, pal, that Brenda was bad news from the first minute."

"Yeah," he mumbled. "Wish somebody would have told me."

She smacked him in the arm. "I did tell you, dummy, and not just once. You chose not to listen. I have to think she possessed some skills that kept you thinking with the wrong head."

No shit. Easy to see it now. At the time, it hadn't occurred to him she had him by the balls, and even if it had, he wouldn't have wanted to hear. In guy-speak, she was a tiger fucking his brains out, and it did wonders for his ego. Most of the time, he was a fairly intelligent guy. But sadly it had taken a while to see past the sex to the reality of his entanglement with a crazy woman.

He opened his mouth to argue and then snapped it shut. The jig was up. Meeting her eyes he said, "I'd argue, except when you're right, you're right."

This time she smacked him on the back of the head with an open hand. "I know I'm right."

Rubbing the back of his head, he muttered, "Humble too."

She smiled and shrugged. "I do what I can."

A crash made him spin and the heavy scent of coffee drifted into the air. A red-faced deputy had dropped a full mug of coffee and was busy trying to clean it up off the floor. Those around clapped and laughed.

Paul turned his attention back to Diana. What the hell, he'd gone this far. Might as well spill it all. "She doesn't want to let it go and she's driving me insane."

"Anything I can do?" All the cockiness in her voice was gone.

Take her out? Arrest her and throw her in jail? Burn down her house? He pushed the thoughts away as quickly as they flashed through his mind. He was a cop, and cops didn't do things like taking out old girlfriends or throwing them in jail on manufactured charges. They were not firebugs. Well, most of them anyway. There was a guy a few years back…no, he wasn't going there. He wasn't that guy and never could be.

What could she do? Nothing. He just shook his head.

"Come on," Diana said. "We need to run out and talk to the K9 handler. We'll discuss this in the car without any of our friends around."

He protested. "Nothing to talk about."

"Let me decide. Come on."

"Yeah," he said and grabbed his jacket. "Let's take a ride."

He might as well talk it out with her because once she was on something, she wouldn't give it up, and frankly, she had a point. Too many ears here.

In the car, Diana driving, of course, he stared out the side window. The trees grew thicker as they made their way out of the city and headed north. Houses thinned, although not as much as he remembered from the last time he was out this way. Urban creep, he thought, and for some reason he felt sad. A city boy through and through, he still appreciated the nature so near the urban center. How many people could journey just a few minutes from downtown and see eagles, deer, moose, and porcupines all in the same drive? It would be a sad day when houses pushed the wildlife from their homes.

Diana's eyes were steady on the road, though he felt she was waiting on him. No sense in trying to avoid the conversation so he picked up where they'd left off in the squad room. "Sooner or later she's going to have to give it up and realize whatever we had is long gone, if it ever really existed at all. I'm beginning to think the whole thing was a figment of my imagination."

"She is a looker. That certainly wasn't your imagination."

He turned to stare at her and then laughed. It felt good and seemed to break something loose inside him. She was the only one he knew who could take whatever he said, turn it around, and make him laugh. "Yeah, she still is. Who knew crazy could package up so pretty."

Diana made a tsking sound. "Ah now, partner, crazy isn't politically correct. She's mentally ill."

"Oh, without a doubt she's one hundred percent mental. It's more than that though. I still think she's pure old-fashioned crazy, PC or not." He'd bet the farm on it.

"Maybe she is or maybe it's more simple that than. You broke her heart, partner. Once she gets over it and moves on, this will all fade away."

Man, he hoped that was true, but deep in his heart, he didn't believe it. Diana might be taking the optimistic route, but he wasn't. At this point, it would take a lot to convince him Brenda was anything except crazy. Plain, old-fashioned, bat-shit crazy, and he was the dummy that let himself get suckered.

He was still thinking about the future and fantasizing about one without Brenda in it when Diana pulled the car into a long, tidy driveway in the area north of Spokane known as Suncrest. The small bedroom community sat on the shores of Long Lake, although this house was up on the bluff away from the expensive waterfront properties. Might not be right on the lake but it was no starter home either. He liked the massive expanse of green grass and tall Ponderosa pines that spread out in front of the two-story home.

They were still getting out of the car when the front door flew open and a woman stepped out. For a moment he wondered if they'd pulled into the wrong driveway. It wasn't Circe Latham. He didn't know who she was, but for the first time today, thoughts of Brenda disappeared.

"Hi," she said as she strode forward with her hand outstretched. "I'm Lisa Roma. Circe said you were coming by. She went out to run Zelda through a little problem and will be back in a few. You must be Detective Erni?"

Diana nodded and took the outstretched hand. "Call me Diana."

After Lisa shook hands with Diana, she extended her hand to him. His big hand dwarfed her little one, but he felt strength in her grip and it was nice. She wasn't anywhere close to being the classic beauty Brenda was, yet he felt an immediate draw to her. He was pretty sure she felt it too because when his fingers closed around hers, he saw a flash in her eyes. It was gone as fast as it appeared. Still, it was there.

"I'm sorry," she said with a smile. "Circe didn't tell me anyone else was coming."

"Paul," he told her. "Detective Paul Garland."

"I can call you Paul?" Her smile lit up her eyes.

He nodded. "Please." She could call him Paul anytime, anywhere. Especially if she was holding onto his hand and gazing into his eyes like right now. Reluctantly, he released her grip.

She inclined her head toward the open front door. "Come on in. Like I said, Circe and Zelda will be back any minute."

She moved with the grace of a seasoned athlete. He liked it. A lot. "Do you live here?"

With a nod, she answered. "Yes. I'm in grad school at GU and rent the downstairs apartment from Circe. I love it out here and she's a fantastic landlord. I got real lucky the day I met her."

Gonzaga University wasn't known throughout the country just for its championship basketball program. It was a highly rated academic university as well. He'd considered GU when he was ready to go to college but ended up at Eastern Washington University instead because the scholarship they offered was too good to pass up. If Lisa had crossed his path back when he was making his college decision, he was certain he'd have waved good-bye to that scholarship and his diploma would now say Gonzaga University.

Circe was always amazed how much better she felt after an evening with a good friend followed by a great workout with Zelda. They'd started with a four-mile run around the neighborhood. Before the run even began she'd planted two jars out in the woods of the state park a couple miles from the house. She'd removed both jars from her freezer marked HAZARDOUS FLUIDS, and one held blood and fluids while the second contained a piece of blood-soaked cloth. Marked and inventoried, each sample, or source as they referred to them, was on file with the sheriff's department. Staying certified required constant training, and so she used the various sources she had in her freezer to keep Zelda's skills sharp. Well, and her skills as well. After all, they still worked as a team, even if she could see the dead.

She'd set them out earlier so the scent would have time to move and pool before she let Zelda run the problem. It was warm this morning and the southwest wind light. Still it was enough to move the scent and give Zelda a good exercise.

Both were ready to go by the time she parked the car off Tormey Road. Though Zelda was trained and field certified, Circe still tried to set her up for the best possible chance of success. She worked her into the wind, running her grids east and west so that Zelda's nose picked up the wind coming from the southwest.

She'd intended at the start to work for an hour, but Zelda didn't share the same timetable. By the time they'd worked for a little less than half an hour, Zelda's ears went up, her back straightened, and her head whipped to the right. No doubt about it, she was on scent.

No more than ten minutes later she had alerted correctly on both sources.

With Zelda waiting in the SUV, Circe had gone back into the field and retrieved the sources. Now they were on their way home. She was feeling pretty great, thanks to both the run and the workout she got following Zelda in the field. Zelda'd calmed down too. The success of her search had satisfied her earlier drive to begin working. Zelda loved the job, and her joy showed on her contented face as they drove home.

Circe regretted that she hadn't discovered working with a search dog earlier. How much better would her world have been if she'd have been side-by-side with a dog even ten years ago? She wasn't going there because it didn't matter. It was enough they were together now, and she was grateful every day for what Zelda brought to her life.

She was smiling as her house came into view. The car in her driveway surprised her a little. She was expecting detective hottie, as she'd called earlier and asked if she could stop by. It had taken her about two seconds to say "come on out," and she'd said it with a smile. But she wasn't expecting Diana would be here so early. She hated to greet her visitor with sweat-soaked hair and a shirt sticking to her back. Then again, she sensed that evidence of a workout wouldn't offend Diana.

Had the other detective come with her? It made sense they'd come together, though when Diana had called her she hadn't mentioned if he wanted to interview her as well. To be fair, she was paying attention to Diana's request to visit, and that's pretty much all she heard when she called. The rest of the details sort of flew right by.

Actually, if she was into guys, Garland—she thought that was his name—wasn't bad-looking. Oh, who was she kidding? He was really good-looking, and even she could appreciate the level of studliness in the guy. It was a sucker's bet Lisa would notice too. When she thought about it, they would make a striking couple. Lisa wasn't that cover-girl pretty most guys went for. What she had was something better. It was an aura of beauty and passion so natural it was irresistible. It was particularly strong because Lisa was so unaware of it. If Garland had come along, she'd be curious to see if the detective was pulled into Lisa's orbit like everyone else was. People were just drawn to her, which was one of the reasons Circe knew she'd be an exceptional psychologist.

As soon as she stepped inside the house and saw the three of them sitting at the table she almost laughed. No need to wait for the answer to her question; it was right in front of her face. Lisa was working her magic on the man, and whether he realized it or not, he didn't stand a chance.

Of course, Lisa was quite adept at avoiding romantic attachments. Somewhere along the line something had happened, and her lovely friend put a new spin on the term "gun-shy." Curious as she was about what caused her to steer clear of romantic involvements, she tried to respect Lisa's privacy and never asked. She had the sense that someday, when the time was right, Lisa would share.

So far, Circe had managed to stay out of her love life, or lack thereof. Until right this second. All of a sudden she had a really good feeling about this guy, and it was high time for her much-too-serious student tenant to let loose. It was time to let go of whatever in her past was holding her back and take a good hard look at what the future had to offer. Good old intuition was guiding her on this one, not a degree in psychology. Lisa might like to default to her education in instances like this, but not Circe. She'd bank on that indefinable feeling any day of the week.

Zelda did what Circe called a "drive-by," meaning she stopped by each person seated at the table for a total of about three or four seconds and then hit the dog door leading to the backyard. It was her normal routine after a workout. In good weather, she would go outside and nap beneath one of the shade trees in the yard. If the weather was cold, rainy, or snowy, she opted for the sofa. Today was a good day, and by now she'd be sprawled out in the shade.

After pouring herself a glass of water from the dispenser in the refrigerator, Diana took her drink and joined the three at the table. "So," she said after taking a sip. "What's up?"

This follow-up visit was a little unusual. Unless, God forbid, she was called into court to testify in a homicide case, her work in the recoveries ended once the body was located. She and Zelda had found the three women, and the rest of it was up to the police and the sheriff's department. When Diana had called and asked to come by, she was a bit vague on why. Circe didn't question her because... well, she thought a little time around the cute detective wasn't a bad thing. That was a little unusual too. Not that she was totally oblivious to attractive women. Not the case at all. It was more that she chose not to pay attention. Easier to keep all her secrets if she kept to herself and avoided involvements.

Still, her willingness to spend some time with Diana aside, she was more curious about the impromptu visit. What exactly could she help with beyond what they already did? She and Zelda helped bring the dead home. End of story. What else was there to report? That anyone would believe anyway?

"This is going to sound odd," Diana said.

Circe smiled. Okay, it was a good way to lead. She could deal with that. Odd was pretty much the definition of her life. "I'm okay with odd."

Diana nodded and gave her a small smile. "Appreciate that. Here's the deal. I have nothing to back this up, but I'm wondering if you and Zelda would do an unofficial search for me?"

"Unofficial?" Now that was odd and not at all what she was expecting. As part of the county's mission-ready search-and-rescue volunteers, she worked only through Brian. Frankly, it had never occurred to her, even with her special talents, to do anything else. Keeping her life ordered and playing by the rules gave her a sense of being normal. Considering how abnormal she felt before she'd discovered K9 search and rescue, she hesitated to consider anything that could possibly upset the life she'd so carefully crafted for herself. Besides, she loved working with Brian and was not inclined to mess up a great relationship even if the person asking was damned hot.

"I don't know..." She hedged. Her mind was screaming at her to say no. Her heart, on the contrary, had different inclinations.

"Look," Diana said and reached across the table to take one of her hands. "I know this is outside your normal chain of command, and I can appreciate your reluctance to buy in. Here's the deal. I think it's incredibly important or I wouldn't ask. I could do this through official channels, but I just don't want to wait that long. Too many calls, too many layers of command."

The plea in Diana's eyes spoke to her soul. Something in them almost felt like Diana was a kindred spirit, as if she too had a secret she held close. It was enough to make her listen and, she suspected, more than enough to make her say yes.

"Tell me."

CHAPTER FIVE

D iana?"
　　She recognized the barely controlled shock in his voice from their years of working together, though she doubted the rest of them would pick up on it. She didn't blame Paul for questioning her, and in front of Circe and Lisa no less. In normal situations they talked through any plan of action, and on the way over she'd sort of left out a couple of the pertinent details about the reason for this visit. Like the fact she planned to ask Circe to take her dog out on an unauthorized search. If she'd said something earlier, he'd have tried to shut her down, and he was really good at making his case. So, she'd opted for avoidance rather than risk falling prey to Paul's logic.

　　This favor boiled down to gut instinct. The bodies of the three women had been a trigger event for her, and the little voices in the back of her head whispered, and not softly, "She's one of them." They weren't really voices, but that's pretty much how she thought of the niggling and persistent thoughts that hadn't given her even a moment's peace since her discovery of the three lost souls.

　　It would be easy to say they'd started yesterday, except the thoughts weren't quite so recent. The missing-person reports of the young women passing through the department always caught her attention. The fact that her childhood friend Joanna was on that list made it worse. Since the first time she'd come across Joanna's name she'd known something was off. She'd felt it then and could still feel it. Until yesterday, putting a name to it eluded her. Now she felt as though a road had opened up and she was compelled to go down it.

Her great-aunt Lily would say she was following in the footsteps of the special women of her family—those blessed with what they referred to as second sight. She wasn't so sure she could buy into the explanation. She preferred to think of it as her cop-trained intuition, of the skills she'd learned from her dad.

Whatever it was, she wanted to explore it further, and given Circe and her dog's amazing record for finding the lost, she was ready to gamble. It wasn't really outside the chain of command. Honestly, she was willing to talk to Brian to get his permission to use one of his search teams if Circe insisted on going that route. At the same time, it seemed important to get Circe's buy-in before she even approached Brian.

"I know." She turned and looked at Paul. "It's irregular."

"Ya think?" His words were cool, his eyes were hot. Getting blindsided did not please Paul.

She turned her gaze away from his angry eyes and back to Circe. "Look, I could talk a good story and make this all sound nice, logical, and like regular police work. I'm not going to do that because it'd be a crock. I don't want to start off on the wrong foot and I don't want to lie to you."

Circe leaned forward, her elbows on the table, her chin resting on her hands. Her eyes were dark and serious as they held Diana's. "Good to know. Now you have me interested. Tell me more."

This was going to be a little touchy. Too big an audience, to be frank, and she was about to share with them something she should have told Paul a long time ago. They were partners, and good ones at that. Beyond partners, they were friends, and it wasn't fair to spring this on him in front of other people. Until now, it had been easy not to say a thing, not to explain. Even as much as she trusted Paul, she just didn't like to talk about this kind of thing. Ever.

Diana knew she was a good cop and that the brass respected her. She wanted to keep it that way. No one ever questioned her work or her clearance rate because she was good at what she did.

There was, however, a little more to it, even if she never put voice to it. Today, she felt compelled to throw it out there. In Circe's eyes she saw something that screamed trust. It drew her in, and if she tried to say she didn't like it, she'd be lying.

Paul was firmly in her circle of trust too, and she didn't fear telling him. He would have her back no matter what and deserved her confidence. But she should have made time to share this with him before they came out here, and the fact she didn't might undermine their relationship to a certain degree. He would be hurt, and she had no one to blame except herself. It was too late though, and she was just going to have to see it through. Damage control would be high on her list after today.

Turning her gaze to Paul, she put a hand on his arm. "I should have shared this with you before, but I didn't want you to think less of me."

His brow creased. "Not gonna happen."

"Hold the sentiment until after you hear my confession." She returned her gaze to Circe. "I don't exactly know how to explain this."

This time Circe put a hand on her arm. "Just say it."

For some strange reason, Diana felt as though Circe already knew what she was going to admit. She blew out a long breath and said, "I sense things."

"Like?" Paul said from beside her.

"Like when bad things are going to happen or when bad things have happened at a certain place."

"You're psychic?" Surprise was threaded through Paul's question. Circe's hand tightened on her arm.

She shook her head. "No, nothing like that. It's more a feeling of dread, like a sick ball in the pit of my stomach. When it hits, I can't shake it until I figure out the what, where, when, and why."

"You felt it out there beside the bodies of the women, didn't you?" Circe asked.

Diana nodded slowly. "The second I stepped out of the car it hit me like a hammer to the mid-section. Because of your discoveries, it only lasted a moment and then I was calm again."

Paul was looking at her like he'd never seen her before. At least it was more an expression of surprise than horror. As much as she trusted him, she'd still worried he would view her as something akin to crazy. He was already dealing with one crazy woman and didn't need to have one as a partner too. "This happen every time we go to a crime scene?"

Slowly, she nodded. "Yeah, afraid so."

"And you never told me." He drew the words out.

"What could I say that wouldn't make me sound like a nutcase?"

He seemed to consider that question for a moment, and then his expression cleared and a hint of a smile turned up the corners of his mouth. "You got a point. So why tell us now?"

"Joanna." The name would mean nothing to anyone except Paul.

The faint smile disappeared and for a moment he looked confused. Then his face cleared. "You think she was a victim of this same killer."

She nodded and was grateful he got it. "There's more to it than the feeling this killer got to her too. For months now, every time I go out for a run in Seven Mile, I get so uneasy I can't shake it for hours. I've run every trail in the area and I don't see a damn thing. Yesterday it hit me after we left the crime scene. Perhaps Circe and Zelda can do what I've been unable to. Maybe they can uncover whatever it is that sends my senses into hyper-drive."

Just thinking about those runs sent chills rippling along her skin. Something was out there, and though she had no way of pinpointing where, she was compelled to try to find the source of the feelings. Maybe it wasn't Joanna, but she was absolutely certain it was somebody, and she was determined to find them one way or the other. With or without Circe and Zelda's help.

Despite the ominous sensations brought on by reliving those difficult runs in Seven Mile, she experienced a feeling of peace also flow over her. This was the first time she'd ever shared this thing she'd never put a name to with anyone outside her immediate family. No one disbelieved or discounted of her feelings, like she'd expected. Surprises came in the most interesting moments.

Circe stood up and looked her square in the eyes. "I'm in."

Lisa jumped up from the table and grabbed a jacket from a hook by the back door. "Count me in too, sister."

❖

Paul knew it was dumb to feel excited that Lisa was coming along. She was a civilian, and even though this search mission of Diana's was leaning toward unofficial, it wasn't exactly proper to have her in the field with them. Too many opportunities for something to get screwed up if, by some long shot, they actually found something. On the flip side, he wasn't about to discourage her. An extra set of eyes was never a bad thing when it came to searches, and he'd have no problem making that argument if it ever became an issue. If push came to shove on this deal, he had her back. In fact, the way it worked out, Diana rode with Circe and Zelda, while Lisa came with him. As his younger sister loved to say, "Cool beans."

"So, you're a grad student." Jesus, exactly how lame could he be? Apparently pretty damn lame.

She smiled, and even out of the corner of his eye he could see how her expression lit up her face. Maybe his attempt at small talk wasn't as bad as he thought. "That I am."

"What's your field?" Now that, he decided, sounded a tad more intelligent. Asking about her field sounded way savvier than simply asking her what she was studying. Yeah, he was getting his cool back.

Excitement came into her voice as she answered. It was an affirmative; he definitely had his cool back. "In less than six months, the gods willing, I'll hold a doctorate in neuropsychology."

"No shit?" So much for his coolness factor—easy come, easy go.

Her laughter was light and pleasant. "No shit."

"Sorry." Time to give it up because he was bungling the whole thing. Might as well just be himself. If she liked him, great. If she thought he was a total dud, oh well.

She laid a hand on his arm, and he felt the tingle all the way to the fingers he had wrapped around the steering wheel in a death-grip. "No worries. I've heard all the cuss words. I even know what most of them mean."

Now he laughed too. Pretty and with a sense of humor. "I suppose you have and I bet you do. Why neuropsychology, if you don't mind me asking?" He had a vague sense of the field, as more than once he'd been in a courtroom during testimony given by a psychologist. To say he understood exactly what they did would be a stretch.

"I can thank Circe for the push, or actually her best friend, Vickie, who's a neuropsychologist. Circe introduced us, and I was so fascinated by what she does for a living, I started asking her a million questions, and well, here I am."

"I'm impressed."

"Don't get too impressed yet. I still have a lot of work to do finishing up and passing my boards."

"You'll do fine."

She squeezed his arm. "Thanks for the vote of confidence. I'm going to need all the positive energy I can get. So, that's my story. What's yours?"

Lisa had freely shared with him and now it was his turn. Fair was fair, although he didn't intend to share everything. He just needed to keep it simple, and really, how much trouble could he get into? Unfortunately, he remembered thinking the same thing when he met Brenda and look how that turned out.

He went for it anyway. "Not too exciting in my case. Classic underachiever. Mom's an attorney, Dad's a third-generation newspaper man. I'm the family's black sheep. Didn't go to law school and didn't dig journalism. Being a cop isn't what my family had in mind for me, ever."

"You like it though."

"Yeah, I do." And he liked the way she didn't make a question out of it as if she understood where he was coming from.

"You good at it?"

He laughed a little and actually appreciated the question. His family, while ultimately supportive, still didn't really get what it was he did, and nobody ever asked if he was any good as a homicide cop. "Yeah, I am."

She gave his arm a little squeeze. "Then you did the right thing."

"That shrink talk?"

Her laugh was light and golden. He could listen to that sound forever, he thought rather irrationally. "Absolutely."

"Good to know. Next time the family gives me shit, I'll tell them I'm not crazy for being a cop 'cause I've been tested by a very good shrink."

❖

Diana directed Circe to an area off Seven Mile Road in north Spokane County. Definitely outside SPD jurisdiction. She didn't mention the fact, considering Diana undoubtedly knew exactly where they were. In the asphalted circular area that marked one of Riverside Park's trailheads she parked the car. This wasn't far from where she lived, and she and Zelda trained here now and again. They didn't come here often because it was a favorite area for people to walk their dogs. She preferred low-usage areas where she and Zelda had the place to themselves. As much as she craved the runs, she craved solitude and peace as well.

As she looked around, Circe found it an odd place for Diana to pick as a search area, given its high use. And since she and Zelda trained here a few times a year, they certainly would have come across something, or someone, in their training exercises. Of course, the park consisted of thousands of acres, and no way had they covered even a fraction of it while training.

"Where's Paul?"

Circe whirled around. A man with white hair and a white beard stood at the back of her car, hands in the pockets of his jeans. Medium height and at least fifty, he appeared to have been expecting them.

Diana came around the back of the car. "Hey, Will. He's on his way."

"He know I'm here?"

Diana shook her head. "No. Figured the surprise would be better. Circe, this is Duane Willschem."

He put out a hand. "Call me Will."

She took his hand and shook it. "Will it is. I'm Circe and this is Zelda." She popped open the back hatch and Zelda stood up. Circe took a step back and waited. It was always interesting to observe Zelda's reaction to people. It told her a lot about the person in about five seconds.

Zelda immediately wagged her tail and licked his face. Will had just passed the Zelda trust test, which was good enough for Circe.

"Will's a retired homicide detective," Diana told her.

That explained why he might be here with them, though why did his presence need to be a surprise for Paul? And why would Diana call in a retired officer when both she and Paul were active on the SPD? Then again, according to Diana this wasn't an official search, so why not bring in someone no longer official?

As if reading her mind, Diana said, "And he's Paul's ex-partner."

"Trained the guy," Will said with a smile. "Taught him everything I know, which of course explains why he's so good at his job. Uh-oh, it's showtime."

At the sound of an approaching vehicle, Circe turned to look. It was Paul and Lisa. It was interesting how quickly Lisa had jumped at the chance to ride out here with the attractive detective. It was great she was finally showing some interest in something besides school, but for Lisa to be so interested after only an hour made her a little nervous. Reminding herself Lisa was a smart woman and that just an hour ago she was thinking how great they seemed together, Circe decided there was no harm in innocent attraction. She couldn't say too much anyway, given the immediate draw she felt toward Diana, unless she was willing to live with the old adage "do as I say, not as I do." She'd rather not and would keep her mouth shut.

Paul was scowling as he got out of the car, and it obviously had nothing to do with his passenger and the drive over here. "What the hell, Diana. It's bad enough you arrange this off-the-books search, but we can't even do it without your uncle's supervision? You're just full of little surprises today, aren't you? Fucked-up surprises."

"Your uncle?" Now, that was interesting. Diana had failed to mention that small fact during introductions.

Diana nodded. "My uncle, Paul's training partner, and one hell of an investigator." She turned and looked at Paul. "If I'm right about this, I thought he could give us some additional insight."

"She's right," Will said. "She always is, and you know I'm always happy to put in my two cents."

The dynamic going on among the three was interesting, and Circe wished she had some of Lisa's psychology background. She was dying to understand what it all stemmed from. Though Paul might resent what he obviously considered an intrusion, she was accustomed to having observers along during searches, so she and Zelda wouldn't even notice if Will joined them. Besides, if Zelda was okay with him, so was she, and extra eyes were never a bad thing.

As Paul, Diana, and Will talked quietly to each other, she slipped on her chest harness and then her waist pack. Both water bottles went into her pack, and she attached Zelda's electronic tracking collar. By the time she was ready, the conversation didn't appear to be going any better than when it started. Paul was still scowling while Will just shook his head. If she waited on them, they might never get started.

"If you guys are so disposed, I'd like to get going." That stopped the talking and they all turned to look at her. She raised an eyebrow. "We're set to go if you are." Though she couldn't hear their conversation, she had the distinct sense it wasn't about the search they were about to embark on.

"You're right," Diana said. "Let's not stand around here making snarky remarks about things that don't matter in the big picture. Let's give this a try and see where it takes us."

"Fine," Paul snapped. He stuffed his hands in his pockets, his face still dark. His words said fine, his body language something quite different.

Will clapped him on the shoulder. He was smiling and confident, Paul's clear irritation at his presence apparently of no great concern to him. "Come on, Paulie. You know you've missed me."

"We don't need a babysitter," Paul said in a low voice.

Shaking his head, Will told him, "Not here for that, Paulie. I'm here as another set of eyes and I'm here for Joanna. That's it. Don't get your shorts in a twist over this."

"Yeah, whatever. Let's just get this done." He turned away and went to Lisa's side.

Later, Circe intended to find out what this was all about. Judging by the exchange between Will and Paul, they had a history of the contentious kind. Bound to be interesting, given Paul's emotional response. She didn't know the man well, but she had the sense this wasn't his typical mode of operation.

By the same token, whoever Joanna was, she'd left a lasting impression on not only Diana, but Paul and Will too. The three of them were quick to set aside obvious tensions in order to try to find the woman. She'd get the scoop on all those stories another time. Right now she just wanted to get started. The charge of energy flowing through her was growing stronger the longer they stood here. Diana was right about one thing. Something, or someone, was close by.

"Where do we start?" Circe said when no one took the lead.

Relief washed over Diana's face. Circe got the impression she was grateful to be drawn away from the confab that had started the moment Paul got out of the car. "The strongest vibes I've gotten are to the northwest near the river." She waved toward the steep slope to their right.

Circe took a hard look around. The circular parking area lay on a bluff. In this part of Riverside State Park, to the south, flat fields bordered a great distance of an asphalt path that wound for miles throughout the park. On the north side, the land sloped sharply toward the Spokane River below. Much of that area was wooded, though every so often fields of wild grass, spring golds, sagebrush buttercups, and camas dotted it. In the springtime it was a dichotomy of flowering beauty and allergy-inducing pollen. Didn't matter to her though, because she loved it here.

Circe leaned down and pressed the button on Zelda's collar to sync it with the GPS. Though they didn't have a defined search area, she readied her GPS unit nonetheless. Once they started, she planned to have her track manager on. The tracking function would allow them to view a map of the area and know exactly what ground they covered. Nobody had to tell her it was compulsive behavior; it was simply her way.

She took the lead, and as they started down the steep slope in the direction of the river, everyone quieted. Zelda was on lead until they reached the flat ground below the bluff. Once there, Circe unclipped the lead from her collar and ran her hand over her silky head. "We'll head north first," she explained to the others. "And then we'll grid east and west, as the wind is coming from the south. Working Zelda into the wind gives her the best chance of picking up a scent cone."

After instructing her posse to stay behind both her and Zelda, Circe leaned close to Zelda and whispered in her ear.

One thing she'd learned about German shepherds: they like to work and at a clipped pace. The second she gave her the command, Zelda was off. Circe ran most days of the week to keep in shape and to gear up for long treks with Zelda. While she didn't have to run to keep up with her, she wasn't in for a leisurely walk either. If she didn't work to stay in prime form, she'd drop behind Zelda in minutes.

With a wave of her arm, she directed Zelda toward the river, and once they reached the bank, she turned and began to walk west. Zelda, who always had one eye on Circe, saw the change in direction and changed her pattern as well. Along the riverbank, the trees were sparse and the view unobstructed. It seemed unlikely anyone would be able to conceal a crime here—too great a risk for exposure. In fact, as she looked, she realized from here she had a clear view across the river.

Still, to be thorough, she and Zelda covered the open area. After trekking about four hundred meters along the river, Circe turned south and walked another fifty meters, then turned east. From experience she found fifty-meter grids worked perfectly for her and Zelda. Despite roaming a good twenty-five to thirty meters away, Zelda saw the turn and made her own. Soon she was roaming ahead of Circe again, still intent.

If Diana and the rest of the crew were talking as they moved, she didn't hear them. Like Zelda, once they began to work, she kept her eyes on Zelda and at the same time surveyed the surrounding area, looking for anything out of the ordinary, like the appearance of the dead. Everything else, like people talking, became a low murmur of background noise.

As they moved through each grid line, the trees became thicker, the view from the open fields and river banks more obscure. Sunlight punched through the trees, giving the ground a green-and-gold-dotted appearance. The air was clear and fresh. It was beautiful, yet suddenly tendrils of unease wrapped around her. Diana's instinct about this place was right.

Zelda's ears twitched and her body stiffened. She was on scent. Then, only moments after Zelda's telltale signs of scent, she noticed the woman.

Sitting on the ground with her head down and her hands folded in her lap, she was far different from the women they'd found yesterday. Her clothing was expensive, and when her head came up, despite the blood on her neck, she was pretty. Briefly her eyes met Circe's and then she was gone.

Circe's heart ached and she was certain the woman she saw was Diana's friend. All she had to do now was wait for Zelda to do her job. Zelda kept working as Circe's pace slowed.

After circling a piece of ground three times, Zelda proceeded to alert. Well, that didn't take long, not that she was surprised. It was only one of the reasons they made such a great team. Circe was always able see the dead just as Zelda was always able scent them. Circe stopped, pulled a flag from her pack, and put it in the ground next to where Zelda was holding her alert. Then she pulled the toy from the waist pack and rewarded her.

Turning to look behind her, Circe said to Diana, "Zelda says there are human remains here."

CHAPTER SIX

His day was going very well until the evening news came on. Then everything blew up and the rage that filled him was hard to contain. It was all over the news, the discovery of another body by a K9 team, this time in Riverside State Park near Seven Mile Road. He knew exactly how near to Seven Mile Road because he was the one who'd put her there. She was his first after he'd returned home and was special because of it. His welcome-home present to himself. She was the one who'd made him believe, because if he could make her disappear, then what he had to do was going to work out well.

What the hell had been going on the last few days? All things considered, what he was doing wasn't wrong. It was necessary. It was also important and needed to continue. How his work was being uncovered baffled him. God knows he was incredibly careful. Okay, well maybe the three down near People's Park were less careful and more fun, but overall he took great pains to keep everything tidy and well hidden. Now, interference by the cops could mess things up, and he couldn't afford for that to happen. He was too close.

On the news clip tonight, he caught sight of two familiar faces, the same two detectives from yesterday. He didn't recognize the woman, but he knew the guy, and it made him groan. What was his name? Paul something or other. He'd made his acquaintance and didn't care for the guy.

This was so frustrating. If he didn't talk to someone he was sure to go nuts. In a pinch he knew one person he could always talk to about anything. Eve. Of all of them, she was the steady one. Nothing ever seemed to rattle her, and she had a way of talking to him that ultimately gave him a sense of calmness. Typically, she was close by, which was another thing about her he found comforting.

She didn't disappoint him today either. "Hey, handsome, what's bothering you?"

What wasn't bothering him at the moment? Distilling it down to its essence, he told her, "I'm worried they're going to track the dead women back to me before I have a chance to finish things."

"You've been careful, right?"

He nodded. "I'm careful. Extra careful. It's not like I'm stupid."

Her voice was soft and soothing. "You are definitely not stupid. This will all work out."

"I want to believe it will."

"It will. You have a support system that others would kill for, and you have the book. Nothing can derail what has to be done. Look at the rewards you've reaped so far."

She was right. Since the book came into his hands and he began to follow its teachings, his life had changed dramatically. He had money, love, and respect. The final ritual and all he needed to make it happen were close. Afterward the power and vast wealth promised to him within the pages of the text would make everything that came before inconsequential. She was right; he had no reason to panic now. If he continued to follow the path, everything was bound to work out.

Besides, how in the world could they connect any of those bodies to him? Except perhaps the one found in Seven Mile. He didn't want to admit to Eve why that one was different or why he had selected her when he had known of others more suitable. Really, if he thought about it, the risk was small that the investigators would link her back to him, so he didn't see the need to tell Eve. No, he would keep that particular secret.

He smiled and leaned back in his chair. "You know, it will all come together. You're right, Eve."

"Aren't I always?"

"Yes, you are."

It was dark by the time Diana found herself on Circe's front porch once more. Earlier she'd promised Circe she would update her on the body that turned out to be exactly where she said it was. If she harbored any doubt about Zelda's ability as a human-remains detection dog, her discovery this afternoon had put it firmly to rest.

To her it seemed a logical conclusion that this body was Joanna's, unless some other missing person wore a small silver pentagram, that is. For her friend it wasn't a satanic symbol but rather a testament to her belief in Wicca. The pentagram didn't embody evil. No, its five points represented fire, water, air, earth, and spirit. Diana had never shared Joanna's beliefs, but she respected her right to practice the faith of her choosing. More than anything, she hoped the spirit of that symbol had taken her to a place safe from harm. She really wanted to believe that because it hurt her soul to think of her out in the wilderness for all those months, cold and alone, and buried beneath the dark, rich earth.

She pushed the doorbell button. From deep inside she heard the echo of the bell, followed immediately by a barking dog. Zelda, of course. Despite the roar of the bark, Diana found it welcoming. She was beginning to really like that dog.

"Come in," Circe said as she opened the door.

Diana didn't need to have the invitation offered twice, and she stepped on in. The search for Joanna was all her idea, and finding her was a relief on many levels. Despite that, the reality of her death was depressing, and she had to acknowledge a small part of her really hoped she was wrong. The one bright spot in the day was the opportunity to spend time with Circe. From the moment they met yesterday, she'd felt drawn to her. Some people were like that. No rhyme or reason why, but they were special and the feeling of kinship was immediate. That's the way it was for her with Circe. It was as if they'd known each other for years.

Now how Circe felt about her was a mystery. While she was friendly to Diana and amenable to doing her a favor today, Diana still didn't have a clue if she felt that pull of friendship.

Or even, at the very least, the beginnings of friendship. Diana was all for becoming friends, and if it ended there, great. Who ever had enough friends? Except, truthfully, it was more for her. The tingle of interest went much deeper than making a new friend. She recognized the thrill of attraction, despite her less-than-active dating life these days, and hoped she wasn't alone in the feeling. Today, in particular. Finding Joanna was a double-edged sword. She was grateful to be able to bring her home, though finally knowing that her dear friend had lost her life at the hands of another also broke her heart. She wanted, or perhaps needed, something to bring hope back into her heart.

In the living room, Circe motioned for her to sit on the sofa, and Diana sank to the cushions at one end. On a low table in front of the sofa she saw a ceramic teapot and one china teacup painted with delicate blue flowers.

"Do you drink tea?" Circe asked.

Diana started to shake her head, then stopped herself. Not usually especially this time of night. A beer, sure. A nice merlot, absolutely. Tea in a delicate bone-china teacup, never. "Tea would be nice." Who the hell just said that?

"Give me a sec," Circe said as she disappeared down the hall. A minute later she returned with another teacup and saucer. This teacup was covered with pale-yellow flowers.

As Circe poured tea into the cup, the rich scent of bergamot filled the air. Darned if it didn't smell fantastic too. She might have to rethink that beer and wine. Could she possibly be evolving into a tea drinker? There were worse things.

It tasted as good as it smelled. She liked Earl Grey tea, but she'd never brewed a cup this good. Her style of nuking a mug of water and slapping in a tea bag that had been sitting in her cupboard for a couple of years obviously lacked a lot. Clearly she didn't possess the touch and would have to find out what Circe's secret was. She might drink the stuff more often if it always tasted like this.

When Circe sat down on the far end of the sofa, her legs tucked up beneath her and her teacup held between both hands, neither of them said a word for a few minutes. It wasn't an uncomfortable silence; in fact, just the opposite. Diana appreciated the easy companionship. The peaceful silence was nice and something she needed right now.

"It's her, isn't it?" Circe finally asked. "Your friend, I mean."

Diana thought she had it under control. When they went out there today, she'd mentally prepared herself for the possibility of finding Joanna's body and had managed to hold it together all day. Still, hearing the words out loud suddenly made tears prickle at the back of her eyes, and for a minute she was afraid she might lose it. Not something she wanted to do. She wasn't the kind of woman who cried—at least not in front of other people. Then again, the way she was feeling, Circe wasn't "other people," and tough as she was, even she was entitled to moments of being human.

Taking in several slow, long breaths, she stared down at her tea without answering. When she felt a little more in control, she said, "It was her. God, yes, it was her."

Circe slid closer and took her hand. "I'm so very sorry. Tell me about her."

Talking about Joanna might be the thing to break her, and she wanted to keep it together. Or maybe she did need to share. What was the right thing to do? A knot sat in the pit of her stomach so heavy it hurt, and the feel of Circe's hand in hers helped. "Joanna Decker was the first friend I made when we moved to Spokane. The Deckers lived across the street, and the day we moved in, she was in her yard. She walked over, said hi, and that was that. From the fourth grade on, we've been friends."

"Then she went missing."

How could she explain her pain at losing her friend encompassed more than the months of not knowing whether she was alive or dead, or the cruelty of today's discovery? The roots of her despair had come far earlier when she realized Joanna had been going through something she didn't want to share with Diana, or anyone else, that she could tell. From what she'd been able to piece together at the time, it seemed to have been a mid-life-crisis type of event, and Diana had tried to be there for her. But for whatever reason, Joanna wouldn't talk to her. It was like they were strangers instead of the kind of friends who'd shared all the important events in their lives. For a while, she kept tabs on Joanna and continued to try to convince her to confide. Whatever it was, Diana believed she could help. At the very least, she could be there as the friend she really was. Then life got in the way. Diana got busy on the job and didn't check in for a good long while.

That was the part she regretted more than anything else. It had been so easy to let it go, to tell herself Joanna would get over it and be back to normal soon. She was busy, her career was taking off, and she pushed the needs of her friend to the back burner. Days went by. Then it was months. One day Joanna's father called her, and only then did she get the full picture. Joanna was missing, and Diana, the one person who'd promised to always have her back, had let her down when it mattered the most.

Difficult as it was, she dredged up the words to explain all of this story to Circe. Being honest about what had happened was easier than she'd anticipated. Even to her own ears she came off as an uncaring bitch. When it counted she hadn't come through as much of a friend.

She was afraid to look up, to see in Circe's face what she felt in her heart. When she finally raised her gaze, surprise washed over her. Diana didn't detect even a tiny trace of disapproval in Circe's clear hazel eyes. What she saw instead was compassion and empathy, which made her like Circe even more.

❖

Paul dropped into his favorite chair, an old recliner he'd bought for his very first apartment. Pretty much everything else from the early days of being a bona fide adult was long gone except the well-used chair. Back in the day it'd cost him more than he could afford, but he'd allowed himself this one luxury. These days it didn't match any of the rest of the furnishings and contrasted with the contemporary furniture he'd put together for this house. It didn't matter to him. This beat-up chair was his place of comfort, and for whatever reason he was always able to think better when he relaxed in it.

Tonight, his heart was heavy for Diana. Despite his cop instincts that had told him Joanna was probably dead, he'd held out hope that she'd simply gone away to start over. He knew Diana had hoped for the same thing until the moment Joanna's body was lifted from her makeshift grave.

If he closed his eyes he could still see Joanna, with her short black hair, bright blue eyes, and petite body. Nervous energy had always poured from her in an infectious way. Diana had set Paul up with Joanna not long after they became partners. It was a good thought because he and Joanna got along great, just, as it turned out, not in the romantic sense. They tried a couple of dates, figured out pretty quickly they didn't have any sparks between them, and became really good friends. He loved her even if he was never able to fall in love with her, and he knew she felt the same way toward him.

But he, like Diana, knew something was troubling Joanna before she disappeared, even as she tried not to show it outwardly. Whatever her torments were, she never shared them with him or Diana. When she dropped out of sight, he tried to tell himself she just needed time to exorcise those secret demons. In the back of his mind he'd worried about her, but at the same time, he kept his thoughts silent, because by then he'd become involved with Brenda. He'd sensed that Brenda would not have taken kindly to his concerns about the welfare of another woman, particularly when that woman was pretty and friendly. If he hadn't been so caught up in the lust of the moment, he'd have seen what a big red flag Brenda's jealousy really was.

Now he felt nauseous, a bone-deep sickness that threatened to buckle his knees. He shouldn't have let it go. A good cop would have followed his gut and pushed. A good friend would have too. Both he and Diana had dropped the ball on this one. The only one who didn't was Will. Why was it so hard for him to take guidance from Will? To follow his lead? Like his refusal to give up on Joanna. Whenever he had spare time, he kept looking for her.

Well, he'd found her now, hadn't he? Just like that gut feeling had been screaming at him for months. Dead. Beautiful, soulful Joanna, dead, and he hated himself for getting so caught up in his own drama that he'd failed his friend. He hated that once again Will had been right and he'd failed to listen.

With both hands on the arms of the recliner, he pushed up to his feet. While he wasn't much of a drinker, this moment demanded a scotch to take the edge off his guilt. If he couldn't deal with the guilt, he might as well mask it.

As he closed in on the door to the kitchen, he heard a noise from inside. He slowed and reached around for his gun. The safety off, he inched toward the open doorway, holding the gun with both hands out in front of him. As he caught sight of movement, he tightened his grip and moved his finger to the trigger.

He rounded the corner and stopped just short of pulling the trigger. Slowly he brought the gun down and held it in one hand at his side. "What the fuck are you doing here?"

CHAPTER SEVEN

Circe understood what Diana was feeling tonight. She hadn't lost close friends, but the dead populated her whole life. She not only saw them, but she also felt the anguish that seemed to follow them to the great beyond. The tragic words the dead spoke to her were too often full of regrets, and it didn't matter whether their deaths were natural or homicidal. Those regrets came through loud and clear to Circe, and she longed to be able to ease their troubled souls.

With the exception of a rare few, the dead who came to her were strangers. That fact made no difference at all in the way she felt about them. Each one weighed heavy on her spirit, and that's why it had become so important for her to find a way to use her unwanted gift. Whatever or whoever had decided that she was the one to see through the veil separating the living from the dead must have had a reason, or why would they gift her with the power?

At least that's the conclusion she'd reached when she was old enough to start reasoning through the thing that set her apart from family and friends. The only way this thing made any sense at all was if she used it for some higher purpose. Once she embraced that rationalization, she found a peace in her gift that until then had wholly eluded her.

Except for Vickie, she never talked about it with anyone because no rational explanation for what she could do existed. Beyond explanations, she still harbored no desire to spend time at the local mental-health facility in Medical Lake, and if she told people what she could do, that's exactly where she'd end up. So on many levels, she understood how Diana was feeling.

Looking into Diana's eyes, the color of bellflowers, she felt a tug of something special. All her life she'd kept her distance from all but a very select few, but not because she wanted to. She'd learned this method of self-preservation when she was very, very young. Her safety and freedom hinged on her silence. Even now, she didn't have an urge to share her deep, dark secrets with Diana or anyone else. They had more of an unspoken kinship she hadn't felt with anyone else. It was nice.

"You aren't responsible for your friend's death," she said quietly.

"I should have done more."

Circe laughed wryly. "You know, the word *should* needs to be tossed out of the English language. It's quite destructive and leads to very damaging emotions."

"Sounds like you speak from personal experience."

If Diana only knew. When she was ten she should have told someone about the boy she saw in the woods and maybe his family would have found peace much sooner. When she was fourteen she should have told someone about the woman buried in the neighbor's flowerbed and perhaps a serial killer would have been stopped sooner. Should have. Should have. Should have. God, how she hated that word.

Yet if she'd done any of those things, where would she be now? Medical Lake? Yes, that would be an affirmative, and so she'd learned to deal with the guilt that came with every one of the *shoulds*.

Circe blew out a long breath. "Let's just say a situation or two might have gone a different way had I opted for a different course of action. I finally realized that if I got stuck on what I should have done, I would have drowned in my own regrets a long time ago. I can't change the past and am not sure I would even if I could. Instead, I try to look forward. I found a way to make a difference and that's what I focus on now."

"With Zelda?"

She smiled and glanced over at her companion, where she lay curled up asleep on her big plush dog bed. Snoring softly, she was oblivious to the conversation that turned her way. "Yes, with Zelda. She's changed my life in so many ways."

"From what I hear, what you two have done has changed a lot of lives and given many families, if not peace, then at least closure."

She shifted her gaze from Zelda back to Diana. "Peace and closure are both important. It's not just a one-way street, either, because I've gained a great deal as well." No words could ever explain what her partnership with Zelda meant to her. Zelda filled a part of her heart she hadn't even realized was empty until the small puppy came home with her. What they were able to do together was even more incredible and gave her the kind of peace she'd never believed possible. She couldn't even try to imagine a life without Zelda.

Diana's blue eyes studied her, and as Circe gazed into them her heart did a little flip. Softly, Diana asked, "I've heard K9 officers say the same thing. They talk of the closeness they share with their K9 partners."

Circe nodded and smiled. "It's a bit like that, yes." Once more she let her eyes slide to Zelda, who had shifted on her bed and now lay on her back with her legs up in the air. It always struck her as funny to see the big dog upside down yet still snoring. "It's more than being close, so much more…"

Diana's head tilted as she studied her. "How so?"

How could she explain without spilling her secret? Every moment she spent with Diana a little piece of her protective shell was chipped away, but not enough to crack her book of secrets. She wasn't quite ready to do that…yet. The best thing she could do right now was to stay as close to the truth as possible without telling all of it. The strategy had been working for her for years and no reason it wouldn't work tonight.

"Ever since I was a child, it bothered me when I'd hear about someone who was lost or missing. I would think about them out there lost, cold, and alone. Even if I thought they were dead, I hated the idea of them being alone. It scared me and I felt horrible because

I couldn't help. Then through a friend I learned about K9 human-remains detection and suddenly my whole world changed. I could help make a difference, and I could do it with a beautiful, intelligent dog at my side. Working together as a team is a journey hard to describe. Every time we bring someone home and reunite the lost with their loved ones, I'm grateful. You have to understand that it's not just for the families. It's for me too." She put her palm against her heart. "It brings me peace."

Because, she added silently to herself, when I bring them home, the dead leave me alone.

❖

"Brenda, what in the fuck are you doing here?" Paul asked for the second time.

He couldn't believe his eyes. Gorgeous in a cornflower-blue dress, her hair flowing down her back in golden ripples, Brenda was standing in his kitchen putting together a plate of cheese, crackers, and fresh fruit. Reusable grocery sacks were on the counter, and a big bowl filled with ice held numerous brown bottles.

She smiled and inclined her head toward the platter. "I know you've had a terrible day, and I thought something to eat and a nice craft beer would be exactly what you need. Finding that poor woman was all over the news, and I was just certain I needed to be here for you. A man who's been through what you have today should be able to come home to good food and a cool drink. You can always count on me. I hope you know that."

His hands were clenched into fists as he held them tight to his sides. "How did you get in my house?" Blood warmed his palms as his fingernails bit into flesh.

Brenda didn't have a key. He'd taken it out of her purse himself. She shouldn't have been able to get in here when he wasn't around, and even if he was here, no fucking way would he let her inside. A fortress was the last place he wanted to live, yet all of a sudden barred windows and doors held a particularly enticing appeal.

Her expression was serene and unbothered in spite of the distinct irritation in his voice. He didn't know how much clearer he could be. "I still have a key," she explained patiently.

"I took it from you."

Her laugh was light and happy. She was arranging and rearranging the food on the platter as if each piece had to be perfect. "You took one." She shrugged. "I have another." Without looking at him, she went to the refrigerator and pulled a mug from the freezer. At the counter, she grabbed a bottle from the bowl of ice, popped the cap, and poured the amber beer into the mug.

God damn it! Every time he turned around she was pulling some kind of shit behind his back. The ripple effect of some mistakes was beyond imagination. Some detective he was. A good one would have anticipated the psycho bitch would figure out another way to stay in his life. She was like a bad rash that wouldn't go away.

After he wiped the blood from his palm on his pant leg, he held out his hand and forced himself to stay calm. "Give it to me, Brenda. Now."

She pouted and motioned to the frosty mug of beer and the beautifully arranged platter that she finally stopped fussing with. "Oh, come on, Paul. You and I both know this thing we have runs deep. A little quarrel now and again isn't going to keep us apart. Great couples always argue and they always make up." She smiled as if he'd just invited her to move back in.

Good God, how was he going to get it through her thick blond head that they were over? When he slapped a restraining order on her, maybe? That would be priceless, and even though he didn't voice the threat, they both knew it would never happen. If it did, he'd never hear the end of it because the entire force would find out a crazy, albeit beautiful, stalker had suckered him. This kind of thing did not happen to guys like him. No legal channels to help him out on this one; he was on his own.

"Brenda." He said her name slowly and managed to keep his voice calm. "We did not have a little quarrel. I told you I don't want to see you anymore, and I meant it. I don't want to see you, I don't want you in my house, and I don't want you dropping by. That's about as clear as I can make it. Now, I want the key and any other key if you have it, and then I want you to leave."

Darkness flooded her face, and everything that was beautiful about her flowed away with it. How had he never seen the darkness in her when they were living together? He hated to think he was so superficial that he took good-in-bed as a character reference. Denial wasn't a defense he could use because the woman standing in front of him was proof that he could, indeed, be that shallow. "It's that woman, isn't it?" Ice crystals seemed to hang on every word.

What in the world was she talking about now? She was the only woman causing him grief. "What woman?" This whole situation made him bone weary. It had to end.

"The one I saw you with on the news clip. I could see how you leaned into her, and the little bitch was just a step away from hanging on you. Both of you should be embarrassed." Her voice dripped with what he could only describe as venom. Great, a jealous stalker. He'd believed things were as bad as they could possibly be. Now he wasn't so sure.

"Woman?" He repeated the word, still trying to figure out what the hell she was talking about. Then it hit him. Lisa had been the woman standing next to him when they were at Seven Mile. The ever-present media, which could make it to a crime scene faster than law enforcement, must have filmed them together. "Brenda, you don't know what you're talking about. The only two non-law-enforcement people at the scene were the K9 handler and her roommate."

"Whatever," she said as she dug into her purse. Her hand whipped back out with a key between her fingers, and she threw it at him. It bounced off his chest and dropped with a clang to the floor. "A whore is a whore."

"You need to leave." He found it hard to say the words calmly and quietly. Any patience he might have clung to evaporated. He wanted to walk over, grab her by the collar, and toss her out the door. The thing was, he'd be the one assaulting her at that point, and he didn't need this situation to get any worse than it already was. The best thing he could do was stay calm and focused. Get her out of the house and then, well then, he'd change the locks.

Instead of leaving, she flung the platter across the room, fruit, cheese, and crackers flying in every direction. "You never appreciated me," she screamed. The platter hit the wall and shattered, broken pieces of pottery dropping like tiny bombs to the tile floor.

"Leave, please." He kept his expression neutral. He wasn't planning to engage in the tantrum she was working up to. Been there, done that.

After a scream, she shoved the bowl of ice and beer to the floor, where it too shattered in an explosion of glass and ice. Without looking at him again, she stomped to the door. The click of her high heels was like the shot of a nail gun, and it raised the hair on the back of his neck. At the door, she wrenched it open and whirled. "You're going to be sorry," she hissed. Then she was gone.

❖

Jesus, she was in a bad mood, and he didn't have time for her moods. Bipolar was the term he liked to use for her dramatic up-and-down emotions. All in all her condition was wearing, and not just on him, but on Eve as well. If the three of them weren't so close he'd tell her to go to hell.

He was forever following her and cleaning up her messes. She screwed something up and he fixed it. With Eve's help, they always found the solution to whatever problem she came up with. Or, to be more accurate, created. She was a walking disaster on three-inch designer heels. After all this time he should be used to it, and in many ways, he was. It was just that drama-free for a little while might be nice. A guy could dream anyway.

Still, he had to admit, in some ways her drama was fun. His own life was fairly routine, and if not for the constant attention to her crises, it would be boring. And, if he was being brutally honest, she was the one who'd found the *De Nigromancia*. Of course, he took credit for the find and didn't feel the least bit guilty about doing

SHERI LEWIS WOHL

so. After all he'd done for her over the years, he was absolutely vindicated in embracing this one small lie.

The best part about the text was that he could use it to help her, and that's what he planned to do now. By the time he climbed the stairs to his attic office and his precious book, he was smiling and feeling wonderfully motivated. For an hour he pored over the pages until he found just the right spell. But he didn't have one of the ingredients. His shelves downstairs were decently stocked, but given the unique nature of his work, he occasionally found himself facing holes. This was one of those times.

He walked back downstairs and checked his gear. It was important to make sure everything he'd need was in the kit and ready to go. The house was quiet as he worked and he appreciated the solitude. Peace and quiet always helped him get ready for a hunt. He loved feeling the items in his kit. The sensations made his fingers tingle, and he couldn't keep the smile off his face.

Sometimes the requirement for one of the spells was unique. In those instances, he carefully selected the subject for their special qualities. It often took him days, if not weeks, to discover just the right one. Not so tonight. While the ingredient was missing from his stock, any number of potential donors would work just fine. All he needed to do was cruise the night streets and check the livestock. The right one would reveal herself to him, and voila. He would have what was necessary to complete the spell.

Different parts of the city gave him different stock to choose from. Some required more finesse, while others were so easy it was laughable. Tonight, easy was on the agenda. It wasn't that he didn't like the challenge of the more difficult areas. No, he just wanted to get this done, and simple made it quick and efficient.

At this time of night, Second Avenue was a sure bet, and he wasn't disappointed. During the daytime this was a bland stretch of the city populated by old churches, several shelters, and small but thriving businesses. As the sun set each day over the mountains to the west, the tide changed and the business people disappeared to be replaced by those who often slept the day away. These were the people he came looking for.

He started at Division and drove in the middle lane all the way down to Maple Street. Satisfied by the product selection, he circled around and retraced his drive, pulling to the curb just a couple blocks shy of Maple. Nights like this made his entire body buzz, and when the cute little hooker with the pink-tinted hair opened the passenger-side door and climbed into the car, everything inside him came alive. He could hardly wait to get back to the house.

CHAPTER EIGHT

Circe leaned against the open front door while Diana stood on the porch. This was as far as they'd made it after finishing their tea. Diana didn't seem to be able to get her feet to move any closer to her car. For ten minutes they stayed here still talking while she rubbed the small whistle on her keychain between her fingers.

"I really should get going." As much as she liked spending time with Circe, it was a long drive back into town. At least that's what the rational part of her mind was saying. The other part, well, that part could easily stand here all night.

"I know." Circe's smile lit up her face. "I feel a little guilty that you drove all the way out here again today. You could have just called to tell me about Joanna."

Diana shrugged. The thought had occurred to her too, and just as quickly as it did, she dismissed it. Circe had done her a huge favor by trusting Diana's instincts and sending her dog out to search for her friend's body. She'd done what no one else had been able to so far, and that meant a lot to her. The least she could do was come out here and tell her in person. Besides, if she was honest, the drive was worth it so she could spend a little more time with Circe. "No big deal."

"Oh, it was indeed a big deal. Just know that I appreciate it." Circe put a hand on her arm. Her fingers were warm against her skin, and Diana wished it would stay there.

The contact did little to help her step away. In fact, it made her want to step closer, a lot closer. Even from here she could smell the scent of vanilla—soap, perhaps, or shampoo. Whatever the source, it was sweet and lovely. She wanted to pull her close and breathe it in more deeply.

Instead she did what she needed to and stepped closer to the stairs leading to the driveway and away from Circe, whose hand dropped away as she moved. All the warmth went with it. "It's no big deal considering what you did for me."

This time Circe shrugged and gave her a shy smile. "Zelda and I are happy to help any way we can. I'm sorry your friend was murdered, but I'm glad we could help bring her home."

Her thoughts turned to Joanna, and her heart grew heavy, pushing away the sweetness of being near Circe. "You have no idea how much I appreciate your help and the fact that you took a chance on my gut feeling. Joanna's family will be forever grateful to you and Zelda for finding her."

A cloud crossed Circe's beautiful face. "It's why we train and why we go out in the field."

"Thank you anyway. You have no idea what this means to her family and to her friends." She stepped down to the driveway.

Diana was just opening the driver's door when Circe's voice stopped her. "I'm glad you came."

For some reason those simple words touched her heart, and tears almost blinded her as she pulled out of Circe's driveway. She wiped them away and concentrated on the road. She never considered herself to be an emotional woman, though at the moment it would be hard to deny. Finding Joanna and spending time with Circe had made her emotions bounce all over the place. She was glad for at least a little while that she was by herself. It would give her time to pull it together.

The highway curved along the river, and at this time of night traffic was light. It was a peaceful drive and the water was glassy smooth, reflecting lights from the homes scattered along the shoreline. She could easily understand what brought people out to live this far from town. Even as she braked for a couple of deer racing across the highway in front of her, she still decided this was a drive she could get used to. Or maybe she could get used to it because of who was at the end of the drive.

As she pulled into her own driveway, her lights swept across the garage doors. Or they should have anyway. Instead, her garage was wide open. She stopped the car and stared as her car lights cut through the darkness. Everything was in chaos. Plastic bins that had been on shelves when she left this morning were open with their contents thrown across the garage floor. Someone had slashed open a bag of fertilizer and poured it over everything. Not one thing in the garage was where it had been when she backed out of the garage earlier.

"What the hell?" Putting the car in park, she turned off the ignition and opened her door. Slowly she stood and the same time unclipped the gun in the holster at her waist, though she didn't pull it out, for now. Stepping over broken jars, shattered Christmas decorations, and yard tools, she scanned everything as she moved through the chaos. With each step something cracked and crushed beneath the soles of her shoes. At the door leading into the house, she took hold of doorknob. When it didn't turn, a weight seemed to fall from her shoulders. It was still locked and, from the looks of it, hadn't been tampered with. Thank the gods for one small favor.

At the wall switch located next to the door into the house, she clicked on the overhead light. Words failed her and all she could do was stare. Who would do something like this? More important, why? Who the hell did she piss off so bad they would come in here like a tornado? Stupid question really. Given her profession, a better question might be who didn't she piss off? Blowing out a long breath, she clipped her gun back in the holster and pulled out her cell.

"I need you," she said when Paul picked up. "How fast can you get over to my house?"

The alarm in his voice was clear. Here she thought she had it all together, but considering his reaction, she guessed not. "What's happened?"

"Just get here. You have to see it."

"On my way."

She started to say thanks before she realized she was talking to dead air.

❖

Paul stood in the middle of Diana's trashed garage and did a three-sixty. "What in the fuck…"

"I know, right?" During the time it had taken him to get here she took a good long breath, got her bearings, and kicked into professional mode. She had taken pictures from every angle of every broken box, destroyed yard tool, and slashed bag. The chaos was everywhere, and she was determined to get clear evidence of it all.

"Who did you piss off?"

She was shaking her head. "Damned if I know. Since I called you I've been thinking over anyone and everyone who might have done this, and I've come up blank. I've put away plenty of people, yet nobody pops out at me. No threats or anything like that. This is so random."

In all the time they'd been partners, this was the first time he could recall her being rattled. She was putting on a good front and probably thought she was pulling it off, but she wasn't. He could see through her like a pane of glass.

That she called him first was no surprise. If the shoe were on the other foot, he'd have called her before anyone else. Now, however, it was time to take this to the officials. This wasn't some practical joke or kid-like vandalism. It seemed like targeted violence. "We need to call this in."

She sank to the step leading into the house. "Yeah, we do. I just wanted you here before I made the call." Running her hands through her hair, she studied the mess. "I still don't get it, Paul. Nothing I'm working on would generate this kind of reaction, and my personal life is at an all-time boring low. I can't think of a soul angry enough at me to violate my personal space like this."

He spent every day with this woman and was fully aware of her current lack of a social life. His own was pretty messed up, but unlike Diana, at least he had one. In fact, he could actually do with a little less personal life. Or a lot less actually. Brenda needed to get the hell out of his life. But he wasn't going down that path right now. This was about Diana, not his stalker problem, and yup, he was at the point of acknowledging the very ugly truth: he had a stalker. She didn't share his problem, at least as far as he knew. When he thought about it, though, maybe she had her own secrets. He was managing pretty well to keep his Brenda problem close to the vest. Who was to say Diana didn't have something similar going on in her life?

He put a hand on her shoulder and squeezed gently. "I'll phone the station." Walking outside, he stood in the driveway and called it in. When he ended the call he figured they had about half an hour before the crew arrived. As soon as they got there, he and Diana would be out of the loop. They were too close, and no way would the chief let them work it. The investigator in him didn't like that scenario even though he understood the reason for it. So, if they were to find anything, they needed to do it during the next thirty minutes.

At his car, he grabbed a high-powered flashlight out of the glove box. Back in the garage, he shined it on the floor as he walked back and forth in a straight line. Broken Christmas decorations, hiking gear, snow shoes, yard tools, and trash. As the beam of his light swept the floor he hoped for something, yet nothing unique or special jumped out at him. It was a good, old-fashioned mess of huge proportions. Someone had spent plenty of time throwing everything around as if in a blinding rage, like a spoiled child pitching a tantrum.

He clicked off the flashlight and tapped it against his leg. "Nothing, damn it."

Diana stared out across the mess, a frown on her face. "Maybe it was just random vandalism."

She almost sounded hopeful and he didn't blame her. The situation sucked big-time. Still, if it was random rather than personal, it hurt a little less. He could understand her wanting to gravitate toward that conclusion even if he couldn't buy in. The way he saw it, this was far from random. No, he was reading personal in this mess.

Not wanting to make her more upset than she already was, he said, "Could be. Do me a favor and shut the door. Whoever did this needed to have the door shut while they were trashing the place, or one of the neighbors would have seen it and called it in. So, let's take a look at it from the vandal's point of view."

It was one of the first things Will had taught him: get inside the head of the perp. He might get annoyed with Will when he felt like he was being micro-managed, which was most of the time when they were together. It didn't mean he didn't respect Will or appreciate what he'd taught him over the years. The guy was a great detective, and he was generous with sharing hard-earned knowledge.

"Good thought." Diana reached up and pushed the button that controlled the electric door. It whirled and slowly closed.

Once the door was down, Paul clicked on the flashlight again and shined it on the inside of the door. For a moment after it closed all the way, they were both silent as his flashlight played across the panels of the door.

"Oh, shit," he murmured as he read the single word written in red spray paint: BITCH.

❖

He was whistling as he sprayed down the walls and floor of the workroom. Red water flowed to the drain, where it swirled and glistened under the glare of the overhead light. A faintly metallic scent wafted through the air. The night had gone well and he was now ready to make it all happen. After everything was neatened up, that is. A tidy workroom is a happy workroom. He laughed and kept spraying. The water spiraling down the drain set in the middle of the floor faded from red to pink, but only when it ran clear did he shut off the water.

It was too late tonight to do much beyond gathering supplies and disposing of the leftovers. A shame. At the shelves lined with jars, he gazed longingly at the tidy rows. Each treasure was a little different, each one special in its own way. Tonight's jars were next to each other almost glowing in their freshness. His fingers itched to give it a go and see how powerful the magic turned out to be. So far the book had not failed him. Each spell he'd used brought him more wealth and power, and this one promised even more. Ah well, tomorrow would be soon enough to make it happen.

He wound up his hose, used the squeegee to push the last of the water down the drain, and then headed upstairs. At the top of the stairs, he snapped the padlock closed on the latch to the basement door. It wasn't like anyone really came here, but it didn't hurt to be cautious. Then he turned and looked at the kitchen counter. Fury shot through him. Why did she have to be such a damn slob? On the counter sat a wineglass and an open bottle of Merlot. He knew it was Merlot even though the label was facing the other direction because the ruby wine was spilled all over the counter.

All she had to do was take five minutes and clean up her mess. Someday, he was going to reach the point where he couldn't take it anymore. She would have to go and he would make her. That was a day he looked forward to.

For now, he gritted his teeth and tried not to breathe in the stink of the alcohol as he picked up the bottle. The remainder of the wine he dumped down the drain and put the empty bottle into the recycle bin. He put the wineglass into the dishwasher next to the other three he'd picked up from various drop points throughout the house, wondering if she even knew they had a dishwasher. After wiping down the counter, he looked around at the kitchen that was once more clean and shining. Nodding his approval, he clicked off the overhead light and walked out.

Now he could concentrate on the rest of the night's duties. If he'd tried to leave the mess for her to clean up it would have bothered him to the point of distraction. From long practice he knew the best thing—the only thing—he could do was to tidy up. He crawled behind the wheel and backed out of the garage. Tonight he drove toward Sunset Hill, not thinking about the body wrapped in the camouflage-printed tarp in the back.

One of the really nice things about living in this part of the country was the abundance of nature. It was an urban city sprawling for miles in all directions. The sprawl didn't damper the natural landscape, and no matter what direction he drove, he found mountains, forests, rivers, and lakes. In short, plenty of places to take out the trash.

The spot in Peaceful Valley he'd used for his three latest subjects was daring. He'd known it when he chose it. The area around the Sandifur Bridge was heavily used, and the chance of discovery was relatively high. It was the one thing that made it so fun to use. He liked the edge of danger to it.

The women were discovered far quicker than he liked, and that was tragic. Not game-stopping, just tragic. He would have preferred for others to leave the bodies right where he put them. That way he'd have been able to stroll through the area anytime he wanted, remember every little detail, and no one would have been the wiser. Now, it was all spoiled. People did not have the right to undo what he so carefully orchestrated. Then again, he'd made the decision to roll the dice when he'd put them there, and he'd lost. All part of the gamble.

Tonight he drove past Peaceful Valley, where yellow crime-scene tape was still stretched between trees. He had to work hard to ignore the urge to stop and rip down all the yellow tape. He managed to take the high road and kept driving. If he were to drive out to Seven Mile, he was certain to find the same picture there and would feel the same way. The news reports were hinting at a serial killer, and that actually made him laugh. That was the last thing he considered himself. In fact, he wasn't a killer at all, at least not in the true sense of the word. He was more of an alchemist. Yes, indeed, an alchemist. He liked the sound of that.

Halfway up the Sunset Hill, he had an intriguing thought. After pulling into the parking lot of a restaurant near the airport park-and-ride, he turned around and headed back the way he'd just come. Why he hadn't thought of it before was beyond him. It was perfect.

CHAPTER NINE

Circe always turned on the news in the morning. It was more background noise than anything she seriously watched. Even so, one story had her racing to the set: a quick blip about the vandalism of a cop's house. No name was mentioned though no name was necessary. The chill that raced through her body as she gazed at the television told her everything she needed to know. It wasn't just any cop's house; it was Diana's.

"Lisa," she said into the intercom system installed between the main floors of the house and the downstairs apartment.

"What's up?"

"Come up for a sec."

"On my way."

A minute later, Lisa was in the kitchen and, before Circe could say a word, was making herself a latte from Circe's espresso machine. "So, what's up?" she asked again, her attention focused on the stainless carafe filled with milk she was holding under the steamer arm of the machine.

"Did you catch the morning news at all?"

When Lisa shook her head without looking up from her espresso project, Circe continued. "Vandals hit Diana's house last night."

Lisa stopped steaming the carafe of milk and turned around. "Say what?"

"It was on the news. She came home to find her garage trashed. That's about all the news reported."

Setting the carafe down, Lisa said, "You should probably call her."

"You think?" She wanted to, badly. Was it the proper thing to do? After all, they really didn't know each other well. That didn't change how she felt. From the moment she met Diana she'd felt a draw to her like no one else she'd ever encountered. Calling her felt like the right thing to do, especially after Diana had made the effort to come all the way out here to give her the positive ID on Joanna. One good deed deserved another in return.

"Yes, I definitely think you should. She likes you, Circe. I could see it in her eyes, and you like her. That's what people do when they like each other." Lisa poured the steamed milk into two mugs, then picked up both and held one out to Circe.

She took the latte Lisa handed her and held it between her palms. It smelled wonderful and the warmth of the mug was reassuring. Lisa was telling her exactly what she wanted to hear. Always nice to have friends with good instincts.

She took a sip of the perfectly prepared drink and said, "Speaking of liking someone, I couldn't help but notice a little spark of something between you and detective tall, dark, and handsome."

Lisa's smile lit up her face. "He is definitely tall, dark, and handsome."

"You like him." She'd lived with Lisa long enough to be able to read her. Like Circe was drawn to Diana, Lisa was drawn to Paul.

For a second, Circe thought Lisa would deny it. Then she nodded slowly, her eyes intently studying the latte she held. "I do."

"But what?" The hesitation in her voice gave her away.

Lisa shrugged and frowned. "I don't know. I have the distinct feeling he's interested in me, but I'm sensing something of a shadow there too."

"Now you're starting to sound like me."

"Probably because I've lived with you for so long. You must be rubbing off on me."

Hopefully they only sounded alike. She wouldn't wish her little gift on anyone. Coming face to face with dead people every time she turned around was wearing on the soul. She couldn't ignore them, and often she couldn't help them. What she existed for were days like the last couple where she and Zelda truly made a difference.

"Probably," she mused. "Either that or we really are related and nobody ever told us."

The frown disappeared, replaced by a bright smile. "Nobody has to tell us anything. After everything you've done for me, you'll be my sister for life."

Circe put down her latte and hugged Lisa. "You'll always be one of the family."

Stepping back, Lisa looked at her and smiled. "I think we forego the call and just drive on into the police station. Don't you think an up-close and personal visit is appropriate under the circumstances? I think your lady cop could use a sympathetic friend right now."

Another reason she loved Lisa. The woman possessed a knack for knowing what was in Circe's heart and putting a voice to it. "Why yes, I think that's absolutely what we should do."

❖

Paul made the decision to come clean. After what had happened at Diana's house last night, it didn't feel right to hold back. She had a serious problem and so did he. Partners didn't hide things from each other. Not real partners anyway.

"Need to talk with you, D." He motioned his head in the direction of one of the small conference rooms. He might have decided to tell Diana, but that didn't mean he wanted his secret to be public knowledge. Sharing with a partner was one thing, blabbing to the entire department something altogether different.

She gave him a curious look. "Okay." Getting up from her desk, she followed him into the conference room. It made him love her all the more when he noticed she carried a file folder in one hand. Until he saw it in her hand he didn't think about how odd it might look if they were heading to a conference room without any case information. That was the kind of thing that would make talk buzz. By carrying a folder, any folder, she made it appear they were sitting down to discuss an open case. Once again, Diana rocked.

After they were both inside with the door firmly shut, he put his hands on the table and studied them for a long moment. His nails were trimmed and tidy, the hands of a guy who worked at a desk. He tapped his fingers and wondered where to start. Out at his desk it had all seemed simple and straightforward. Just blurt it out. Here, alone with Diana, it wasn't nearly as simple or straightforward. This was going to be harder than he thought. He finally looked up and met her eyes, and what he saw there gave him courage. "All right, here's the shit. You know I broke it off with Brenda."

"Of course."

"Well, I broke it off but she didn't."

"Meaning?"

"Meaning the crazy bitch is stalking me."

She wrinkled her forehead and studied his face. Not hard to follow her train of thought because it had all run through his mind when the nightmare first started. He could almost predict what she was about to say, and when she spoke, he wasn't wrong.

"Brenda? She seems so normal. Well, normal in the way-too-focused-on-her-looks way."

"Yeah, well, I'm telling you, she's gone off the deep end and I can't shake her. Every time I turn around there she is. I go to take the trash out and she's standing in my driveway with cookies. I stop at the grocery store and big coincidence. There she is *casually* shopping. Last night was the crowning glory. I got home from the crime scene out at Seven Mile and she was in my kitchen. She was in my fucking kitchen."

Diana blew out a long breath. "You got your house keys back from her, right?"

That was almost insulting. Of course he did and she should know that. In her defense, she was treating his problem with the same professionalism she brought to everything, and after the first flush of irritation at feeling like she was treating him like he was stupid, he appreciated it. "Did that when I had her move out, but little did I know the sneaky bitch made extra copies. I about had a coronary when I found out. Made her give me the one she used last night, and even though she said it was the only one she had left, I don't believe a word that comes out of her mouth. I'm telling you, Diana, she's bat-shit crazy. Got a guy coming out this morning to change all the locks and install a few more deadbolts."

Diana nodded as she studied him for what seemed like a really long time, and emotions he couldn't name played across her face. He had no idea what she was thinking, but something was definitely going on inside her head. Exactly what he had been trying to avoid all these months and exactly what he needed. Avoiding the truth hadn't done him any favors, and it was time to get help from the person he trusted the most. If anyone could figure out how to get rid of Brenda without anyone ending up in jail, it was Diana.

"Paul," she said slowly. "If Brenda really has slipped into the realm of stalker..."

"She has." There was no maybe about it despite the delusions he'd tried to embrace earlier. Along with his decision to come clean with Diana was the decision to be realistic about the situation with Brenda.

"Okay, she has, she is. What do you think the odds are she sees me as a rival for your attention and affections?"

"What?" That came out of left field. What did Diana have to do with Brenda stalking him?

"Me. Do you think she sees me as competition?"

Diana? No way. He'd never been anything besides professional with her. He loved her in many ways, but not in the way that would be important to Brenda. Even if things were different, he simply never would or could have a shot with her. Undeniably he wasn't her type, so the idea Brenda would perceive Diana as a threat was far-fetched.

Or was it? A rational person wouldn't perceive Diana as anything other than his partner and good friend. A person who'd ditched rational and embraced crazy was something altogether different. Suddenly the emotions that played across Diana's face made perfect sense, and a chill raced up his spine.

"I want to say no, but you and I both know you could be onto something. It's pretty coincidental your place gets trashed right after Brenda and I duke it out, verbally, that is. She's crazy enough to do something like that. You should have seen the way she chucked a tray of cheese and crackers across my kitchen and smashed a bowl of ice and beer on my tile floor. I'll be sweeping up shattered pieces of platter and beer bottles for months."

"What time did she leave your house?" She was obviously still working a scenario in her head.

"I don't know, wasn't looking at the clock. Too pissed off that she got into my house to begin with and even more pissed off at the mess I had to clean up." He shrugged. "Eight, maybe, give or take a few." Not checking the time was a rookie mistake. Just another sign of how out of sync he got when Brenda was around.

Diana pursed her lips and then said, "I didn't get back home until almost ten."

Shit. Now his problem was becoming Diana's. He sure didn't see this coming. All his grandiose ideas about keeping the Brenda problem to himself and finding his own solution just went up in smoke. "Plenty of time for her to do the damage at your place."

Diana screwed up her face. "Yes, except how did she get into my garage? I mean, I think we've established she's unbalanced enough to do it, but she'd still have to gain access somehow. I keep everything locked up tight."

He didn't have a quick answer on the how, but one thing he did know: Brenda was a sneaky bitch and one with money enough to get whatever she wanted. Though he'd asked her about its source on more than one occasion, she'd managed to avoid answering every time. Once she'd made a vague reference to a wealthy family, and maybe that was what set her up initially, but he was pretty sure she made as much or more herself. "Who knows. Diana. If she stole my key, why not one of yours too? Let's just say when she's motivated, she seems to find a way to do whatever she wants."

Diana was tapping a pen on the table, a telltale sign of her concentration. He'd seen her do that a hundred times as she worked through problems. "We need to explore this a little more. God knows I've pissed off more than my share of folks in this city and in reality it could be any one of them."

"Except you don't think so."

Slowly she shook her head. "No, I don't, and that's why we have to dig into this."

His heart sank as he realized how true her words were. He'd been going along fat, dumb, and happy, thinking Brenda was his problem alone. So wrapped up in his own troubles, he'd apparently missed the forest for the trees. "I think we have to. I don't believe in coincidence."

Her eyes were on his. "Neither do I."

❖

Diana walked out of the conference room, her mind whirling, and stopped. Sitting next to her desk was Circe. The sight made her heart tighten, and she had to work hard not to smile like a kid on her birthday. Good Lord, she was falling fast. It felt good. It felt wrong. She ignored wrong.

"Is there a problem?" Despite her happiness at seeing both Circe and Lisa at her desk, she didn't believe for a moment their visit was just to say hello. And, to her knowledge, no one else had contacted the sheriff's department to borrow Circe and Zelda for another search. So why were they sitting at her desk?

Circe stood and Diana's gaze swept over her. She looked fantastic in jeans, a figure-hugging blue shirt, and red kicks. Why couldn't it be five o'clock on a Friday night so they could leave here together for a night on the town? How much fun would it be to go dancing with her in that outfit?

Circe was shaking her head as she took one of Diana's hands. Like before, the shock on contact was amazing. Amazingly good that is. "I heard what happened at your house last night."

Diana didn't get it. The news vans had showed up right after the investigation crew, but no way would her name have been mentioned. No reporter worth their salt would have dared put her name out there if they wanted to keep on good terms with one of the city's best detectives. "How did you know it was me?"

Circe shrugged, her expression open. "I just knew. Can't explain it."

"You didn't hear it on the news?"

"Oh God, no. I heard about the break-in and I knew it here." She touched her chest.

"She does that kind of thing all the time," Lisa added. "She has that weird sixth-sense thing. A bit on the creepy side at first, and then you get used to it after a while."

Diana noticed that Lisa's eyes were on Paul as she spoke, and Diana almost smiled. Had Paul noticed? Not quite yet. Interesting development.

"Are you okay?" Circe asked. "That had to be frightening." The genuine concern in her eyes touched Diana.

When was the last time a woman besides the women in her family or her good friends had really worried about her? She couldn't even remember, it had been so long. Sad story on her part though exciting now to think someone would reach out to her like this. It felt really nice, and for just a moment she was going to let it warm her. It suddenly didn't matter how Circe knew she was the victim; it only mattered that she'd come to her.

"I'm fine, though I opted to stay at my dad's place last night."

Something like relief played across Circe's face. "I'm so glad to hear that. When I saw that news report all I could think about was you in your house alone. If I'd known last night, Zelda and I would have tracked you down to make sure you were okay."

Wow was all she could think. Even when she was out there dating, no one ever stood up for her like that. She was the big tough cop who looked out for everyone, and suddenly here was someone looking out for her. Circe was special, and it wasn't just her hormones talking. If she was this kind so soon after they met, what would she be like later? She wanted to find out.

"I appreciate your kind thoughts. I was safe and I will be safe."

As Circe studied her face, Diana wondered what she was searching for. Was this what subjects felt like when she sat across from them in interrogation? Well, maybe not quite like this because Circe's scrutiny made her feel warm, and she was pretty sure that wasn't the vibe she gave off when questioning people, innocent or guilty. Whatever Circe searched for, when a tiny smile turned up the corners of her lips, Diana was pretty sure she was satisfied by what she saw in her face. She dropped Diana's hand and got up from the chair by her desk. As she stepped away, she said, "I was going to call, but Lisa thought we should come down and see if we could do anything. This is much better than calling, particularly as it somehow feels like my fault."

That stopped her. For a brief second she watched Circe walk away, before she started to follow Circe's retreat. "Your fault? Why on earth would you feel like that? The vandalism at my house had nothing to do with you."

Circe stopped, put her hands in her pockets, and looked down. "I disagree. You made a special trip out to my house, and if you'd simply called me, you would have been at home and it wouldn't have happened. No one would have been stupid enough to trash your garage if you'd been there."

Diana thought about the conversation with Paul. Given what he'd told her, Circe's theory was only partially right. It might not have happened, or it could have been much worse if, in fact, Brenda had trashed her garage. If she'd do that in her misguided quest to secure Paul's love, what would she have done if they'd come face-to-face?

This time Diana shook her head. "It had absolutely nothing to do with you, Circe, I promise. We might have a lead, although I can't really say too much more at the moment."

Relief showed in Circe's face as she looked up to meet Diana's eyes. "I still feel responsible."

She hated that this beautiful woman believed she was responsible for last night's violation of her home. "You're not. Our lead is a million miles away from you and no one you'd have any reason to know."

"You're sure?"

"Positive."

"All right. You're the professional and I trust your judgment." With a nod, she started toward the door again before stopping once more. "You will stay at your dad's until you know for certain though, right? I hate to think of you there alone, even though you are a big-time detective."

She smiled. "Absolutely. Dad would have a coronary if I went back home before we arrest the ass who broke into my garage."

Circe's smile made her eyes light up. "That's good. It means I won't have to worry about you."

"No, you don't. I'll be just fine."

"Oh, I know, and I know one other thing."

"And that is?"

"You'll get her."

As Circe spoke, she caught movement out of the corner of her eye. As her gaze shifted to the doorway, two questions hit her all at once. How did Brenda get into the squad room, and why did Circe say they would get *her*?

CHAPTER TEN

Fucking A. It didn't seem to matter what he did. Paul couldn't catch a goddamn break. When he'd first walked out of the conference room and saw Lisa at Diana's desk with Circe, he thought his whole day was starting off on a great note. He felt good about coming clean with Diana. He felt even better seeing Lisa. It was the first real burst of optimism he'd experienced in months.

Now it was all blown to hell in the space of a few seconds. Whatever dumb-ass let Brenda up here was going to be sorry. He would personally see to that. He put a hand on Lisa's shoulder and spoke quietly in her ear. "Sorry, love, give me a second."

He tried not to let the fury show on his face or in his body as he crossed the room and stopped Brenda from getting any closer to his desk or the three women behind him. As she always did, Brenda looked great. Wearing slim black slacks that showed off her long legs, a flowing blue shirt, and with her hair cascading down her back in golden waves, she had every guy in the place staring at her. The hotness factor probably played into how she was allowed upstairs without checking with him first. One lesson he'd learned the hard way—she was a master manipulator. She was so smooth, she'd get her way before the unsuspecting even realized they'd been had. He'd be sure to clue them all in later.

"Hey," she said, smiling as if their conversation last night never happened. Or the shattered platter or the key launched in his face. Or Diana's trashed garage.

Without pausing, he took her arm in a firm grip and turned her back toward the door, knowing he held her too tight. Leaving marks on her arm wasn't a good idea. Neither was having her linger in his office. "What are you doing here," he spat close to her ear.

"Came to see you, silly." Her smile was wide and made her look even prettier. That is if one didn't see the brittle craziness beneath it.

"Brenda, what part of *get lost* did you not understand from last night?"

"You are so funny." She laughed and leaned into him, apparently oblivious to the death grip on her elbow. "I understand how tired you were last night and how my timing wasn't the best. After I left I realized that once you got a good night's sleep, everything would be better. All is forgiven. So, here I am."

"For what?" By now he'd pushed them both through the front doors of the PSB and they stood outside in the bright sunshine. Somehow in the daylight some of the superficial beauty was wiped away and what he saw in her face chilled him. God, how did he get himself into this fucking mess? "What do you want from me?"

The look on her face shifted to one of pure confusion. She touched his cheek with one finger. "I don't understand your question."

He kept his voice low as he jerked his face away from her. He didn't want to make any more of a scene than he had already by propelling her like a train out of the PSB, and he didn't want her touching him. "It's simple. I made a mistake when I thought you and I could be together. A huge mistake. We can't be together. Not now. Not ever."

The same darkness he'd witnessed last night flowed over her again in a fraction of a second, the speed of the change chilling. Any lingering prettiness vanished. "It's that woman, isn't it?"

"There's no woman," he said, letting the weariness she caused him to echo in his voice. Anger didn't get through to her. Rational reasoning didn't either. Nothing seemed to penetrate the shell of her insanity.

"I saw you touching her, whispering in her ear. Whore."

His reserve snapped and anger roared back in with a fury that frightened him. He didn't dare lose control. Not here, not now. "Stop it, Brenda. Stop all this crap. It's not her. Not any woman. It's you I can't stand. You get me? You!"

There, he'd said it and managed to keep control. It took everything he had not to explode. Truthfully, he didn't know how much clearer he could make it. She was the problem, the whole damn problem, and he wanted her out of his life once and for all. He'd already paid plenty for this mistake.

Color rose in her cheeks, and her eyes narrowed like those of a cat ready to strike. Her voice was low and full of menace. "You'll be sorry, Paul. You'll be really sorry."

He still held her arm tight and pulled her closer. "Trust me, sweetheart, I'm already sorry. I know what you did, Brenda, and I'll prove it. You hear me? You're going to end up in jail, I promise. Now leave me and my friends the fuck alone."

She yanked her arm away and stepped back. Her charming smile was back on her face, all bright and full of sunshine. "You screwed the wrong girl, Paulie. You can't and won't prove anything against me, and I am not going to jail, yours or anyone else's. *Capisci*? You're the one who needs to watch his back."

❖

When he walked in, he was surprised to see the jar sitting on the kitchen counter. He wasn't surprised to see the dirty coffee cup sitting there too. Once again she thought only of herself. She needed coffee, made it for herself, and then left the mess. She knew how much he hated messes, but that never stopped her. He suspected she took perverse joy in getting on his nerves. Correction, he didn't suspect. He knew. Nothing was off limits if it was going to piss him off.

The jar, almost glowing on the counter, was obviously a gift from Eve. She was forever doing things like that for him. Some days he was so tired it was hard to work up enough energy to even get out of bed. On those difficult days, it wasn't unusual to find special gifts left for him on the counter by the ever-thoughtful Eve. She was not only smart and rational, but she was also kind, and that was a pleasant change. She seemed to have a sixth sense about when he needed encouragement.

Now, he picked up the jar and turned it around in his hands. The light coming through the kitchen window made the reddish liquid almost glow. For a second he wasn't sure what it was and then he knew. He smiled.

While he slept, Eve had obviously been up in his attic office reading through the *De Nigromancia*. Funny, he didn't even know she could read Latin. Like him, she must have attended Catholic school. What other type of school shoved Latin down the throats of the pupils? One of these days, he would have to ask her about her experiences. They could compare notes. Or would that be horror stories?

For the moment, he was happy to hold her precious gift in his hands. How had she known this was the exact potion he was planning to make today? No need to follow through on the question. She always seemed to know what was going on with him. It was a little bit like she was psychic—just one more thing that made her supremely cool in his eyes. The fact she always had his back comforted him. Nobody else did.

But would it work? He laughed. Of course it would. The combined effort between him and Eve was at genius level. How could it not be perfect? The text hadn't steered him wrong yet, and he didn't believe it would with this one either.

It would be incredible if he could use it right now, but the time wasn't quite right. Soon enough all the pieces would be in place. Then, and only then, would he use it. Everything would be his once he put his plan into motion.

"Thank you, my darling Eve," he said to the empty kitchen.

He opened the refrigerator and put the jar inside. Maybe it would be fine sitting on the counter, but he didn't want to take any chances, given the precious nature of the ingredients. It would be just like her to blow through and, in her frenzy of movement, knock the jar to the floor. She'd look at it, laugh, and walk away. Potion ruined, mess left, and not a shred of remorse. No, he refused to take any chances with Eve's thoughtful gift. Best to put it out of the path of danger.

Inside the sterile refrigerator with the mostly empty shelves, the small jar seemed to glimmer. The sight made him smile even more widely. The magic inside the jar was hard to miss. It was a sign if he'd ever seen one. All the years of standing on the sidelines were about to end. He was on the path to true greatness.

Oh yes, soon everything would be his.

❖

After Lisa and Circe left, and Paul had sent Brenda on her way, Diana dragged a reluctant Paul out of the station and over to her car. He'd come back in from his confrontation with Brenda wearing an expression as dark as she'd ever seen on his face. It didn't bode well. He was typically a really steady guy, and she sensed his control slipping. "Come on."

"Where are we going?" He followed, though not exactly enthusiastically. It appeared he preferred to sit at his desk and simmer. They were going to have to do something about Brenda and fast. She didn't want this situation to get out of hand, and the way it was looking, that wasn't far away. Whatever it took, she'd keep her partner out of trouble.

"We're going to my house."

"Why?"

Talk about sounding like a little kid who was pissed off about not getting his way. This was worse than she thought, and they needed to solve this quickly.

"You'll see. Now get in the car."

The idea had occurred to her earlier, and it seemed like the best way to keep Paul's stalker problem on the down-low. She realized what it cost him to come to her about Brenda, and he'd hate for his problem to become common knowledge. She could think of one way to solve the problem and keep it close to the vest. When she got to her house, Will's car was already parked at the curb.

"Really?" Paul grumbled when he noticed the dark-blue sedan. "You called your uncle? Again?"

Expecting this reaction, she was ready to deflect. "I did. Come on, Paul. This is a good way to start if you want to keep this situation unofficial. Let Will do his magic, and if we can't solve your problem this way, we'll have to bring in the cavalry. You know he's good at what he does. He was exceptional on the force and he's just as good as a PI."

He stared out the window at Will's car. "Yeah, he is. Doesn't mean I have to like it. I don't need a damn babysitter."

"But you know I'm right."

"Yeah, yeah, yeah. Might as well call in Maddie too."

She glanced at him out of the corner of her eye. He wasn't going to be happy. "Already called her."

"Oh, for Christ's sake. Will and Maddie? I don't know about them working together. It'll be like mixing water and oil."

"They'll be fine."

Maddie, a retired professor from Eastern Washington University, was Paul's godmother. Tall, tough, and out-spoken, Maddie was a world-class computer researcher who through the years had done a fair amount of consulting work with federal law enforcement. The way Diana saw it, putting Maddie and Will together on this made perfect sense. If anyone could get to the bottom of the Brenda problem it was those two.

Before Paul could get out of the car, Maddie drove up and parked behind them in the driveway. She got out looking as relaxed and genial as ever. In jeans, an EWU sweatshirt, and hiking boots, she looked like a typical retired woman. Underneath the casual appearance was a beautiful mind with mad computer skills.

"Hey, Will," Maddie said in her boisterous voice. "Long time no see."

"You two know each other?" Diana looked from Will to Maddie.

"Oh, hell yeah," Maddie said. "Spokane's a small town really. Didn't matter if you were SPD, sheriff's department, FBI, or any other agency with a bunch of letters. I got to know them all. Willie here was one of the good guys, although I don't like to say that out loud. Gives him a big head and all."

"Still am a good one," Will said with a wink.

"Too bad," Maddie said, winking back. "I like my guys a little bad."

Really, they were flirting? Maddie and Will? "Guys, we have an issue we need help with."

Maddie inclined her head toward Paul. "Diana says our little boy has run into a little trouble."

"First," Paul barked, "I'm not your little boy, and second, I don't have a little dilemma. I have a big fucking problem. Brenda."

Will put his hands in his pockets and asked, "The gal you lived with for a few months?"

"Yeah, that's her. Biggest fucking mistake of my life."

Diana raised a single eyebrow and said soberly, "I have to agree with him. I think this Brenda is turning into a serious predicament, and hopefully you two can help. It's just a hunch, but I think she may also have been the one who trashed my garage."

Maddie cocked her head. "Why would this woman come after you? It's not like you're a threat to her."

"No, I'm not, at least not to a rational person. But remember, guys. I don't think we're dealing with rational here. She's stalking Paul, and people who have it together do not stalk. In her head, just the fact that I'm a woman and I'm Paul's partner may be enough for her to perceive me as a threat."

Will was making notes. "Diana's right. I've seen it happen before. These folks don't think like the rest of us, and she could fixate on Diana as being the reason Paul's not interested in her. If she does come to that conclusion, or already has, Diana could be in real danger. This could escalate in a hurry."

That thought had already occurred to her too. Initially the vandalism of her garage had just pissed her off. Then as Paul related what had been going on in his life, her thoughts about the threat level had shifted. While she'd never personally handled a stalker case, her dad had, and sadly it had ended badly. At the time she'd been in college, and even now she could still see the shadows that haunted her dad for months afterward. Whatever it took, this was not going to be a repeat performance.

"Okay." Paul jumped in and all his former irritation seemed to be gone. She was relieved to see it. They were going to need him clear-headed and thinking like a cop. "Can you two check it out, see what you come up with, and maybe find a solution, because I'd really rather this not go beyond us."

Will put a hand on his shoulder. "All kidding aside, Paulie, this is serious. These people can be dangerous. They're like the Energizer bunny. They keep going and going and going."

Paul shook his head. "I know that's true some of the time, but I don't see Brenda like that. She's a little crazy, and she's definitely narcissistic, but she wouldn't hurt me or anyone else. That's just not in her. I may have looked past the crazy part of her personality, but I wasn't so far gone I'd have missed a violent streak."

Diana wanted to believe that was true, but she didn't. Paul undoubtedly bought in because he was in denial. Who could blame him? She couldn't image how it would feel to discover the person you thought you loved was someone else entirely. Love might be a stretch in that relationship, although certainly he'd believed he was in "like" when he invited her to move into this house. Throw in his profession as a police officer and he was certain to think he should have known better. Why did cops always think it wouldn't happen to them?

At this point, Diana didn't have a problem bursting his bubble. He needed to be present in the real world. "You don't really know what she's capable of, Paul. You think you know her, but you didn't see this coming. What else are you blinded to?"

His shoulders slumped. Her mark had hit home. "You're right. I didn't see it, and who knows what else she's capable of. Come on, Will, Maddie. Take a look at Diana's garage. It'll give you an idea of what I'm dealing with."

Will stood outside the open door and surveyed the chaos. He whistled and then turned to look at Paul. "You're screwed, buddy."

Chapter Eleven

Circe was late for the Sunday-morning run, and everyone else was already on the course. Normally she popped right up when the alarm went off. This morning, she turned off the alarm and went back to sleep, unusually weary. Fortunately she woke up with enough time left to be only a few minutes late, though tardy enough that her friends had started ahead of her. These Sunday mornings were important to her and she hated missing any of them. She enjoyed the camaraderie as much as the physical exercise.

Today her weekly group of running buddies had decided to start from a great downtown bakery and follow the seven-and-a-half-mile course of the annual Bloomsday run. One of the largest road races in the country, Bloomsday was a Spokane jewel, and her group liked to practice on the course now and again. Especially this time of year as the race was only about a month away.

She parked the car in one of the diagonal parking spots at the side of the bakery and then popped the back for Zelda. She loved coming along not just for the joy of racing along the city streets but to see the rest of Circe's friends. Circe had the sense Zelda believed each and every one of them came to see her and the run was secondary.

Because they were in an urban area, Circe clipped the lead on Zelda's collar, even though she knew how much she hated it. Zelda was reliable off lead, and a simple *come* was all it took to get her to comply. Still, this area had too many busy roads and too many people who were potentially frightened of big dogs. Zelda didn't protest, just gave her a disgruntled look before they settled into their easy run.

From the coffee shop they headed west on Riverside. The road tapered down before heading back up a gentle slope toward Government Way. Both she and Zelda paused at the bottom of the Riverside hill and glanced right toward the Sandifur Bridge. It would be a long time before either of them could go by here and not think about the three bodies recovered just a few days ago. She hated the killer for taking something so beautiful and tarnishing it. It was an unfortunate by-product of both her gift and what she and Zelda did.

From Government Way they ran north. It was a pretty stretch, bordered on both sides of the road by cemeteries. Some might think that made the course morbid. She didn't. To her it was beautiful and peaceful. The grass was meticulously maintained, and fountains, stone entries, and blooming flowers dressed up the place. Despite her unique ability, she knew that the dead rested peacefully here and she could run by like any other normal person.

Until today.

Circe saw her at the same moment Zelda's ears snapped and her body went rigid. Zelda stopped running and tugged at the lead.

"Oh crap," she muttered as she also stopped and leaned down to unclip the lead from Zelda's collar. Quietly she whispered in her ear, even though no one else was nearby.

The moment Zelda heard the one-word command, she raced around the wrought-iron fence on the east side of the road, her nose close to the ground. Once around the tall fence she followed it north again for about a hundred meters. The woman stood just beside where Zelda alerted.

"Good girl." Circe, who'd been running behind her, stopped and reached down to rub her ears. Then she took her cell phone out of the pocket of her hydration belt. She wanted to call Diana but opted for regular protocol and instead called Brian.

When he answered, she said, "Houston, we have a problem."

❖

Paul was grateful for the call. It took the focus off him and onto something more important. Will had been on the phone asking a thousand questions, which sent his anxiety level sky-high. After his initial apprehension about bringing in Maddie and Will, he'd realized Diana had made a good decision. They were the perfect people to check out things before he took the official route. He needed their unique skill set.

If they could make Brenda see things his way and just go away, all the better. At the same time, having to dredge everything up for Will was pretty uncomfortable, even if they'd once shared everything. Spending as much time together as they had in those early days had brought them close. Some partners hated each other and tolerated each other only long enough to do the job. He and Will had genuinely liked each other, even if Paul always felt like he was working with a perpetual teacher waiting to grade his work and got pretty pissy about it.

He knew that was why he got ticked off when Diana had brought Will along like she'd done out at Seven Mile. It was like he'd flunked a class and the tutor had to come in to bring him back up to speed. It wasn't what Diana was doing; it just felt that way. His reaction had been childish and he owed her an apology. Probably Will too.

Now, when Will was doing everything he could to help him, Paul had to let go of his feelings of inadequacy. That's not what any of this was about. He could do it too, even if he wasn't quite ready to go so far as to apologize.

Even so, when he had to cut Will off so he could leave to meet Diana at the cemetery, the timing couldn't have been better. He was ready to give it a break. Besides, over the last couple of days, he hadn't seen or heard from Brenda. Maybe the worst was over and he didn't need to waste Will or Maddie's time. Maybe it was the light of the very dark tunnel.

Police presence was in full force by the time he pulled up at the cemetery. Diana's car was there and he could see Brian talking with Circe. Frankly, he was surprised to see her here. Diana hadn't mentioned they'd called in the K9 team. Then he noticed what she was wearing: running tights, running shoes, and a black and yellow hydration belt. She certainly hadn't come out to search in that get-up. So, what the hell had happened here?

"Brian, Circe," he said when he walked up to them. "What have we got?"

Circe didn't answer and instead deferred to Brian. "We have murder...again."

The techs were already at work uncovering what appeared to be a tarp. Diana was standing behind the techs watching intently as they worked. He had a very real sense of déjà vu. Didn't they just uncover another scene like this less than half a mile away? Only this time someone had a really warped sense of humor by burying the body on the fringe of a popular cemetery. That was fucked up.

Circe looked tired even though it was barely nine. "We were out for a run when we found this." She waved her hand toward the makeshift grave. "What a way to mess up a perfectly good morning."

"I'm sorry," he said as put a hand on her shoulder. He noticed that Zelda eyed him as he touched her but apparently decided he was no risk.

"Circe?"

He whirled at the sound of Lisa's voice. She came hurrying toward them with a patrol officer at her heels. "She said you were waiting for her?" the officer said in a rush as he tried to keep up. His cheeks were red and he was breathing hard.

"Thanks, Steve," Brian said to the young man. "We got her."

Relief washed across the policeman's face. "You sure?"

Brian. "Yeah, it's all good.

The young uniformed man pivoted and returned to his post on the tape line.

"Thanks for coming," Circe said. "I appreciate you taking Zelda home."

Lisa gave her a tentative smile and put an arm around her shoulders. "You know it's no problem. I'm happy to help. I'm just sorry this happened to you. Are you sure you don't want me to stay with you?"

Circe shook her head. "No. I'll be out of here before too long. I just didn't want to keep Zelda here if I didn't have to." She handed Lisa Zelda's lead.

Paul couldn't believe how excited and happy he was to see Lisa, even though they were at a very unexpected crime scene. Something was wrong with him.

"I'll walk you back to your car," he offered when Lisa turned to leave.

"You don't have to." She was holding Zelda's lead and biting her bottom lip. This obviously wasn't the kind of scene she was comfortable in. Not many people were.

So yeah, he did have to walk her to the car. "I know. I want to. I'll keep the looky-lous away from you. Trust me, the second they realize you were allowed beyond the tape, they'll hit you hard to try and find out anything they can. They can be relentless too. With me by your side, they'll leave you alone."

She nodded and relief softened the lines in her face. "Thanks."

He put a hand on her lower back as he guided her through the mass of officers, tech staff, and on-lookers. His hand felt natural there. A couple of the loitering press started their way, but he cut them off with a look and they had the good sense to back off. Too bad that look didn't have the same effect on Brenda.

Her car was parked at the end of a line of patrol cars, and Zelda jumped into the back when Lisa opened the door. She circled once and lay down, obviously very comfortable. He held open the driver's door for Lisa. She got in and buckled her seat belt.

With an arm on the roof, he leaned in through the open door. "Will you be okay?"

She looked pale and shaken. Though she lived with a team that routinely went out on human-remains detection searches, her body language showed her discomfort with this type of situation. If she could be anywhere else, she would be.

Lisa nodded and gave him a small smile. "I'll be fine once we're away from here. This," she waved a hand in the direction of where Brian, Diana, and Circe stood talking, "is a little much for me."

It would be a lot for anyone to take. The fact she didn't hesitate and came for her friend said a great deal about the kind of person she was. Her selflessness spoke to him and drew him closer. He wanted to know so much more about her. He wanted to know everything about her.

"Can I call you?" he said before his mind had a chance to engage. The second the words were out of his mouth, he inwardly cringed. Only an ass would ask something like that at a time like this. Yeah, he was some kind of ass all right, and truthfully, he wasn't sorry. She was a special woman and he had to spend more time with her.

Without hesitating she held out her hand, her expression serious and her eyes bright. "Give me your phone."

He didn't pause to consider whether it was a good idea. Instead, he quickly pulled his phone out of his pocket and put it in her palm. With her head down, she nimbly punched in her number and then handed it back to him.

"Call me anytime." She flashed him a quick smile. Her face was still pale, but that tiny smile sent warmth coursing through him.

Again, without giving himself enough time to think about it, he leaned in and kissed her on the cheek. "Count on it," he whispered into her ear. Then he closed the car door and motioned for the officers manning the barricades to let her through.

Seriously? They'd found her? How in the bloody hell did that happen? No way should she have been discovered, yet there they all were with their yellow tape, crime-scene techs, and big brass who thought it would give them good press if they were to be seen here. One big damn sideshow.

Jesus, it pissed him off. He didn't like his work disturbed, and he didn't like local law enforcement getting too geared up. That was bad. Too much scrutiny, which made it more difficult to tidy things up after a night of hard work.

He was close to having everything he needed, particularly after the beautiful gift from Eve. The thoughtfulness she'd displayed in preparing that for him put him way ahead. The way he calculated it, give him a week, two, tops, and he'd be ready. Between the spell and the potions created from the sacrifices of the women who came to his special room, he would be free for the first time in his life.

That is if everything else stayed in line. The cops had to stop finding his women. In the big picture, he didn't worry about their being dug up. He didn't like it much and would prefer they stay where he put them. No, it was more about the spotlight issue and that he needed to be unobtrusive. Once he was done, for all he cared they could dig up each and every one. New and old. Of course, he doubted they would find any of the first ones, and even if they did, they'd play hell connecting them to him.

She was his other problem. Lately she was more moody than usual, and when she got this way, she could be a giant pain in his ass. If he could get rid of her, he would. It wasn't that simple and never had been, and so he was stuck with trying to soothe her ruffled feathers in an attempt to keep her content. When she was happy, everyone was happy. As soon as he completed his task and put the magic in the book to good use, he could cut her loose and be by himself once and for all. He could hardly wait for the day.

In the meantime, he would just have to be patient and stay the course. He could keep an eye on things and then simply be extra careful. No harm, no foul.

The tall officer he'd seen in Peaceful Valley days before was walking a pretty woman and the dog, the damn dog, to a sedan parked at the back of a line of police cars. Why it bothered him the man was walking so close to the woman, he couldn't imagine. Yet it did. An uncomfortable feeling washed over him as he saw the man kiss the woman. Everything in him screamed *danger*. Didn't make sense and yet the feeling refused to be pushed aside.

Shifting from foot to foot, he swept his gaze across the group of people surrounding him. It was easy to stand here and blend in with the crowd of onlookers. No one paid any particular attention to him. He should just stay here and not draw any unwanted attention to himself.

He couldn't. Trouble whispered in the light breeze that blew through the trees. The scent of something rotten was wafting through the air. Unease turned to fear. Trying not to be conspicuous he meandered away from the crowd and toward his own car parked at the church up the road from where the crowd gathered. Once out of sight of law enforcement, he ran and jumped into his car. He spied the little sedan as it sped by the church and had it in his view a minute later. Pressing the accelerator, he smiled. A few minutes ago everything felt wrong, and now everything felt right.

CHAPTER TWELVE

Circe's heart ached for the young woman whose body they pulled from the shallow grave. Wrapped in a tarp, she was buried about four feet down. Someone had done a respectable job of concealing her location, especially considering how close to the road they had placed her. The grass had been replaced so carefully, a casual observer would have never noticed the spot for the grave it really was.

The beautiful wrought-iron fence probably made the difference. The ivy crawling up the six-foot fence would have hidden someone from the glancing view of a passing vehicle. And, if the culprit had timed it right, there would be little to no traffic on the road at all. Plenty of time to do the deed and be gone before the daylight made an appearance. Someone had thought this through with an eye toward every detail. Sad, really, that a person would spend such time and energy on an endeavor so evil.

Like the three from Peaceful Valley, this woman was pretty yet carried an aura of sadness that made Circe wish she could do more than simply take her home. She longed to give her peace as well and knew she was powerless to do that.

The sun had moved across the sky and was now high overhead. It warmed her face, and she wished it could warm the ice in her heart. The police no longer needed her to stay. All their questions had been asked and answered. She could have left hours ago and chose not to. Instead, she made her way to the basalt-rock wishing well just inside the cemetery entrance. It was large and beautiful, with a three-foot ledge surrounding the water and flowers blooming all around. Sitting on the ledge, she watched and waited.

It was well past lunchtime when Diana came over and sat down next to her. "I'm so sorry this had to happen to you."

So was she, although she suspected they were thinking of two different things. Circe just wanted to be able to go for an innocent eight-mile run and experience nothing more than tight muscles and heavy breathing. What Diana didn't realize was that every time she went for a run, or anywhere else for that matter, she always ran the risk of locating the dead. They were always there waiting for her, often in places she believed were safe. That was really a misguided belief because of one thing she'd learned: there was no safe place when it came to seeing the dead.

She ran her hands through her hair and looked off over the acres of manicured grass. All was quiet, at least for now. Her work, for the moment, was done. "Better me than someone without the proper training." More training than Diana could ever imagine.

Diana nodded. "You have a very valid point. Still, it sucks to have a beautiful morning ruined by death. You were probably looking forward to a nice, peaceful run, not hours filled with this." She waved a hand toward the spot where a few officers still remained. The young woman's body was gone, as were most of the techs. Workers from the cemetery were there with their own equipment, putting the patch of land back to its former grassy expanse. It didn't take away any of the sadness the discovery filled her with.

How many of her beautiful mornings had been ruined by death over the years? More than she could count, and a lot more than she was ever able to tell anyone. Somewhere, sometime, she was going to find that special person she could share her secret with. Beyond Vickie, that is. Vickie was her best friend, bar none, and without her Circe would have been committed years ago.

Even with that kind of friendship, she longed for more. No one she'd met so far had been able to fill the place in her heart that always felt empty, and maybe it was because so far she hadn't met anyone she trusted enough to share her secret. It wasn't that love completely eluded her.

On the contrary, she'd fallen in love a time or two, and she took full responsibility for the demise of those relationships. Loving passionately was one thing. Loving unconditionally was another. The fault was hers. She hadn't found the courage to step across that line...yet. It would be nice to be able to look across a pillow at someone and share the truth.

She took one of Diana's hands. "I love my Sunday runs and was looking forward to tackling the Bloomsday course this morning. Finding the body of a young woman was the last thing on my mind. It is sad, but you know it would be even sadder if she was left there without anyone ever knowing what happened. She needed to be found, and Zelda and I were the ones who needed to find her. Funny how the universe works sometimes."

Diana's fingers curled around hers and squeezed. "I love the way you take a worst-case scenario and turn it positive. Not very many people can do that."

Circe shrugged. "I've had a fair amount of experience."

"I think you're more than just your experiences." Diana turned Circe's hand over in hers and stroked her palm with her thumb. Her head was down as she spoke. "Circe, this going to sound odd given where we are and most likely really inappropriate..."

Circe's heart sang a little at the stumbling words. She sensed where this was going, and it shoved away the gloom of the morning's discovery. "I like you too."

Diana's head snapped up and her eyes met Circe's. "Really?"

"Yes, really." Diana's eyes reflected everything she'd been feeling, which made her heart sing.

Maybe she'd underestimated this day. Maybe it was going to turn into a really good one after all.

One thing about this Sunday, it went by fast. Paul was so focused after Lisa left, everything flew by with incredible speed.

Diana seemed to be in the same mode, and they worked side by side for hours, exchanging only a few words. Another one of the reasons their partnership worked so well.

Everyone believed the same person had killed all the women they'd discovered recently. The medical examiner and the forensics would have to confirm that theory, but a room full of cops all with the same gut instinct said a lot. Four victims discovered in less than a week. As much as Paul hated to admit it, from all appearances, they had another serial killer in the area.

That thought made him sad. The city had never fully recovered from the reign of Robert Yates and would never be quite the same. So many lives were lost and trust in law enforcement shaken at its very foundation. If this got out of hand…he didn't want to consider the ramifications. This was a great city, in a great state, and it didn't deserve to be plagued by the kind of evil that created killers this heinous.

Rather than focusing on the negative, he opted to focus on solving this string of murders. They would stop this bastard before anyone else lost their life. He refused to allow another serial killer to make Spokane his playground. When he came into law enforcement he took an oath to serve and protect, and by God, that's exactly what he planned to do. It was important to him that his family, friends, and neighbors trust in him and in those he worked with. Stopping this killer quickly would go a long way toward earning that trust.

Diana was the first one to call it a night. She stood, stretched her arms over her head, and sighed. "Time to quit for the day," she said to him. "My brain's fried. The body's willing but the brain isn't."

Paul pushed back in his chair and put his arms behind his head. As he rolled his head from side to side he was dismayed by the snaps that testified to how long he'd had his head bent toward the computer. "With you on that one, D. I'm pretty sure my eyes are bleeding from staring at this screen for so long."

She took a drink from the coffee mug she picked up off her desk and made a face. Putting it back down, she said, "We need fully firing synapses for this."

"You know they'll create a task force." He could see the handwriting on the wall. Oh, they'd be part of the multi-jurisdictional task force, of course. But they would most certainly not be leading it. The job would go to someone with much higher political aspirations than either he or Diana possessed. It was the American way.

Her tired eyes looked even more tired. "I give them twenty-four hours."

"Sucker's bet."

"Come on." She grabbed her jacket off the back of her chair. "Let's get the hell out of here. At this point, we're not doing anything helpful."

She was right. At some point fatigue takes a toll on the body and the work. A few hours of shut-eye would do wonders. As much as he'd loved to stay here and power through, his body was screaming for him to rest. "Meet you back here first thing in the morning."

He was just getting up to join her when his cell phone rang. Diana kept walking toward the door. She waved and said, "See you tomorrow."

The name displayed surprised him. "Will?"

"Hey, man, we need to talk about your girlfriend."

For the last couple of days, they hadn't had any Brenda sightings, and he was beginning to think maybe he and Diana had overreacted. Maybe she wasn't stalking him and didn't trash Diana's garage. When he'd gotten the call out this morning and had to cut Will's inquisition short, he was really hoping he was right. Brenda had finally gotten the message and was moving on. The confrontation outside the PSB had finally done the trick. The tone in Will's voice seemed to counter those beliefs.

"She's not my girlfriend," he snapped, even though he knew Will was baiting him. His former partner and mentor was trying to help, and he needed to keep that in mind. Easier to do when he wasn't bone-weary.

"Whatever." Will, as always, took his moodiness in stride. "I have to say, pal, I'm not surprised you got suckered by her looks. She's one beautiful woman. I am surprised, however, that you didn't do your homework before you moved her in. You're slipping, buddy. See what happens when I'm not there to watch your six."

He didn't need a lecture, especially tonight. With four murdered women on his plate and a potential stalker on the home front, a come-to-Jesus talk from his former partner wasn't on the agenda. Just the facts, that's all he wanted.

He managed to keep his irritation in check. Either that or he was finally learning to be more like Will and take things in stride. "Will, I'm dead tired and want to go home so what is it?"

"Oh, man, like I said, you messed this one up big-time. Me and Maddie have come across some real interesting shit on your little woman."

His newly found easy-going nature wasn't holding. Will was getting on his last good nerve. "Fine, you win, I screwed up. Care to explain how?"

"Be delighted. Did you know your little gal pal spent some serious time in a mental institution?"

❖

Circe stood next to Lisa and simply stared at the broken front window in her house. Thanks to a thunderstorm that had rolled through about an hour ago, not only was her beautiful big bay window shattered, but her carpet was filled with glass shards and was also soaking wet. It was the kind of mess that made her want to cry.

"I swear to God, Circe, I was gone maybe twenty minutes. I ran over to Rosauers to pick up some kale and came right back. When I got back the window was smashed and the lock cut off the back gate."

Circe cut her gaze to the side gate that was now closed, but a broken padlock was hanging from the latch. They always kept the walk gates locked for safety reasons. That and the fact that Zelda was a really smart dog who figured out how to unlatch the gates so she could go on unguided walkabouts.

Today Zelda must have decided this wasn't the time to tour the neighborhood because, according to Lisa, she was sitting on the front porch when Lisa pulled into the driveway. Now Zelda was leaning against Circe's legs.

"Who on earth would do something like this?"

Granted, all neighbors had suffered some type of vandalism at their houses, and hers certainly wasn't exempt. One of things she loved out here was that it was low on the problem scale. While it was just a few miles north of Spokane, it seemed to be a separate little town. The community was small and tight-knit. Everyone knew everyone, and neighbors looked out for each other. People didn't go around cutting padlocks and smashing windows. Around this neighborhood, kids usually tossed empty beer cans in the yard or dented mailboxes with baseball bats.

That someone had been able to come into her yard, cut the lock on the gate, and smash her front window without anyone seeing a thing wasn't just unusual; it was unheard of around here. Flat-out crazy.

Straight-up scary.

Right after she called the Stevens County Sheriff's Department, she gave in to impulse and called Diana. Her home was not only outside Spokane but in another county as well. Diana had absolutely no jurisdiction here, but the petty details didn't matter. Over the last couple of days her intuition had grown steadily stronger when it came to trusting Diana. Something about her radiated a special connection, and given what had transpired throughout the course of the day, she could use the connection.

The Stevens County Sheriff's Department wasn't likely to appreciate her calling in the SPD, though frankly she didn't care. It wasn't a case of her questioning their skills; she wanted a skilled and knowledgeable friend at her side. Diana, if anyone, could appreciate the way she was feeling right now. Her call was as much personal as professional and, if she was being honest, heavy on the personal side.

The deputy sheriff and Diana pulled into the driveway at about the same time. Given how far Diana needed to travel to get here, she obviously hadn't driven the posted limit. The time it took for the deputy sheriff to get here told her he'd come from somewhere north in the county and hadn't been nearby. This was a large county with a law-enforcement presence often stretched very thin. With the ground they had to cover, they did a decent job.

Without acknowledging the deputy, Diana bounded out of her car and raced directly to Circe. Not hesitating, she pulled her into her arms. Against her hair, Diana said, "I'm so sorry. Are you okay? Is Zelda okay?"

It felt so great to be held like this that Circe almost cried. Top that off with the fact she asked about Zelda, and it was a miracle she didn't burst into tears. She wanted nothing more than to melt into Diana and forget about dead women and broken windows. "I'm okay. We're all okay. I'm so glad you're here."

Diana let her go and stepped back, studying her face. "Do you have any idea who would do this?"

Circe shook her head as she glanced over at the deputy, whose eyes were narrowed and stuck on the badge at Diana's waist. She held out her hand to him. "Deputy, I'm Circe Latham, the homeowner."

Though he shook Circe's hand, he kept his attention focused on the badge at Diana's waist. Slowly his gaze came up until his eyes met Circe's. "Ma'am, I'm sorry if there's some confusion here, but this is Stevens County jurisdiction. SPD doesn't have authority to investigate here."

Diana took a step back from Circe and held out her hand. "No worries, Deputy. I'm not here to intrude. I'm here only as a friend. I'm Detective Diana Erni."

From the expression on his face, Circe wasn't convinced he believed Diana. "She's my *friend*," Circe said. "I called you first and Diana came up only as moral support."

His body language said he wasn't happy, and she guessed she could understand the appearance of interference by someone from a larger, outside agency. That wasn't why she'd called Diana, and somehow she needed to convey that to him.

He studied her face before his eyes cut to Diana's. Whatever he saw in their faces seemed to satisfy his reservations and he nodded. "All right, tell me what happened."

An hour later, Circe, Diana, and Lisa stood in the driveway and watched the sheriff's cruiser pull out of the driveway. Once he decided Diana wasn't there to interfere he was all business. While she couldn't say what Diana thought, she was feeling pretty confident the Steven's County Sheriff's Department would investigate fully.

As the deputy pulled out onto the street, Paul pulled into the driveway. Circe raised a single eyebrow and glanced at Diana. "Don't look at me," she said, shaking her head. "I didn't call him."

For a second she was confused and then Circe smiled. All of a sudden it made perfect sense. Of course Diana didn't call him. Why would she? She turned to Lisa. "You called him, didn't you?"

Lisa nodded and looked a little sheepish. "Figured if you could call a friend, so could I. Besides, this whole thing gives me the creeps, and a big strong guy around can't hurt. Right?"

Well, well, well, things around this household were certainly getting interesting. Somebody appeared to be pissed off at them, she was finding dead bodies right and left, and both she and Lisa appeared to be falling for a couple of cute cops. All and all, it could be worse.

CHAPTER THIRTEEN

The lights were low in his attic office, and once more he pored over the pages. A cinnamon candle flickered on the corner of the desk, the pleasing scent filling the air. His hair dripped, and for the third time, he picked up the towel and rubbed it over his scalp before it fell onto his precious book. He should have taken the time to dry his hair, but he'd been in a hurry to get to his book. His hair felt much drier now and so he tossed the towel to the floor. A twitch hit his left eye as it occurred to him how much that action reminded him of her. She would walk off and leave a wet towel on the polished hardwood and think nothing of it. True, he had dropped it on the floor, but he would pick it up when he was finished here and take it to the laundry. The twitch receded and he continued to read, no more drops of water threatening the pages.

His own needs put aside for the moment, he continued to search for something in particular. Things had to change around here, and now. The book held the answer, he was convinced of it. All he had to do was find it.

When he got home earlier, he'd found a pile of wet and muddy clothing discarded on the bathroom floor. She didn't even make the effort to put them in the hamper. As usual, he picked them up and then had to clean the mud from the tile floor. The mess was incredible, even for her. His fury grew with each swipe of the mop.

Year after year he'd hoped she would change. Year after year she'd let him down. Lately, she seemed to be worse than he'd ever seen her. He couldn't keep turning a blind eye. They'd been together so long, loyalty kept him bound to her, but that loyalty was being tested beyond tolerable limits. One of these days she was going to create a mess he couldn't clean up. Then where would they be?

Right now he couldn't afford her unpredictability. Dealing with the day-in and day-out irritations were one thing. Threatening the safety of all of them was something entirely different. She was putting the padlock on her own cell. Surely he could find something in the *De Nigromancia* that could keep her in line. He didn't want to get rid of her exactly, just rein her in so she didn't create any unnecessary problems.

Once he put his final plan into action, her sloppiness wouldn't be an issue. Until then, however, he needed to corral her. No more doing stupid things, no more creating problems where none should exist. No more piles of muddy clothes left for him to clean up. She simply had no choices left. She was going to behave or else.

Or else what? He smiled and tapped the book. It was here, just as he hoped. A simple little potion, and as he moved his finger down the line of ingredients, his heart grew lighter. Everything he needed was downstairs in his pantry. Twenty-four hours to cure the potion and she'd be locked up as surely as if he'd put her in jail. He could almost hear the click of the cell door. The feeling of relief was almost orgasmic.

Of course, he'd have to keep a close eye on her in the interim. She could be strong-willed when she took a mind to be, and he didn't like dealing with her at those times. If he was careful, he could blindside her and the power would all shift into his hands. He stood, leaned over the desk, and blew out the candle. "Not to worry," he muttered to himself as he headed downstairs. "I'll keep that bitch under lock and key."

❖

Paul jumped out of his car and made it to Lisa's side in four long strides. He pulled her into his arms and felt a rush of relief the second his arms closed around her trembling body. More than that, he felt like he'd come home. How something like this could happen in the blink of an eye, he didn't know and didn't care. He was content to know it just was.

"Are you all right?" he asked close to her ear. He knew she wasn't; he could feel it in the tremors of her body.

Her arms tightened around him. "I'm much better now."

"Ah-hum."

That was a voice he knew intimately. Letting his arms drop, he took a step back from Lisa and turned to look at Diana. Nothing about her had changed since she left the office, meaning she'd come straight here. "Hey, D."

She raised both eyebrows. "You forgot your white horse."

He let his gaze slide from Diana to Circe and back again. "I tied it up right next to yours."

With a small laugh, she said, "Touché."

"Fill me in," he said and put an arm around Lisa's shoulders. He didn't care what Diana, or anyone else for that matter, thought about his quick attraction to Lisa. Could all the recent difficulties have been a prelude to this? He'd like to think fate was finally smiling on him.

Only doubts continued to tap at his skull, trying to shake his confidence, the disastrous relationship with Brenda being topmost. After all, he'd moved her into his house and thought it was all going to be fine. That had turned out to be so far from fine it could have been from another universe. If his judgment could be so lacking in that relationship, he could miss the mark here too.

Despite the tragic results of that decision, this was different. Or at least it felt different. With Brenda, he'd known in his heart that the moment he moved her in he was settling. He might not have voiced the truth but it was there. She'd made it easy for him to settle, and he'd let her. At that point in his life, it all worked in a warped way. But crazy had eventually started making her appearance, and then he'd had to face the consequences of the fact that he'd taken the easy—or perhaps more accurately stupid—way.

On the positive side, Lisa was the polar opposite of Brenda. She was beautiful in a way that was real and heartwarming. Brenda's beauty was superficial, like a glossy magazine cover. But Lisa's had depth and substance and, most importantly, soul.

That's what it felt like to him the moment she opened the door for them—like her soul was reaching out to his.

God, how teenaged-girl that sounded. Good thing none of them could read minds because he sure as hell didn't want anyone reading his at the moment. He would prefer to keep his soul-searching insights to himself, at least for now. That didn't mean he didn't believe it was true because he did. He felt it deeply.

The cool thing was that he could tell Lisa liked him too, and her phone call was certainly a good indication. Unfortunately, he had no idea how she felt beyond liking him. He wasn't full of himself… or at least not too full of himself…but he knew he wasn't a bad-looking guy, and he was in great shape. Women seemed to like him and he always liked women too. It wouldn't be out of the realm of possibility for Lisa to be attracted to him.

But he really wanted to know if it was deeper than mere attraction. Did she feel the same heart pull he did? Could she look beyond the superficial to the man behind the badge? He hoped so, because he had a feeling this relationship held real promise if they were both on the same page. If she didn't feel what he did, it would be awful. His confidence wouldn't hold up under the blow of another misread relationship.

As much as he'd like to just blurt it out right now and find out where he stood with Lisa, he opted to be a bit more reserved. Though it wasn't his natural habitat, he was going to reside in the land of patience. After all, part of the problem with Brenda was that he jumped too quickly. Slow and careful had to be better. Shifting into professional mode, he said, "Tell me what happened."

Circe spoke up for the first time since he'd gotten out of the car. "Here's the down and dirty."

Just as Circe finished bringing him up to speed, rain began to fall again. Before they had a chance to get inside, all four of them were soaked. Circe and Diana stayed upstairs while Lisa tugged on his hand as she led him to her downstairs apartment.

She left him momentarily at the door while she retrieved a couple of towels. With one towel around her neck, she stopped in front of him and reached up to rub the other one across his head. His eyes were on hers, and he saw his own hunger reflected in them. If she didn't feel as he did, she was doing a pretty damned fine imitation. His earlier resolution to be patient and take things slow faded away. It seemed to him that he suddenly knew exactly where he stood with Lisa.

He took her face in his hands and for a long moment stared into her eyes. No, he didn't see any imitation in her eyes. This was very, very real. Slowly he bent forward and kissed her.

❖

Diana stood next to Circe and surveyed the damage. "You have a carpet shampooer by any chance?"

Circe put a hand on her shoulder and squeezed. "Of course I do. I'm very domestic, you know."

The warmth of Circe's hand on her shoulder felt wonderful. She didn't want to move until a hefty gust of wind bringing in a spray of rainwater changed her mind. Moving would be a good thing. "How about a piece of plywood?" They couldn't leave this window wide open. The way the rainstorm was hanging in there, everything in the room would be soaked if they didn't board the broken window up soon.

"No plywood, but would a piece of bead-board paneling work? I have a full sheet left over from a bathroom remodel."

Diana nodded. "That would work great. Tell me where it is and we'll close this window."

"Far side of the garage, and you'll see a toolbox on the bench out there as well. Also nails and a hammer. I'll get the carpet shampooer and see how much of this water I can suck up."

Right where Circe said they'd be, Diana found the panel and the tools. Within half an hour they'd boarded up the broken window and cleaned the carpet. It would take the carpet a while to completely dry, but they'd solved the worst of the damage for the time being.

Circe stood surveying their work and nodded. "Not bad if I do say so. I'll call the window company in the morning and get the replacement taken care of. Hopefully the carpet will be dry by then. Don't really want to replace carpet right now."

"We make a good team," Diana said as she slipped the hammer into the tool belt she'd found in Circe's toolbox. She felt very handy with the belt slung low on her hips, the hammer smacking against her leg as she walked.

Turning her gaze from the repairs to Diana, Circe smiled. "You know," her eyes moved down Diana's body and then back up, "you do a tool belt real proud."

The look in her eyes wasn't that of the friendly dog handler she'd first met out in the field. What she saw now made her flush in a way she hadn't felt in a long time. She liked it.

As she moved her hips from side to side, the hammer thumped against her leg. "Well, you know I'm versatile. A gun by day, a hammer by night."

Circe's eyes darkened at the same time Diana's pulse went nuclear. What in the world was she doing? Obviously flirting and doing it with a style she didn't even realize she possessed. Made her proud, but was it really appropriate?

Why the hell not, her mind screamed. It wasn't like they were coworkers, despite their recent work together. She couldn't see any conflict with a relationship between a cop and a K9 handler. A very sexy K9 handler, who could probably use someone to give her a bit of comfort after a really bad day. Who better to understand than a cop?

Come to think of it, she'd be inconsiderate if she didn't offer sincere friendship. Right? Yeah, right. Like she wasn't feeling so attracted to Circe it was driving her insane. She could call it anything she wanted or try to justify it with every kind of rationale she could make up. It wouldn't change the fact that she wanted to hold the woman in her arms and kiss her until neither one of them could think of anything except each other. Not murder, not bodies, not broken windows.

The corner of Circe's mouth pulled up in a smile that said everything her words didn't. "You feel it too, don't you?"

Only to the tips of her toes. "Yes."

Circe moved very close. "I knew it."

Diana wondered if Circe could hear her heartbeat. It sounded like a cannon in her ears. All of sudden she felt like she was sixteen and just about to experience her first kiss. It was that exciting. Except they weren't teenagers and this was so much deeper than the first blush of love. This had a world-changing feel to it.

Circe took her face between her hands. The sensation of her hands against her cheeks felt so sweet Diana's eyes closed for just a second. When their lips touched she was pretty sure she moaned.

The taste of her was as sweet as she'd imagined and far more hot. Nothing could compare to a first kiss, and this one blew away any other she'd ever experienced, even at sixteen when Suzi Sampson had made her gasp for air. She was gasping for air now too, but for a completely different reason.

She put her arms around Circe and pulled her close. As she did, the hammer poked both of them. "Oh," Circe said as she jumped back.

"Sorry." Diana laughed.

Circe reached around her and unclipped the tool belt. "I don't think you need this anymore."

Diana held her arms out while Circe took the belt. "No, I don't suppose I do."

"No, you don't." Circe dropped the belt on the carpet, her eyes still on Diana.

The look she gave Diana sent her imagination soaring. "You are so beautiful," she murmured. Beautiful and special and gloriously hot.

"So are you."

The woman must be blind, Diana thought. People didn't usually use the word beautiful to describe her. Striking. Handsome. Tall. Beautiful, not so much. Obviously, Circe was blinded by lust.

"You need to turn on the lights," Diana said on a laugh. As much as she liked the idea she could fill this woman with blinding lust, full disclosure was a pretty good idea too. If she was hoping for a beauty to get involved with, she was looking at the wrong woman.

Circe didn't smile. "You don't see what I do. You are beautiful, and more important, you're beautiful here." She put a hand on Diana's chest.

Diana covered Circe's hand with her own. The words brought tears to her eyes. This woman was special. She supposed she'd realized it the moment they first met. Every second since then she'd simply reinforced it. She had so very little to offer in return. Whatever she did have was Circe's.

"Where have you been all my life?" Diana asked.

Circe didn't miss a beat. "Waiting for you."

That was it. She pulled Circe into her arms and kissed her deeply, her tongue skimming over Circe's teeth until it touched hers. The shock was pure electricity. People said it all the time, and she always thought it a crock of shit until this very moment. It wasn't just a flowery phrase. It was as real as if she'd been hit by lightning. Had anyone ever kissed her like this before? If they had, she sure as hell didn't remember because this felt a world away from anything she'd ever experienced.

Diana's hands smoothed up Circe's back as she pressed her close, the feel of her firm breasts against hers making her breath hitch. She would like nothing more than to throw caution far, far away and make love to this woman right here, right now. Electricity should not be wasted.

Except she wasn't that kind of woman and she didn't do things like that. She was cautious to a fault—a really big fault if she was being honest. It was her nature and her comfort zone. She liked to come across as strong and self-assured, but in reality she was just as fragile as anyone else when it came to matters of the heart. She didn't want hers broken, and the woman she held in her arms right now wasn't a one-night-stand kind of person.

At least she could hold her and kiss her. It would be enough. It would have to be.

CHAPTER FOURTEEN

Circe couldn't believe what was happening. She was all over
Diana like she'd never been kissed before. She certainly
wasn't a virgin and had done her fair share of necking. Except she
couldn't recall ever being kissed this like this before. She felt it all
the way down to her toes and it made her hungry. Ravenous, if she
was being truthful, and not just for the touch of any woman. It was
all about this woman.

Diana's fingertips stroked her cheeks, the touch erotic in its
gentleness. The feathery stroke set her body on fire. When Diana
pulled back, Circe parted her mouth in a nearly silent "oh," and
Diana slid her thumb over Circe's lower lip. Before Circe could talk
herself out of it, she slipped her tongue out and lapped the smooth
pad. The sensation made her nipples go taut and her abdomen
tighten.

As Circe swiped her tongue across Diana's thumb, it was
Diana's turn to sigh, and she pressed her thumb inside Circe's
mouth. She sucked it gently and the heat inside her grew. Diana's
eyelids drooped as desire seemed to glow in her eyes.

Circe tried to dampen her excitement. They barely knew each
other, and in the heat of the moment she could be mistaking passion
for a simple case of comforting another after a tragedy. Well, her
broken window wasn't exactly a tragedy, but still, it was the intent
she was worried about. Was Diana feeling the intoxicating draw that

had been building inside Circe since the moment they met or was this simply a case of right time, right place for a little fun? Diana seemed to read her mind.

"You are a witch," Diana said quietly. "A beautiful, sexy witch. I've been feeling you pulling me in since we met. Only a witch could cast that kind of spell on someone like me."

For a second Circe grew cold. Did Diana know what she could do? Had she somehow found out her secret? Then the coldness passed as Diana's hands once more took her face between them. In her eyes all she saw was passion and need. She was pretty sure it was a reflection of what was in her own.

"I could say the same for you," she told her. "It could be you're the witch and now you've put some kind of spell on me."

"If that's true, it's one kick-ass spell and I like it. Whatever magic this is, I don't want it to go away."

In answer, Circe pressed her lips to Diana's. This time Circe didn't detect any gentleness in their kiss, just a deep and hungry need. For whatever reason this woman made her feel alive and passionate. It was a new, wondrous feeling. She wished she could bottle it up so it would always be with her.

"I don't usually jump all over women I've just met," Diana said against her lips.

"I can relate," she said with a laugh.

"You feel it too, don't you?"

Feel the need and the desire? Oh yeah. Feel the perfect compatibility as if they'd known each other for a thousand years? Oh yeah. It was all there wrapped up in a package so fine it made her shudder.

"Yes." She didn't see any reason to deny the obvious. Most of all, she didn't want to.

"I want you," Diana said simply.

Her answer was to take Diana's hand and lead her down the hallway to the big bedroom that hadn't seen another woman's presence for more time than Circe wanted to admit. She sure as hell wasn't a nun. Neither was she the kind of woman who liked hookups. She didn't have to love another to have sex with them. She did have to know them at least a little and like them before she could open herself up to their touch.

Diana was different. She didn't know her well, hadn't known her long. Even so, the connection was deep, as if they had been on this path toward intimacy for months. It all felt right, and she wasn't going to try to analyze it or pick it apart. For once in her life, she intended to close her eyes and let herself flow with the experiences the universe was sending her way.

Inside her bedroom, Diana cupped her face as she leaned closer. She brushed her lips against Circe's, prompting her to open her mouth wider. Gently Diana's tongue teased and tasted, and Diana moaned softly as she threaded her fingers through Circe's hair to pull her closer.

Circe stood still, letting the sensation of Diana's lips and tongue draw heat, the smoldering fire within her body burning hotter and higher. She'd been kissed before and enjoyed it, but it had never felt like this. She wanted so much more.

And it scared the crap out of her.

Eve showed up just as he was getting ready to go out for the evening. He was going out not because he needed more supplies for his pantry. No, it was more, he had to admit, for the fun of it. Somewhere along the line, his mission had turned from working toward the greater good—which meant for him of course—to working for the joy that filled him with each thrust of the knife and each drop of blood that hit the workroom floor.

It was hard to pinpoint when it had morphed into pleasure. Sometimes things got a bit muddled in his mind, though he didn't allow himself to get too caught up in the details. It was enough to feel the joy in his body and revel in the freedom to act as he wished. When he'd discovered the book he'd never imagined all it would bring him. Now that he was beginning to understand the full import of the magic he found in spells the pages contained, he felt joyful and free. Thanks to the wisdom of the book, his wealth grew, his power grew, and best of all, he became untouchable. No matter what he did, whether it was to further the teachings of the book or to simply have fun, no one dared touch him. He answered to no one. So tonight, without bothering to justify what he was doing, he prepared to hunt.

"She's causing more problems," Eve said without so much as a hello. Leave it to Eve to cut through any bullshit and go right to the point.

He sighed and ran his hands through his hair. This was a discussion he didn't really want to have at the moment. The promise of tonight's activities had him feeling high, and he didn't want Eve to bring him down with her insistence on problem-solving. Eve wouldn't give it up, and so whether or not he wanted the discussion, they were going to have it. "I know, and I promise to keep her under control."

"You realize she could jeopardize everything."

He slapped his hands to his sides before curling his fingers into fists. "I know," he snapped. "I know exactly how she can fuck this up."

"You're not keeping a leash on her."

Closing his eyes, he counted to ten. Sometimes Eve acted like his mother, and as much as he loved her, it irritated the hell out of him. The last thing he needed was another mother. Whether Eve believed it or not, he was perfectly capable of keeping her in line. Maybe he turned a blind eye now and again, but overall, he had her tethered pretty tight. It seemed to him that sometimes Eve just liked to look for problems that weren't there. She didn't trust him and that pissed him off.

"I've got it handled," he said as he opened his eyes and stared out the window. "It'll be just fine. Trust me. You know I can keep her in line."

She snorted. "Right."

"Let it go, Eve. I said I'll take care of it, and I will."

"Did you find the gift I left you?"

Her abrupt change of subject surprised him. Usually when Eve got onto a rant she wasn't quick to let it go until he agreed with every little thing she said. He smiled as he continued to stare out the window. Outside the moon shone golden light down on the trees and the grass. A cat zipped across the lawn, little more than a moving shadow in its quickness. The night was going to be a beautiful one, full of promise. A full moon always made him happy. "Yes, and I appreciate your thoughtfulness. It will help me a great deal."

"Of course it will. That's the reason I made it."

A pain shot up behind his right eye. Gently he massaged his brow until the pain faded. Eve could use a dose of modesty. She certainly didn't lack self-esteem. It was another thing about her that sometimes wore on him. Sometimes she would be easier to take if she embodied a touch of humbleness. Not likely to happen. It wasn't her way.

He frowned and grabbed his car keys from the counter. "I need to go," he told her. "I have work to do."

"Tonight? Don't you think you've pushed the envelope far enough lately?"

Far enough? She was crazy if she believed that. He'd just begun to exercise his full power, and all he'd accomplished thus far had just whetted his appetite. Much, much more to do before he reached his full power. If Eve took the time to read the text maybe she'd understand. Perhaps she would never embrace the happiness it brought him, but she might grasp a bit of what it was bringing into his life. Then again, she would never really approve because she wasn't the one in control. He was. She didn't like not being the top dog. Too damn bad. This was his time to shine, and he wasn't going to let Eve or anyone take the joy out of the world he was creating.

"No," he snapped and didn't try to hide his annoyance. "I do not."

Eve sighed. "I don't know why I even try with you."

"I don't either, so why don't you take your leave and give me some peace?" He'd had enough of her mother-knows-best speeches for one night. The thought of his own mother sent another sharp pain behind his eye. Didn't need to go down that alley.

"Perhaps it is best," she said.

A moment later he was alone and was able to relax. In a way he was surprised she'd given up that easily and left. It wasn't like her. Sometimes she could surprise him, though, and tonight was one of those times. He'd take it for the gift it was. Alone, he was able to think through what he hoped to accomplish tonight. Once he had a plan firmly in his mind, he walked out the back door after checking the padlock on the basement door and making sure to engage the deadbolt on the back door.

❖

Paul's heart was pounding so hard he thought it was going to burst. Jesus, it wasn't like this was his first time, yet that's exactly how Lisa made him feel. She kissed him with such heat it gave him an instant hard-on…just like the first time. Smooth way to impress a lady, that's for sure. So, why then did he feel elated instead of embarrassed?

She moved a step away and smiled. One eyebrow rose. "You kiss pretty good for a cop. They teach you that in the academy?"

He tilted his head and studied her face. Humor danced from her eyes and he smiled. "You kiss a lot of cops?"

Her lips pursed and she shook her head. "Not so much."

"How many then?" The teasing was fun, the thought of her kissing another cop, not so much. For some odd reason it made him uncomfortable to think about her kissing anyone else, let alone one of his fellow brothers in blue.

She put her index finger to her lips. "Well, let me count." Tilting her head from side to side she smiled. "Okay, I added it all up and came up with a pretty accurate number."

"And it is?"

"One. I can say with some confidence the tally is one."

"Tease." He couldn't help but return her smile and enjoy the rush of tension leaving his body. He wasn't going to have to bust anyone's chops for messing with his woman. God, even in his head that made him sound like a Neanderthal. A presumptuous Neanderthal no less.

"Going to arrest me?" She raised that one eyebrow again—he was beginning to find that look pretty sexy—and held out both hands in front of her. "Cuff me, Mr. Policeman?"

His hand strayed to the handcuffs on his belt. He'd be lying if he said the idea didn't possess a certain amount of intrigue. Not his customary style, but hey, a guy could change. An open mind was a good thing on and off the job. Then he laughed. "Maybe later."

"Spoilsport."

"You know how we cops are."

"No," she said slowly and moved back in until she was mere inches away. "I don't. Why don't you show me?"

He took her face between his hands and stared into her eyes. Intelligence and humor stared back at him, and damned if that didn't make him even more excited. He lowered his head until his lips skimmed hers. She tasted sweet, her lips soft. They parted as he touched them and he thrust his tongue through.

Her arms went up around his neck and she pulled him closer. The kiss deepened, and every nerve ending in his body seemed to come alive. Maybe feeling like a first-timer again wasn't so bad after all.

He slid his hands down her back and skimmed her backside. Her body seemed to fit his hands perfectly, which made him groan. She smelled wonderful, felt even better, and tasted like honey.

He was going down hard.

This time he was the one to step back. Giving himself a second to let his breathing settle down, he finally said, "You're making me crazy, woman."

"I feel so bad." She laughed and didn't look like she felt bad about a single thing.

"I can tell."

She shrugged. "Sometimes it just feels right."

He couldn't argue the point. He'd been thinking the same thing since they met. "Damn straight. It feels more than right."

Her face grew serious and she took his hands in hers. "It does, doesn't it? What do you think this is between us?"

Paul shook his head. "Damned if I know."

"Have you ever felt this way before?"

For a long moment he stared into her eyes. He'd already got himself into a whole crapload of trouble by rushing something that shouldn't have happened in the first place. Did he really want to jump off the dock again? Yeah, he did. "No."

A slow smile pulled up the corners of her mouth. Damn, but she was beautiful. "I haven't either."

"What are we going to do about it?" He sure as hell didn't know. What he did know was that he wanted to see where this thing with Lisa might go. She awakened something in him that both scared and excited him.

Lisa took his hand, turned it over, and kissed his palm. "We'll take it one step at a time. Who knows? We could be long-lost soul mates."

The thought made him laugh even as the words hit his heart with a seriousness he would never admit to. "Maybe we are, and maybe I should head out before we try to find out a little too quickly."

"Would that be a bad thing?"

She had no idea how much he wanted to stay, but better sense won out. She was special. He'd known that the moment he met her, and he planned to be a big, mature guy and do this the right way. No hook-ups. No going straight to bed because it was the exciting thing to do. The one good thing to come out of the Brenda debacle was the realization he wanted more from life than superficial relationships. No more settling because it was easy.

"No," he admitted slowly. "I have a feeling it would be a fantastic thing."

"But?"

"But I think you're special and I say we do this right."

She closed the gap between them and threw her arms around his neck. Her hug was tight, her breasts pressed against his chest making the tightness in his jeans grow even tauter. "I could fall in love with you."

His thoughts exactly. He kissed the side of her head. "Why don't you walk me out to my car?"

"You're sure you want to leave?"

Not in the least. "Yes. Not because I want to but only because I'm sure it's the right thing to do."

"As long as it's not the thing you *want* to do."

"Oh, baby, you have no idea how it's the exact opposite of what I want to do."

Chapter Fifteen

Outside, Diana heard the soft sound of a car pulling away. It had to be Paul leaving, which actually surprised her. A person would have to be blind to miss the sparks flying between him and Lisa. Good for him, taking the high road and all. Her car stayed cold and steady in the driveway. She wasn't going anywhere.

"We're doing this, aren't we?" Circe's voice was soft, her eyes steady on Diana's.

"Only if you want to." *Please want to.*

The smile Circe turned on her was dazzling. Instead of answering, she proceeded to slip out of her clothes, slowly and with deliberate movements. She had long, muscled thighs and softly curved calves. Her breasts were beautiful, with nipples that hardened as she stared at them. She wanted so badly to feel them in the palms of her hands, to feel the heat of skin against her own.

With her eyes still on Diana, Circe backed up until her legs touched the king-sized bed. She sat down with her back against the headboard and her feet flat, her knees spread slightly. It was the most erotic thing Diana had seen. It made her wet and hot.

"Well…" Circe drew out the single word.

Swallowing hard, Diana began to unbutton her shirt. She was certainly not the vision of beauty she saw in Circe. She was far more like one of the guys she worked with than a picture of femininity. Would Circe be disappointed?

Still watching Diana as she fumbled with buttons and snaps, Circe's hand began to stroke between her legs. "I don't want to have to handle this myself, but if you go any slower, I'm afraid you'll miss out on the fun."

"I'm hurrying," she muttered and couldn't keep the hitch out of her voice. God help her, the sight of Circe stroking herself almost undid Diana.

Any inhibition she harbored fled, and the last of her clothing hit the floor. She sat on the edge of the bed and for a moment simply watched Circe's fingers stroke her own clit. It made her so wet. She grabbed Circe's hand and brought it to her face, inhaling the musky scent on her fingers.

It was too much. She turned, dropped her head between Circe's spread legs, and touched her tongue to the already-swollen clit. Circe's moan let her know she'd hit just the right spot. Sliding her hands under Circe's ass she brought her up and tasted every bit of her. As Circe's moans grew louder, she tongued her clit as she slid two fingers inside. She was hot, wet, and tight.

Circe bucked as Diana slid her fingers in and out. She laid one hand on her flat belly. "Easy," she said as she raised her head. "We have all night."

"Then you have to stop touching me like that," Circe gasped.

"Not going to happen." Diana lowered her mouth again. As she licked and stroked in and out, Circe erupted. Diana continued to stroke her through the climax, loving the way she tightened around her fingers.

"Diana," Circe said on a sigh. "I think I want to marry you."

Laughing, Diana pushed up until she was lying next to Circe. She kissed her hard, a hand on one of her beautiful breasts. Her chest was still heaving from the intensity of her orgasm. "You probably say that to all the girls."

"Oh, baby, you are no girl, and I always figured that when someone could make me see heaven, she was the one I'd marry." She turned on her side and gave Diana a wicked smile. "But now that I've seen heaven, I think it's time to make you see it too."

She rolled over on top of Diana, and any argument she might have had disappeared the second Circe's hand slid between her legs.

❖

"Where have you been?"

Paul's hand flew to the gun at his waist and he had it halfway out of the holster before recognition settled in. Slowly he lowered the gun back into the holster. Son of a bitch, she'd blindsided him again. When he'd pulled up in the driveway he didn't see Brenda sitting on the back steps. Of course she was wearing all black, and even her pale hair was pulled up beneath the dark hood of her sweatshirt. Come to think of it, kind of a weird outfit for the woman who liked to look as though she'd just stepped out of Talbots. Pretty functional threads for a stalker though.

The glow he'd enjoyed since his kiss with Lisa vanished in an instant. "Oh, Jesus Christ, Brenda. What. Do. You. Want?"

All he could think about right at this second was Will's call with the news that blondie had spent time in a mental institution. He'd made a huge mistake the day he opened his home to her, and ever since it appeared he was going to pay for it forever. He'd give anything if she'd just go the hell away permanently. Whatever institution had unlocked her door had made a big mistake.

"I asked, where have you been?"

The tone of her voice cracked his already brittle nerves. "None of your fucking business."

She jumped to her feet and the hood of her sweatshirt dropped away. Her hair was a mess and he couldn't recall ever seeing it that way. She looked like another person, a stranger with wild eyes and tight lips. "You've been with her, haven't you? I can smell her on you."

Standing a good three feet away, he ran his hands through his hair. Rage roiled inside him and it took tremendous effort to keep his words calm. He refused to give her the satisfaction of knowing she got under his skin. "Look, Brenda, you have to stop this. You can't come around here." He wasn't going to get into it with her. Never again.

"That's just stupid. Of course I can come around any time I want to. You just have to stop seeing that woman. It's not fair to me and it's not right. I deserve to be treated better." She rubbed the back of her hand over her eyes, smearing black mascara across her pale skin. It gave her a raccoon-like appearance.

"You don't deserve anything because this has nothing to do with you. We're over and have been for a long time. You need to get that through your head." He tapped the side of his head with one finger. "We're over. In fact we never really were."

She was pouting and he didn't think any of this was getting through to her, so he pushed harder. "If you don't stop coming by here or my office, or anywhere else I'm at, I won't have any choice except to get a restraining order. I don't think you want me to do that."

She pushed her hand through her tangled hair and bit her lip. "You wouldn't do that to me. You love me." For the first time she sounded unsure. Her black-ringed eyes blinked and blinked.

He closed his eyes, counted to ten, and then opened them again to stare at her. He had to go in for the kill if this thing was ever going to end. "I do not love you, Brenda. I have never loved you and I never will. It was huge mistake to move in together, and I blame myself for that one. I'm trying to correct the mistake now and be honest with you. I don't love you. The sooner you make peace with that fact the easier it's going to be. Stop coming by here or I will take legal steps."

Her eyes stayed on his as she moved from the steps to the walkway. Her confidence seemed to have returned, her posture erect, her voice firm. "It's her, I know it is, and soon you'll see that I'm right."

The tone in her voice chilled him and Will's words came back to him. "She was in a mental institution." God, what he wouldn't give to send her straight back.

"Are you threatening me?" His hand strayed to the gun at his belt once again.

She actually looked surprised and her words softened. "Threatening you? Of course not. I love you and I don't care what you say. I know you love me too." Her smile was tinged with what he could only describe as craziness.

He moved his hand from his gun to the cell-phone pocket clipped on his belt and wondered if maybe he'd let this go too far. He couldn't reason with Brenda, not when she was in this state of mind, and people like that could be volatile. It might be time to let go of his ego and call it in. While he didn't want to believe she was dangerous, how did he know for certain she wouldn't do something violent? The answer was simple: he didn't.

"You need to go, Brenda. Now." All he needed to press were three little buttons: 911.

For a moment he thought she'd keep arguing. The expression of stubbornness was all over her face, and he'd dealt with her like that before. Suddenly her face cleared and she shrugged. "We'll talk later when you've had a chance to see I'm right."

She walked away without looking back, and even though she was gone, he couldn't shake an uneasy feeling that something bad was going to happen.

❖

Circe came awake slowly. At first she was confused by the warm weight next to her, and then she smiled as it all came back to her in the glow of recollection. She reached out and brushed the hair from Diana's sleeping face. Just the memory of their lovemaking sent warmth flooding through her body.

She was no virgin by any stretch, yet she couldn't remember anything that even came close to what they'd shared. It went beyond intimacy and that was new to her. Scary as hell too. She had so many secrets.

A sound made her turn her head, and as her eyes adjusted to the darkness of her bedroom, it was all she could do to stifle a scream. Four women stood near the doorway, the same four women whose bodies they'd discovered just this week. Around them a pale light glowed as if the setting sun was shining down up on them. Their faces were clear in the otherwise darkened room.

She pushed up to a sitting position and stared. This couldn't be possible; it had never happened before. Four sets of eyes stared back at her, proving to her how wrong she could be. It was very possible. One stepped forward. It was Joanna, Diana's friend. "Help her." The two words were clear and said in a voice soft yet full of pain.

Fear shot through Circe and this time she couldn't suppress the gasp. It wasn't the appearance of the women alone that sent fear coursing through her. It was their plea. She wanted to ask who needed help yet knew it was pointless. They never heard her even though she could hear them.

"Help her," Joanna said again. The intensity of the anguish in the two words tore at Circe's heart.

This time, Circe couldn't stop herself. "Who?" she cried. "Who do you want me to help?" Maybe, just maybe they would hear her now. If the rules of her gift changed and the dead suddenly came to her, then perhaps for the first time they would also be able to hear her.

Diana shot up from the bed and reached for her gun. Earlier, she'd laid it on the nightstand and now it was in her hand. The reaction had been one fluid motion from sleep to armed combat.

"What's wrong?" she asked without even a trace of sleep in her voice.

Circe's heart was still pounding and a tear traced down her cheek. What could she tell her? How could she make her understand or even believe what just happened? The moment Diana came out of the bed, Joanna and the women who stood quietly behind her vanished. In the doorway now was nothing but empty darkness and the echo of a heart-wrenching plea.

"Nothing," she lied and wiped away the teardrop with the back of her hand.

Diana did a three-sixty before she slowly laid the gun back on the nightstand. She flipped on the bedside lamp and sat down next to Circe. With one finger under her chin, she turned Circe's face until she was gazing into her eyes. Circe could tell she wasn't buying the lie.

"Try again," she said. Her dark eyes were intense as they studied her.

She couldn't come up with an explanation that would make sense. This situation went way beyond her reality of being able to see dead people. What had just happened was a new wrinkle to her so-called gift. The spirits of the departed did not show up in her bedroom, not once, and she'd been seeing them for a very long time. If she couldn't explain it to herself, how exactly could she explain it to Diana without giving her a credible reason to commit her? Not quite the way she wanted to start a beautiful new relationship. Diana was sure to think her certifiable.

And maybe she was. Seeing dead people out in the world was a little insane all by itself. Having dead people show up in her bedroom went beyond crazy. Now she was bringing them home. No, she couldn't tell her. Out of the question.

"Tell me," Diana demanded. Her words were firm, but her eyes held a softness that let Circe know she was safe. "I know something's going on inside that beautiful head of yours. Remember, I'm a trained professional. I know when people want to confess."

Diana might be offering her safety in return for confession, and still she couldn't summon the courage to bare her soul. Instead, Circe opted for distraction. After all, she was stark naked, and it was hard to think about what had happened when she felt so exposed. She got up and, from the back of the bathroom door, grabbed her fleece robe. Diana didn't appear to suffer from the same feeling of exposure. She was still totally naked and staring at her, waiting patiently. Again, she couldn't concentrate.

Diana rested her back against the headboard and patted the bed next to her. "Sit down, take a breath, and just tell me." Her request under normal circumstances would be quite reasonable. Normal wasn't exactly a realm she existed in.

"It's not that simple."

"Oh yeah, it is."

Easy for her to say. Diana wasn't the one who spent her entire life surrounded by death. She didn't walk down the street and come face-to-face with the recently departed. She didn't go for a hike and find a lost soul wandering among the pines.

For the first time in a really long while, she felt like maybe she was losing her mind. While it had taken most of a lifetime, she'd managed to carve out an existence that made sense and life had been going along pretty well. All it took was a serial killer leaving bodies all over her city to turn her life upside down. Somehow she needed to make sense of everything happening.

Her hands were trembling and her heart pounding. She could keep everything bottled up and slowly lose her mind, or…

She stared across the room at Diana, wishing she could see what was in her heart as clearly as she'd seen the four women standing in her bedroom. Sharing might not hurt, and maybe, just maybe, it might help. Taking Diana up on her invitation, she sat on the bed, turned so she was facing her, and crossed her legs. For a minute she stared at her clasped hands, not having the courage to look into Diana's eyes. "All right, I'm going on faith here, and I need you to keep an open mind."

"I will." Diana put a finger under her chin and drew her head up so their eyes locked. "Tell me."

"I don't think you understand. I need you to keep a *very* open mind."

Diana tilted her head as she studied Circe's face. Circe could almost see the wheels turning inside. "I'm a pretty open person. You can trust me."

How she wanted to. In her life she'd had so few she could truly trust, and it was a lonely place to live. Lonely and tiresome. To be able to talk about the things she saw would be huge. In fact it would almost make her feel normal.

She was standing on the edge of a cliff with two choices: turn around or jump. "All right."

Diana put her hand over Circe's clasped ones. "I'm not kidding, Circe. You can trust me with *anything*."

With a trembling voice, she jumped. "For as long as I can remember, I've been able to see the dead."

CHAPTER SIXTEEN

Paul picked up the phone and hated the fact that his hand was shaking. "Will, tell me you've got something."

"She show up again?"

One thing he'd always admired about Will was his uncanny ability to feel out the big picture. The day he retired, the SPD lost one of its best, although given his private work, the community still benefitted. Right now, he wanted and needed that expertise. He wanted someone to help him make it all go away.

Though he often helped people in exactly the same position he found himself in now, until it happened to him, he didn't really understand how awful it was. Now he did, and the reality was more frightening than he ever imagined. Experts could teach this stuff in seminars and throw psychobabble at them all day long, yet it still didn't give anyone the true perception of how invasive it felt to have someone do this.

Making a wrong turn in a relationship shouldn't be a life sentence, yet that's exactly what was happening. She was not going to stop. He'd seen it in others when he'd arrested them, had glimpsed the intensity that shone in their eyes like beacons in a lighthouse. It was in her eyes too, and regardless of how desperately he wanted to believe it would all go away, he knew better.

She would never go away.

"She was sitting on the porch when I drove up. Jesus Christ, Will, I just told her to stay away, yet tonight it was like we'd never talked. She's certifiable, I swear to God."

"If you recall, I've already confirmed that particular tidbit, my boy. You should see the info Maddie pulled up on her. You'll want to be sitting down when you read that report."

Paul ran a hand through his hair. A headache was starting to build, a steady thump, thump, thump behind one eye. "I don't think I even want to see that. I'm freaked out enough as it is." With his fingertips he massaged his right temple, hoping to ease the growing pain.

"Okay, my man, you take a look at it later. Here's what we're going to do starting tonight. I want you to go about your normal business except vary things a bit. Take a different way to work, don't go to the same places for coffee, lunch. Don't shop at your normal grocery store. You feel me?"

No problem. Like he was hungry. Just the thought of Brenda banished his appetite in a flash. He wouldn't need to go to a restaurant or pick up groceries. Food was the last thing on his mind. Too bad he couldn't package that; he'd make a million on the diet market.

"I feel you."

"Good. Tell me you installed an alarm in your house."

Ever since Will had taken on private security, he'd been like a dog with a bone. He'd been after Paul for at least a year to get a security system installed. Of course he'd ignored him. He was a cop; why did he need a security system when he was licensed to carry a gun? Not to mention he still had that you're-not-the-boss-of-me thing going on with Will. Someday he'd probably grow out of it. Possibly.

"Not yet."

"Boy, I could come over there right now and kick your ass."

"But you won't."

"No, I won't, but get it done before she goes all *Fatal Attraction* on your ass."

"Huh?"

"Movie. Michael Douglas. Glenn Close. Do you ever do anything besides read books?"

"Not much into movies."

"Forget it, just get the damned system installed."

"What are you going to do?"

"Time for me and Maddie to do a little divide-and-conquer. We'll figure out what your sick princess is up to and come up with a plan to diffuse the situation before it goes nuclear."

"Will..."

"Yeah?"

"Do it soon."

"Copy that."

He closed his phone and shoved it back into his pocket. He liked living here and enjoyed his home. Until now. Tonight every shadow jumped out at him. Every moan or squeak sounded like a cannon shot that raced up his spine. It wasn't fair. One mistake shouldn't destroy his life.

From the refrigerator he pulled out an icy ginger ale. Most guys would probably go for a beer. He liked cold, tangy, and full of fizz. In short, ginger ale, a comfort food of sorts. Not very manly but it worked. He filled a glass with ice and poured the ginger ale over it.

The overhead light was on and he flicked the switch to turn it off, plunging the room into darkness. He took the tall, iced glass and stood next to the window that looked out over his big backyard. Leaning his head against the glass, he stared out. The shadows of the red maples he'd planted when he first bought the house shifted and quivered as a light wind moved through the night. The shadows made it look as though small creatures were scurrying through the yard. His mind turned to a creature not quite so small.

For all he knew she could still be out there somewhere staring in and hoping to see him as he went about his life. In the dark room she would be able to see very little, and that made him feel somewhat safe. Somewhat. That was the kicker. Big strong cop, cuffs and a gun at the ready, and he was nervous as a cat in his own home. That was fucked up on all sorts of levels.

His phone buzzed in his pocket and he pulled it out. A text message. He couldn't help the smile when he glanced at the phone. Lisa. The text was short, "Sweet dreams," followed by a set of red lips. Her timing was perfect. Just what he needed.

His heart felt lighter and he stood up taller. Holding the glass of ginger ale out toward the window he said, "If you're out there, fuck off." He tapped the pane with the lip of the glass and then turned to walk away.

He spun back to the window when he caught movement out of the corner of his eye. The glass in his hand dropped to the floor and shattered.

❖

Diana got up and slipped on her pants and shirt. It was easier to think dressed. "You want to run that by me again?"

"Dead people. I see them. You know, like in the movie with the little boy."

She sat in the chair opposite the bed and stretched out her legs. After the initial shock had passed and as hard as it was to believe, she was actually giving what Circe had told her serious consideration. Any other time she'd run like hell because someone saying something like this would make the reading on her nutty meter go sky high. With Circe, the needle was barely moving. She'd seen her work, been around her, and observed her. She wasn't a flake.

"Dead people?"

"Yes."

"As in ghosts?"

Circe moved her head from side to side. "Not like ghosts exactly. I just see them like I can see you. They're solid and usually can talk to me."

Diana was rolling that statement through her mind when one word hit: usually. "They talk to you?"

"Yes. Some do. Some don't. I've never really figured out what compels some to speak to me while others don't. I just listen and do my best."

"That's what happened tonight? They talked to you?"

Circe's gaze dropped and she put her head in her hands, massaging her scalp. "Tonight something happened that never has before. They came to me here. In my own home."

"I don't understand."

"As long as I can remember, it's happened one way. I find them. They don't come to me. They don't appear in my home. They sure as hell don't show up unannounced in my bedroom." The way her voice trembled told Diana how much this troubled her.

Diana leaned forward and put her elbows on her knees. So many things were racing through her mind that she didn't know where to start. "The first three women, you found them, not your dog, right?"

With a shrug, Circe said, "Sort of. Zelda really is a trained and certified human-remains detection dog. It's true I saw the women before Zelda alerted, but she did her work too. She would have found them even if I hadn't been there. That's what I trained her to do."

Diana was watching her closely, and with a flash she understood. Sitting back in her chair, she said quietly, "It's why you became a K9 handler."

Relief seemed to wash over Circe as if a load was taken off her shoulders. "Yes."

"Wow."

"You don't think I'm crazy?" The hope in Circe's voice made her heart hurt. To even consider how life would be if you were trying to hide something like this and pretend to be like everyone else boggled her mind. Diana wasn't sure she was strong enough to have carried a secret so powerful for a lifetime.

Diana got up and moved back to the bed. Taking Circe's hand in hers, she stared into her eyes. "No, I don't think you're crazy. I think you're freaking incredible."

❖

God, that was fun. In fact, it made him feel like God. He couldn't pinpoint exactly when this thing had shifted from mission to entertainment, but damned if that wasn't exactly what had happened. He should have started much sooner. The fun he'd missed by waiting so long. No worries. Now that he understood what he could do and how much he enjoyed it, no one could stop him.

Not that anyone had a clue. They were all running around looking for some horrible person, and that's exactly why they wouldn't catch him. He wasn't some big bad bastard; he was just a regular guy—the next-door neighbor who was quiet and polite, and who kept to himself. He didn't cause any problems and didn't do anything that brought attention his way. Nobody looked twice at guys like him and it worked beautifully. He did what he wanted, took who he wanted, and no one was the wiser.

Now, however, he needed to figure out what to do with the leftovers. He'd had his fun, and though he hated this part, he was nonetheless going to have to take out the trash. But where?

He'd thought he was so smart when he tucked the last one away on the perimeter of the cemetery. It was a perfect hiding place because it was right in plain sight. A great plan too, except it didn't work out so well, thanks to that stupid dog showing up. The mutt all but dug her up. Considering that the odds of not having the body discovered were on his side, that one ticked him off in a big way. That piece of trash should have been safe from discovery for, well, forever.

So now he had to come up with a place a bit more private. No running trails and no place that pain-in-the-ass dog might show up. One more time screwing with him and the dog was going to make the top of his hit list. It might actually be kind of fun to do away with the dog—a little twist on the norm. He smiled, thinking about how he could pull it off. So many tantalizing possibilities.

He drove along Aubrey White Parkway and had an idea. At one of the several pullouts along the scenic road he pulled in and parked, turning off his lights. From here the terrain sloped sharply down to the river. It was hard to make out the faint, lightly traveled paths even in the daylight. The abundance of so many other areas easier to traverse and far more heavily used made the area he studied now a definite possibility.

Traffic on the Parkway was almost nonexistent this time of night, so he didn't worry about anyone discovering him. A tarp and his favorite paracord wrapped up the body in the trunk nice and tidy. Lugging the dead weight out of his trunk, he dropped it on the edge of the embankment. His preferred packaging method made it easy to roll it down the steep embankment toward the river below with a simple shove. In the quiet night air, the sound of snapping twigs and tumbling rocks sounded like a symphony to his ears.

It came to rest against several small pine trees. He followed it down, shovel in hand, his feet sliding on loose dirt and rocks. A couple of times he almost lost his footing. Near where the bundle stopped, he started to dig. The rocky soil cooperated, and soon he had a large hole just the perfect size for his package. Less than thirty minutes was all he needed to accomplish his task. Throwing the shovel into the trunk, he dusted himself off and climbed back into his car. Not a single car passed him by.

Why he'd never thought of coming here before, he didn't know. This was a great place and perfect for his needs. The whole night had turned out to be quite entertaining. When a coyote came racing across the road and he had to stomp on the brakes, rather than curse the wild canine, he laughed. Nothing was going to ruin his good mood.

He could hardly wait for tomorrow.

Chapter Seventeen

It was stupid. Really, really stupid, yet he did it anyway. He still didn't know if it was Brenda in the backyard or if his imagination was running wild. Either way, he was too jumpy to even try to sleep. He cleaned up the ginger ale and broken glass before going upstairs to change into jeans and boots, then slipped on his leather jacket as he went downstairs.

In the garage, he put on his helmet and straddled his Harley. Riding always made him feel better. When he left the house he didn't have a particular destination in mind. His impromptu plan was to simply ride and enjoy the wind in his face and speed. Twenty or thirty miles and he'd be feeling more like himself.

He managed to get a fair amount of wind in his face as he rode along Highway 291. Bugs too, because the highway followed the Little Spokane River until it merged with Long Lake, and this time of night the bugs were in control. Before he realized it, he was in front of Circe's house. He could say he was here to check on Circe, but it would be a big fat lie.

He was here because Lisa lived here too.

Hopefully the loud, obnoxious pipes of the Harley didn't disturb anyone, though that was precisely the reason he had them on the bike. It was important for people to hear him coming. Too many motorcycle accidents happened because drivers had no idea a motorcycle was on the road. In his case, the only ones who wouldn't know he was around were deaf. It was a good thing most of the time.

In the middle of the night when most people were trying to sleep, maybe not so much.

As he killed the engine and rolled the bike into the shadows, he couldn't help but smile when he noticed Diana's car still sitting in the driveway. Whatever was brewing between Diana and the cute dog handler, it was apparently taking off in a big way.

Actually he was glad for his partner. Her career was important to her and he got that. It didn't have to be her whole existence, though, and he'd always hoped she'd find someone to share her life with. Despite his own bad choices, he appreciated what the deep connection with another person could bring.

In fact, that sense of connection had brought him here now. Lisa's spirit seemed to reach out and draw him close. It wasn't necessary to be in the house with her. Just being nearby made him feel calmer and more relaxed. For a little while he would sit on his bike and breathe in the air, let it calm him. The shadows that dogged him at his own house weren't present here. The air was cool and crisp, the sky dark and full of stars. Who wouldn't find peace in a setting like this?

It should have surprised him when he saw a woman come out the front door and walk across the grass in his direction, but it didn't. It made him smile. The night couldn't hide the familiar shape and walk. No, he hadn't known her long, yet he recognized the little nuances that made her unique. He would be able to pick her out in any crowd.

Lisa stopped at the front of his bike and put both hands on the handlebars. "So what's your story, lawman? Bored? Scared? Can't sleep? Had to take your big bad bike out for a spin in the middle of the night?"

"That would be number three."

"Ah, the dreaded *can't sleep*. Been there, done that."

"Speaking of which, why aren't you asleep?"

She smiled and shook her head. "This isn't about me. If you notice," she waved her hand back toward the house, "I'm actually at home. You, on the other hand, are sitting outside a woman's home on a big, noisy motorcycle in the middle of the night. In the shadows no less, as though you think you're all stealthy."

"Cop stuff," he said gruffly.

"Of course it is. Well, what do you say we take this cop stuff inside?"

Her offer sounded great and wrong at the same time. Just the fact he'd ridden here was wrong. He should have gone for a short ride and then returned home. That's what he liked to do when he couldn't sleep. Coming out here was, well, hard to explain, and if he couldn't rationalize it to himself, how was he going to justify it to her?

"Come on," Lisa said again. "You know you want to."

He laughed. He couldn't help it. He did want to go inside. "Maybe."

"Maybe, my ass." Her face grew serious. "Paul, I really would like for you to come in. What happened today has left me feeling uneasy. The truth is I'm glad you came back out. Your being here helps."

He stared into her eyes, looking for a hint that she was just trying to be nice. Nothing like that stared back at him. Instead what he saw made his heart ache. Fear. "It helps me too," he admitted. "Let me pull the bike into the driveway."

A small smile lit up her face. "I'll open the garage. It has enough room for you to park this bad boy inside."

She was right and he was able to park next to Lisa's car, a Mini Cooper. One look at the tiny car and he shook his head. "I don't think I could even get in that thing."

She put a hand to her heart. "You hurt my feelings. I love this car, and do you have any idea of the gas mileage I get in this baby? It's incredible."

"If you say so, but I heard it kinda sucks for a car this size."

"Well, maybe." She smiled. "But I like it so it really doesn't matter." She took his hand. "Let's go inside."

He figured they'd make some coffee, sit around and just talk. Boy, was he wrong. The minute they were in her lower-level apartment with the door shut, she reached for him, pulled him close, and locked lips.

❖

Circe couldn't help it, she burst into tears.

"Oh my God," Diana exclaimed and pulled Circe into her arms. "I'm sorry. What did I say?"

Her sobs began to morph into laughter. "Do you know how long I've waited for someone to tell me that?"

"Tell you what?"

"That they don't think I'm crazy."

"What do you mean, Circe?" Diana looked at her with a questioning gaze that suddenly shifted into understanding. "Nobody knows what you can do?"

With the backs of her hands she wiped away the tears as she nodded. "I have a very dear friend who does, and she's the only one."

"But she thinks you're crazy?"

That made Circe laugh out loud all over again. "Oh, she thinks I'm crazy, but not in that way. No, it's not that. This thing has been with me as long as I can remember. When I was really young my family passed it off as a child's imagination, except it didn't go away as I got older. Then they started getting worried that something was wrong with me. I finally learned I had to keep my secret to myself or I would probably spend my life in doctors' offices or, worse, in an institution. Since then, I haven't shared the truth with anyone except Vickie."

"And now me."

It was hard to believe she'd actually done it. "And now with you."

Diana was shaking her head. "You've kept this bottled up all your life?"

The shock in Diana's voice almost undid her again, and she breathed deep to keep her tears in check. "It's not the kind of thing you can share with people."

"This is new to me too, but I have to tell you, I'm amazed. I've seen some interesting things in my time that defy any rational explanation, and I've always tried to keep an open mind. I've seen what you and Zelda can do. That you could take something that would put most people in lifetime therapy and use it to not only stay sane but to help others is cool on a level I don't see very often."

"Thank you." She hugged Diana.

"So, tell me what you saw tonight."

The innocent request sent chills up her spine. That the dead had come to her here, in her own home, scared the daylights out of her, and considering everything she'd seen in her life that said a lot. At the same time it was hard to explain to Diana what a big deal it was. Might as well just put it out there, and maybe together they could make sense of out of it.

"So like I said, the spirits of the dead women came to me."

"The women you and Zelda found?"

She nodded. "Yes, all four of them."

"Joanna?" She said the name softly, painfully, and tears came into her eyes.

"Yes."

Diana seemed to pull herself together. "They came here and that's not what they normally do."

This time she shook her head. "Not at all, and that's why it freaked me out. They don't show up in my house."

"That sounds bad."

It had struck her the same way when it happened. Now that she'd had a chance to think about it, what really hit her hard was the fear. It wasn't the fact they came to her in her own home as much as the two words they said with such solemnity: "Help her."

❖

He was dead fucking wrong. He'd come home in the best possible mood, and it all went to hell the second he stepped inside. This shit had to stop and stop now.

The kitchen was a war zone: broken glasses, broken plates, trash left on the floor. Something brown and gooey oozed across the tiles, turning them from white to russet. An acrid smell like old vinegar filled his nostrils.

He did a full circle and let the rage wash over him. He'd been putting up with her temper tantrums for years, and he was done. If he could make all those other women disappear, he could sure as hell wipe her off the face of the earth.

His mind made up, he went out to the garage and grabbed the broom, dustpan, and mop. It took him half an hour to clean up all the broken glassware and dinnerware. It was scattered everywhere. He even had to pull out the refrigerator and stove in order to sweep up all the pieces. Pieces of blue pottery at the base of the wall made his blood boil and he carefully retrieved them, hoping to save his favorite coffee mug. It was not to be; the mug, a memento from another place, another kill, was beyond repair. The sticky substance was more stubborn, and he had to resort to hot water and cleanser to return the tile to its pristine white.

By the time he finished, the air smelled of pine and he was calmer than when he first walked into the kitchen, but that didn't dampen his resolve. This was the last time he intended to tidy up after one of her tantrums. He was done. D.O.N.E.

The broom and dustpan back on the hook in the garage and the mop hung up to dry, he returned to the kitchen, intending to call it a night. As he walked past the door to the basement he paused. No, he thought, she wouldn't dare. She absolutely was not allowed to go into his special workspace, not ever, and even she wouldn't be that bold.

He backed up and stared in disbelief at the padlock. It was open, and he knew good and well he'd locked it earlier. Taking hold of the doorknob, he turned it slowly, swung the door open, and flipped on the light. As he descended the stairs a familiar odor assailed him, and the fury he'd managed to tamp down as he cleaned the kitchen began to rise again. At the bottom of the stairs he stopped for a moment before he turned to look.

Fury colored his world crimson. At the end of the room, his shelves were all but empty. Instead of being lined by neat rows of glass jars, each filled with glistening liquid and carefully labeled with name, date, and time, the shelves were a mess, as if someone has swiped an arm across them, sending jars tumbling and flying.

Strewn across his floor, so recently scrubbed and sanitized, were his precious jars, or what was left of them. Broken glass, metal lids, and dark fluids mingled to create a dark, shimmering carpet where only hours ago it had been hospital-clean concrete. If she wanted to get back at him, to punish him, she'd hit the right chord.

His breath caught in his throat and his heart pounded. How could she do this to him after everything he'd done for her? He'd protected her, covered for her, forgiven her over and over again. After the mess in the kitchen he hadn't believed it could get any worse, and once more she'd proved him wrong. This wasn't just worse; it was catastrophic.

She'd destroyed his careful work, his years of accomplishments. The plans he carefully laid were in ruins. It was so clear now. She was out of control, and he wouldn't rest until he destroyed her. This was the last time she would cause him grief.

He whipped around and began to pound back up the stairs. Suddenly his steps slowed. No, he'd changed his mind. He could put her down once and for all, yet that wasn't enough. Before he destroyed her, he wanted her to suffer, and he knew exactly how to make her hurt all the way to her soul. Payback was going to be a real bitch.

CHAPTER EIGHTEEN

I think I'm in love." Paul panted. The first passionate kiss had morphed from making out to mind-blowing sex. His heart was pounding, and he could barely breathe. Not real manly but damned if he didn't feel fantastic.

A little scared too, not that he would ever admit that out loud. Again, not real manly. He couldn't help the way he felt. Lisa was unlike any other woman he'd ever met. He'd been having some of the worst days ever, and out of the darkness came this incredible woman. Made all of it worthwhile.

Her place was amazing too. Warm and inviting, it seemed to embody her generous and loving nature. The minute he'd walked in he felt as though he could stay here forever, and right now that's exactly what he wanted to do. Peace and tranquillity was a great antidote to the darkness touching his life.

Even as wonderful as he felt, a bit of unease rippled just below the surface. The whole Brenda thing had him second-guessing his ability to judge the reality of a relationship.

This was different. When he told her he thought he was in love, he'd said those words only partially in jest. He was afraid he'd tucked a whole lot of truth into them.

Lisa rolled over and kissed him. "You probably say that to all the girls." Her laugh let him know she was joking.

"Only the pretty ones."

"Oh, now I'm flattered. You think I'm pretty."

He slowly ran his hand over her cheek. His eyes met hers. "I don't think you're pretty."

A cloud passed through her eyes. "You don't?"

He shook his head just a little and kept his gazed locked on hers. "No, not pretty. You're breathtaking."

A smile replaced the shadow. "And you're hot…for a cop."

"Careful." He loved to tease her. "Or I'll have to cuff you."

She pressed her lips against his. "Promise?"

"Promise."

Much later, he got up and went to the window. Lisa was asleep, the sheet pulled up, her hair spread out on the pillow. She was beautiful and peaceful, and he was glad she could sleep. He still couldn't.

Outside it was dark, and though it was a residential neighborhood, lights were not plentiful. Only a sporadic porch light broke the darkness of the night. Each home in the area was on a lot no smaller than a full acre, and many were much larger. Bridle trails snaked behind the houses to give people a place to ride horses and mountain bikes, and to walk dogs. The setting was beautiful and private. He could see why Circe was drawn to buy the house.

By all rights he should be exhausted. Instead he was wide-awake. It wasn't that he didn't feel alive and, well, frankly fantastic. It was more what was working underneath all the goodness. He had a feeling like ants crawling up the back of his neck that he couldn't shake. He was really worried those ants had a name: Brenda.

A muffled sound broke the quiet. At first he couldn't figure out what it was, and then he realized it was the buzz of his phone. Someone was sending him a text message in the middle of the night. He found his pants draped over a chair and shoved his hand into a front pocket.

The text was from Will, and what it said sent a chill through him. Though the message said to call in the morning, he didn't plan to wait. Whatever Will needed to tell him, he needed to hear it now. He slipped on his jeans and silently made his way out of Lisa's bedroom.

Will picked up on the first ring.

"What's up?" Paul asked.

"Well, you are, apparently." Will was never the one to pass up the obvious. "Dude, what are you doing up this late?"

"Long story."

"You home?"

"No." He didn't plan to explain where he was. He wasn't ready to talk about his feelings toward Lisa to anyone yet.

"Good."

"Good?" What kind of flipping conversation was this anyway? He was expecting the third-degree from Will. That he was not giving it made the hair stand up on the back of Paul's neck.

"Look, here's my long story, short. Your girlfriend is some kind of crazy."

"I thought we'd already established that."

"Oh, it goes deeper, my friend. Much, much deeper."

Diana didn't miss the fear that flashed though Circe's eyes. Just imagining what she'd endured her whole life and the way she had to keep it bottled up like a secret hurt her heart. Nobody should have to grow up afraid of being locked away. Nobody should have to live a life imprisoned by secrets.

Without giving herself a chance to think about it, she pulled Circe close. "I'm so sorry," she whispered against her hair. "I'm here for you and we'll figure this out together."

Circe wrapped her arms around Diana and hugged her back. "Thank you," she whispered back.

"Thank you for trusting me."

Circe kissed her and then gave her another tight hug. "I'm so glad we met."

"That makes two of us," Diana said as she broke the embrace. "Now, let's figure out what to do with them."

"Do with them?" Circe looked at her with a puzzled expression.

Diana nodded. "Them...the ghosts of the women."

"I don't understand. Do something with them?"

"Yeah, there's got to be a reason why all four women appeared to you here. Think about it. You see the dead where they are buried and they don't move around. So why would they come to you now? What has changed? Some dynamic's at play here, and they're desperately trying to communicate it to you. We've got to figure out what it is. What changed the game, so to speak?"

Circe sat back and stared at her. "You're taking this seriously, aren't you?"

Of course she was. She didn't see any reason not to, despite the distinct note of incredulity in Circe's voice. Circe had shared this with her, yet she had the sense she had fully expected her to run away screaming. To be honest, Diana was a bit surprised she did believe her. After all, it wasn't like people regularly shared things like this with her. And the ones who did typically ended up being referred to the psych ward at the local hospital under an armed law-enforcement escort.

Circe was different. This woman was as sane as Diana; she'd bet the bank on it. So, if Circe said she could see the dead...she could see the dead. It was that simple. She believed her and she was going to act on that belief.

She didn't blink, didn't look away. "As a heart attack."

For a long moment Circe just stared at her, and then the corner of her mouth turned up and she nodded. "All right then. I agree. This change means something. They want me to help her, and so all we need to figure out is who is *her*?"

"Narrows it right down."

The expression on Circe's face shifted and darkness settled over her features. "It's a big city, a big county. Zelda and I could search for weeks and never get close to finding her. I don't know how to help these women."

Diana didn't like the sadness that pulled at Circe. Apparently neither did Zelda, who padded in and jumped onto the bed. She gave Circe a quick lick on the cheek before turning three times and lying down with a groan. Then she closed her eyes and promptly went to sleep.

"We'll figure this out. Together, all three of us."

Circe ran a hand over Zelda's big head, which seemed to impart an instant calm. "I hope so."

"How can we fail? I mean, really think about it, Circe. We have you with your supernatural abilities. We have Zelda, search dog extraordinaire, and then you've got me, super detective. We're a triple threat."

Circe smiled as she looked at the sleeping dog and then brought her gaze up to meet Diana's. "You know, I think you might just have a point."

"Bank on it."

Circe reached over and laid her hand against Diana's cheek. "I trust you, and I'm thanking my lucky stars we were brought together."

Diana got it. She was thanking her lucky stars that she'd met both Circe and Zelda. Sometimes the stars really did align, and all it took was being in the right place at the right time for it to matter. "Believe me, we will figure this out, but I should probably leave and let you get some sleep. We can dig into this more in the morning."

Circe grabbed her hand and held it tight. "Morning works for me. You going home doesn't." That wicked little smile came back onto her face.

❖

Circe came up out of bed fast. Deep sleep had vanished the second icy fingers touched her cheek. Instinctively she knew they didn't belong to Diana, who still slept peacefully, her dark hair in contrast to the cream-colored pillowcase. No, the touch on her skin was otherworldly and lacking anything remotely similar to warmth.

From the back of the bathroom door she grabbed her robe and slipped into it, tying the belt tight around her waist. The carpet was soft beneath her feet, and she soundlessly made her way out of the bedroom. At four in the morning here, cars driving down the street were rare, and rather than people, she was more likely to find a raccoon or a deer or even a moose meandering down the street.

At the big front window she stood with a glass of water and stared outside. She knew who'd touched her and brought her out of a deep and satisfying sleep. What she didn't know was why. Zelda padded out of the bedroom and sat next to her. She reached down and ran her hand over her head.

"You feel it too, don't you, Z?"

Zelda's only response was the thump of her tail against the carpeted floor. Yes, she felt it just as Circe did. Something was off in the universe, and her girls—that's how she was beginning to think of them—were trying to guide her to some kind of revelation.

Out of the corner of her eye she glimpsed a flash of light. Her head snapped around, and for a second she saw nothing. Perhaps she was imagining things, but she quickly realized she wasn't. With a resounding boom, flames engulfed the car sitting in her driveway. She screamed and jumped back, and her water glass went flying. At first she thought her car had just gone up in flames, and then she realized her car was parked inside the garage. The car that had just exploded was Diana's.

She yelled "Diana" before grabbing her cell phone and flying outside. After calling 911, she raced for the hose at the corner of the house and began to spray the flaming car with water. Before long she could hear the sound of sirens in the distance. Thank goodness the local fire station was only half a mile away.

"Holy shit!" Diana was standing next to her, dressed but barefoot. "What the hell? How did that happen?"

A fire truck came screaming around the corner and pulled into her driveway. She stepped back gratefully to let them take over.

"I don't know," she said to Diana. "One minute I was just looking at the window and the next, boom! Your car was a giant fireball in a matter of seconds."

Diana was shaking her head vehemently. "Nothing was wrong with my car. No way could something like this happen spontaneously."

As she'd stood there spraying the car with her ineffectual garden hose, the same thing had occurred to her. "Not without help."

Diana was rubbing the back of her neck with both hands. "I was thinking the same thing." Slowly her hands came down and she turned a full circle, scanning everything as she did.

"What do you see?" Circe could tell by the expression on her face she was searching. Her eyes were narrowed and her face intense.

"Nothing."

Circe surveyed the area too and, like Diana, didn't pick up a thing. In the dawning light of day everything appeared normal, the same sight that greeted her every morning. "I don't see anything unusual."

"You mean besides your car going up in flames?" The voice was Paul's, and Circe turned to see him and Lisa standing behind them. Both were staring at Diana's now-smoldering car. "What in the world happened?"

Briefly Circe wondered how and when he got here and then dismissed the question as inconsequential. She didn't care about the details; she was just glad to see him.

Diana turned and caught his gaze. A look passed between them that Circe couldn't identify. "You take east. I'll take west."

Without another word, they disappeared, leaving Lisa and Circe standing alone with the first responders. At least they'd managed to put out the raging fire before anything beyond the car was affected. A chill ran down her body as she realized how close Diana's car was to her house and how easily it could have been engulfed. If she hadn't been standing there looking at the window when the car went up in flames, at the very least her house could have burned down. At the worst, they could all be dead right now.

In only a few minutes both Diana and Paul returned. Again that look passed between them. "WHAT?" Circe demanded.

"I don't know what's going on," Diana said. "But it appears somebody has a hard-on for you."

"But it was your car." Nothing had happened to anything of Circe's, and besides, who would give her the time of day? She was about as harmless as they came.

"The locks on the walk gates were cut again. All three of your gates were open. I think someone wanted Zelda to take off."

That stopped her, and she dropped her hand to Zelda's head. As in the house, Zelda hadn't moved from Circe's side. "That doesn't make sense."

Diana raised an eyebrow and nodded toward the boarded-up front window. "Does that make sense?"

Circe still wanted to believe it was all just coincidental. "I haven't pissed anyone off."

Paul looked at Diana and she nodded. "No one except perhaps a serial killer."

CHAPTER NINETEEN

Oh. My. God. That was fun. Why the hell he'd never thought to play with fire before, he didn't know. Talk about a rush of adrenaline. Using the bolt cutters to make short work of the flimsy gate padlocks was a giggle, but improvising the explosive device was pure genius. He was going to have to remember the IED tactic in case he got another nosy Nellie like the dog handler and her mutt.

She really was a bother. If he scared her enough perhaps she'd find something better to do with her time than expose his girls. The cops hanging around her house were a little problematic, though rather convenient. He could kill two birds with one stone, so to speak, and efficiency always made him happy. Take out the pain-in-the-ass dog handler and two detectives all in a single effort—it was pure genius.

Standing in the shadows of the neighbor's shrubs he was effectively invisible in the early morning light. No one saw him. No one could. He blended in perfectly, which allowed him to watch the unfolding events from a hideaway a safe distance away.

The funny part was the way the two cops put their serious faces on. Typical cops. Always thought they had the answers and the upper hand. They really thought they'd be able to track him down. He shook his head and nearly laughed out loud. He'd been hiding in plain sight all along, and not once did either of the dimwits get a clue. They never would and that was a beautiful thing.

Maybe, just maybe, before he introduced them to his special workshop, he would let them see. Only after it was too late for either of them to do a thing, too late to stop what was inevitable. Then he would open their eyes, and it would be a glorious moment. He could almost visualize the shock on their faces. That alone was worth every risk he'd taken thus far.

Not on this morning though. This was enough for now. He could tell by their faces that they were starting to understand, and he liked the expressions of dawning knowledge. It reminded them how powerful he was and how unstoppable. The book gave him knowledge and strength. They had no clue what they were up against, and by the time they did, it would be far too late to prevent what he now considered his destiny.

Keeping to the darkest shadows, he moved away from the house where the flashing strobes of the fire trucks created a light show and the yard full of firefighters went about the work of mopping up around the destroyed car. Full daylight was on its way, and neighbors were beginning to come out to their porches to stare at the house on the corner and a burned-out shell of a car. The community was sure to be buzzing with gossip before the sun was high in the blue sky.

He'd parked his car at the grade school about an eighth of a mile away. He got in and pulled out onto the highway. Keeping to the speed limit, he drove toward town. He was smiling and wondering what she was going to do when she heard what he'd done tonight. She wasn't going to like it, and that made his smile grow bigger. He'd been telling her for a long time now to back the hell off, but her penchant for ignoring his advice was legendary.

They were bound to have a war over this, and he looked forward to it. In the end only one winner would emerge, and he was more than confident who that would be: him.

❖

It was too late to go back to bed, and Diana figured none of them would be able to sleep after the fire department left anyway. The Stevens County Sheriff's Department responded after a call from the fire chief, and she spent a fair amount of time talking to the investigator. From the marks on her car, it was pretty clear the fire was intentionally set. A rag stuffed into the gas tank and set on fire.

Now, a rollback was in the driveway and her car on the way to evidence back in Spokane, thanks to a cooperative spirit between the local authorities and her own department. It looked sad up there on the truck bed, black and hollow, smelling of fire and gas.

In her mind this was definitely all related to their active case. They had a pissed-off serial killer on their hands. Just exactly who he was more pissed off at she wasn't sure: Circe with her twice-vandalized house and tampered-with gates or her. Given that her car was the one he torched, Diana couldn't be sure if he was targeting Circe and her skill at locating the dead, or her, and possibly Paul, for being the two investigators on the case.

Either way, this monster knew exactly who they were and where to find them. First, the damage at her house, and now her car while she was at Circe's. Unless someone was following her, no one could possibly know where she was. This was some kind of scary shit.

"Here." Circe handed her a mug of coffee. "You look like you could use a caffeine intervention."

Gratefully, she accepted the mug of coffee served just the way she liked it, strong and black. Nothing she hated more than ruining a good cup of coffee with sugar or cream, or, God forbid, both. "Thanks."

Paul and Lisa joined them, and the four of them sat around the kitchen table in silence. The surreal feel to everything that had happened seemed to hit each of them at the same time. It sure as hell did for her, particularly since her car was now a pile of blackened metal. She loved that car, and it ticked her off that someone would intentionally set it on fire. It didn't even seem possible someone would do something so evil. Who would do that?

It was a stupid question. In her heart of hearts she felt certain it was the same person responsible for killing those women and burying them in shallow graves all over the city. Not just shallow graves. No, this crazy bastard buried them just yards away from popular recreational areas. How incredibly sick. She'd been around killers her entire career. Sometimes she thought she could understand them, or at least what drove them. Not that she agreed with them, just that she could comprehend how they came to be at the point where they took a life.

But not this one. Not the bodies left like trash or the reports from the ME about the amount of blood loss each had sustained or the multiple stab wounds. Not the things that had been happening to her, to Circe, to all of them, really. And she hated it when things didn't make sense. Drove her nuts.

True, people in her profession had to think outside the box on a regular basis or they'd never get the job done. Even so, much of what they did and the things they discovered contained a certain logic. This didn't.

She was still mulling over how to proceed, and she suspected Paul was doing the same, when Circe spoke up. "What should we do now?" She had a mug between her hands and was turning it around and around without spilling a drop of coffee.

They all turned her way and looked at her expectantly. Even Paul stared at her as if waiting for her to impart great answers to them, which surprised her, considering he usually tossed out ideas on investigations first. She kept recalling something her dad was always saying: "Don't be on the defensive." Right now this bastard had them all on the defensive, so they were playing a constant game of catch-up. That was going to stop this instant. Dad was right. Besides, she always liked offense better anyway.

Setting her mug down on the table, she swept her gaze across all three expectant faces. "We're going to track this son of a bitch down."

❖

For a change everything at home was quiet. He would have put a hefty bet on her throwing a tantrum over his night's activities, but she was uncharacteristically silent. He should probably be nervous by her non-reaction, but honestly he was too damn happy with himself to let it bother him. Instead, he opted to view her silence as an unexpected gift and to accept it with grace.

The key from his pocket unlocked the basement door. An unpleasant odor wafted through the air as he pulled the door open, a reminder of her earlier out-of-control behavior. At the bottom of the stairs he took hold of the broom and began to work. As he swept and mopped his workroom, attempting to put it back in order, his fury tried to rise a number of times. Each time it did, he took it down with the gratitude that her absence created. It was simply much easier to work and think when she wasn't around. He so looked forward to the day when that was a permanent condition. If things kept going the way they had the last few days, that permanent situation would arrive sooner than he envisioned.

With every last shard of glass swept up, undamaged jars returned to their rightful spot on the shelves, and the floor once more spotless, he paused to survey the extent of damage she'd caused. Sadly, it was fairly extensive. Yet as he studied the jars remaining it occurred to him that it wasn't as catastrophic as he first thought. He'd be able to restock it all again without too much trouble.

Besides, though he would never admit it to her, tracking down additional subjects didn't upset him very much. During his time away from Spokane, he'd been able to test his skills and had developed much of what he used now. After he had the *De Nigromancia* it had occurred to him that, in a way, he was going to school. Everything he'd done in all the other places was a sort of homework. Then he came back home and everything came together, and it turned out not only was the work necessary, but it was fun. Who knew?

Or maybe he'd been fooling himself all along. At some level he probably always knew he was a natural for this kind of work. What about all those incidents with the neighborhood dogs and cats when he was in middle school? And then in high school, well, nobody talked about that. In at least six cities, many unsolved disappearances took place. It made him smile to think about it even all these years later.

Truth was he'd always been in the game. The book simply gave him focus and an avenue to channel his energies. It promised him the things everyone desired: money, success, power. Everything he'd learned along the way would come together to create rituals that would result in his achieving all his heart desired. The small rituals he'd tested so far had turned out to be huge successes. When he had his shelves restocked, he'd be ready for the mother of all rituals. He would become untouchable. The thought made his body buzz.

Peering at his precious jars he had an epiphany. He needed subjects, he needed to teach her a lesson, and he needed to get rid of one pesky K9 and her handler. The plan was flawless, everything he needed, and it would all come together in perfect harmony.

God damn, he was good.

CHAPTER TWENTY

Paul waited in the living room while Lisa got ready for her classes. Given everything happening around them, he refused to leave her here by herself. Nor did he want her going into town alone. Call him old-fashioned but he was determined to make sure she was safe. He planned to personally deliver her to classes and pick her up after she was done. Until the crazy bastard doing this was caught, he had every intention of becoming her shadow. Any good cop would do the same thing, given this set of circumstances.

Or, perhaps more accurately, any good cop who was totally infatuated would do it.

Then again, did his actions make him different from Brenda? She was always there, watching him, spying on him, and noting his every move. Was he veering into the land of stalker? Or was his insistence of taking Lisa to school and picking her up something different?

Yes, his mind screamed. Yes. Nobody was threatening him. No one had chucked a brick through his window or turned his car into the towering inferno. Brenda was infatuated with him only because he was who he was, not because he was in danger.

He had every reason to be scared for Lisa. Danger wasn't just a theory; someone had threatened her and Circe. That's what set him apart from Brenda. His concern was because of very real, very tangible danger.

But Will's call chilled him even more than what had happened at Circe and Lisa's house. It frankly didn't make sense. Brenda lived by herself. He was sure of it because he'd been there right after she moved out of his house and back into her own. It was embarrassing to admit she'd sucked him in for one lone roll. He'd been weak and, more embarrassingly, horny. It wasn't an excuse; it was just the facts. If Diana knew, she'd say he let the wrong head do the thinking that night. She wouldn't be wrong either.

Except, even given that mistake, what did he really know about Brenda? He'd been in her house and in her bedroom one single time. That was it. He hadn't explored the rest of the house and didn't have a reason to at the time. He'd realized as soon as he'd done it that sleeping with Brenda was a huge mistake. He'd left as quickly as he could, his own personal walk of shame.

He thought about that night and nothing unusual jumped out at him. The house, or what he saw of it, had Brenda's touch all over it. Then again, just because he didn't see any obvious signs of a man living with her didn't mean much. Her decorating skills had been just about the last thing on his mind at the time. The way she was all over him, the idea she was living with another man was pretty far-fetched.

According to Will, a man was, if not living in her home, at the very least staying there. Will had seen him come and go on no less than three occasions. He didn't see Brenda and the man together, so his observation regarding their relationship wasn't clear at this point. But Will was absolutely certain that a man was there.

Even if he had no personal evidence to back it up, Paul had no reason to dispute Will's report and never would. He'd learned much of what he knew from Will and owed him a great deal for helping him become the kind of detective he was today. If Will said a man was living there, then one was. Either Paul simply missed seeing evidence of a man at her house or he'd moved in after that night of poor choice.

God, he was going round and round in circles, and it bugged the shit out of him. Brenda was so unstable he was scared what she might do. Throw in some random guy, and who knew what she might be able to talk him into doing for her. Given everything else they were dealing with, he was worried he might not see her coming. She'd like that.

"What's put that frown on your face?" Lisa kissed the back of his neck, which, in contrast to his dark thoughts, sent chills of the nice variety down his back.

He turned and looked at her, her natural beauty taking his breath away. With no heavy makeup or high-maintenance hairstyle, she was fresh-faced with her long hair pulled back in a clip. Simple and breathtaking. If the hideous experience with Brenda had brought him to this moment, then it was all worth it. He could spin it any way he liked, but it would all come back around to one simple truth: he was falling hard.

❖

Diana stood in front of the whiteboard and studied the marks she'd made. It didn't take an FBI profiler to see the pattern, and she kicked herself for not doing this earlier. Could be she was losing her touch. "This person is comfortable in this particular geographic area." She tapped the marker against the board.

When she got no response from Paul, she turned. He was sitting in a chair gazing off into the distance. He had that thousand-yard-stare thing happening. Something was going on with him, beyond his getting tight with Circe's roommate, Lisa. She actually approved of that blossoming relationship. Lisa was a night-and-day improvement over Brenda. Of course anyone would be an improvement over that nut job, and that had been her opinion even before she knew how unbalanced Brenda was.

It was about time he found a good one. In the past, he'd been drawn to women of less than Ivy League mentality. Way less. His whole approach was foreign to her; she liked to be able to talk with her dates. Obviously he'd never intended to hold intelligent conversations with most of his. But all that had changed a few days ago. Lisa was most certainly a woman of substance. Diana liked her and hoped her partner, whom she loved dearly, didn't screw it up.

But Lisa hadn't put that look in his eyes now. She'd place a bet on it. He was working through some other deeply felt issue.

"Paul. Dude. What's going on?"

His head came up slowly, and for a second, he looked beyond her. Then his eyes cleared and he appeared to be with her for the first time this morning. "What?"

"What's going on in that pretty little head of yours? You're a million miles away."

"Nothing," he muttered. "What have you got?"

Diana shook her head. "No way. You're not evading the question. What's going on with you? I've been standing here talking to myself for at least ten minutes. We have some murders to solve, you know? Where's your head?"

He blew out a long breath and ran his hands through his shaggy hair. "Okay, you're totally right. I've been preoccupied because Will called me late last night."

She raised an eyebrow. Why hadn't Paul said something earlier? Ordinarily he was quick to bitch about her uncle, though his bitching was usually good-natured. He blew a lot of steam though he actually liked and admired Will, and everyone knew it, including Will. "What'd he say?"

Paul shook his head. "That's the weird part. He told me Brenda's living with some guy."

Had she heard him right? "That doesn't make sense. She's been stalking you like a lovesick adolescent. Someone that entrenched in what they believe is true love wouldn't jump to be with another person. No way. I don't believe it."

"I know." He linked his fingers together and rested them beneath his chin. "It doesn't make any sense to me either, and it's driving me fucking crazy. She's driving me crazy. I wish she'd just disappear."

As if their very conversation had summoned her, Brenda walked up smiling. As usual, she looked as though she'd just stepped out of wardrobe and makeup. Diana wouldn't look that good even if she spent all day in the hands of a professional. This woman seemed to do it with little effort at all. For that alone she could hate her.

It wasn't hard to understand how Paul had been sucked in. Brenda had an alluring aura of intrigue and beauty. But after you got past the mask, the real woman appeared, and you didn't see much except the kind of oddness that left everyone around her feeling uneasy.

"Hi, Diana," she said as she gave her a smile that didn't look even remotely warm. It did the moment she turned her gaze on Paul. Her smile was dazzling and her eyes lit up like neon lights. It wasn't right on a whole host of levels. "Hi, Paul," she drawled in what Diana had to think was her attempt at sexy. Sounded just plain creepy to her.

He jumped up as if someone had just hit him with a cattle prod. "What the hell are you doing here?" he snapped. "Jesus, Brenda, I told you not to come back."

Her smile didn't waver as she held out a paper cup from a local espresso stand. "I thought you could use a latte after the night you had." She put her other hand on his shoulder.

Diana and Paul shared an uncomfortable glance. The same thought had to be flowing through his mind: how would Brenda know anything happened last night?

Paul spun away from her. "What *exactly* are you referring to?"

Brenda's face clouded and she appeared genuinely confused. "Why, darling, it was on the Channel 2 news this morning. There you were on video standing in a driveway by a burning car. You, Diana, and your friends."

Was it just her, or did Diana hear an ominous note in her voice when she said the word friends?

"Video?"

Brenda nodded as she tried again to hand him the latte. "Someone's cell-phone video, or so the newscaster explained."

Diana dropped into her chair and quickly pulled up the Channel 2 news on her computer. Sure as shit, there it was. A shaky but relatively clear video of the car in full blaze, and right behind it stood the four of them: Circe with the hose still in her hand, Diana barefoot, and Paul and Lisa, side by side. She looked at Paul and nodded.

He stood his ground, his hands stuffed in his pockets. Diana had the sense he was holding on to his temper by a mere thread, and she didn't blame him. She was also proud of him for keeping calm. "You need to leave," he said simply.

"But I brought you a latte." Brenda's mouth turned down in a pouty frown, again with the obvious attempt at sexy. Diana wasn't going to be the one to break it to her, but it wasn't working. That look would send anyone sane running in the opposite direction.

Brenda stared at Paul for what felt like five minutes, but he didn't say a word. As the minutes ticked by, every trace of beauty in Brenda's face disappeared, replaced by stark ugliness. She slammed the latte down on Paul's desk so hard the lid popped off and the milky drink splashed all over it, soaking papers and running down the desk leg. "You piece of shit," she hissed. "It's her. I know it is."

His gaze never wavered and his voice remained cool. "Leave now."

At first Diana thought she was going to argue. Surprisingly she didn't say another word. Instead, she stiffly left, not turning around as she disappeared out the door. A woman with a beautiful face had walked in carrying a latte. A woman whose face was marked by ugliness walked out empty-handed.

"Okay..." Diana sank to a chair next to Paul's desk. "As much as I hate to say it, you're screwed. That woman should not be allowed to walk the streets unsupervised."

"Ya think?" Sarcasm replaced the calm he'd embraced earlier with Brenda.

"Indeed I do, and I also think we need to call Will."

Paul rubbed his hands across his scalp, making his hair stand up in all directions. "At this point, I'm not sure what else he or Maddie can do. They've pretty much confirmed she's got serious mental-health issues. If she really is living with some guy, and I believe Will when he says she is, maybe we should touch base with the unlucky sap and tell him to keep his girl on a leash."

"Do you have any idea how sexist that entire thing sounded?"

He rolled his eyes. "That's what you're worried about right now? My not being PC? I'm worried about that woman putting a bullet in my ass."

Truth be told, so was she.

❖

Circe had some time to kill before she needed to head over to Gonzaga University and pick up Lisa. She'd promised Paul she'd be there as soon as Lisa's last class was over to give her a ride home. They'd all decided that for a little while anyway, they would make sure they stuck together. Nothing spooked her easily, but right now, she was twitchy and together was a good thing.

Of course, at the moment she was also alone. Well, sort of. She had Zelda to keep her company and keep her safe. Nobody in their right mind would dare harm Circe when Zelda was around. Then again, whoever was harassing them probably wasn't in their right mind, so who knew what this monster might try? Still, Zelda was imposing and tough. Circe always felt safe with her dog at her side.

With an hour left until Lisa's last class let out, Circe had just enough time for some exercise. It would do her and Zelda good to run a short trail, get some fresh air, and not think about anything unpleasant. While she had plenty of great places to run close to home, she decided they might as well start back toward town. The city didn't lack for trails perfect for biking, running, or hiking. They could do their run closer to downtown and then buzz over to GU to pick up Lisa.

From Highway 291, she pulled off the highway onto Rifle Club Road. Where Rifle Club Road met Aubrey White Parkway, she turned into the small parking area and put her parks' parking pass in the window. Technically they were now in Riverside State Park, and without the pass hanging from her rearview mirror, she ran the risk of a ticket if one of the park rangers checked the parking lot.

Zelda was already jumping around in the back of the car. She knew what they were here for and was delighted. Zelda hadn't met a run yet she didn't love. Road or trail, she adored them all. Circe wasn't far behind her. She enjoyed the fresh air, great trails, and the joy of watching Zelda race through nature.

"Just wait," Circe told her with a laugh. "Give me a sec to get ready."

Getting ready consisted of strapping on her hydration belt and tucking her keys and phone into the small pocket on the belt. Once she snapped in two bottles of water, one for her and one for Zelda, she was ready. Though Zelda hated it, Circe hooked her leash to her collar. She was pretty sure Zelda rolled her eyes.

"You know the drill, girlfriend. You're on the lead until we're out of sight of the parking lot and the road." Dogs off leash weren't allowed in the park, and she didn't want to get a ticket for that either, although once they were a fair distance away from the car, she routinely broke that rule. Only, she justified in her head, because of Zelda's dependability off lead. After all, she wasn't a regular dog. She was special, and that entitled her to break the rules. Sounded good in her head, though she suspected it would be a big fail if she tried to use that rationalization with a park ranger.

Zelda was all but dragging her toward the trails. On the east side of Aubrey White Parkway stretched gentle slopes and open fields full of well-used paths. It was a nice area for a workout but a little too traveled and wide open. Zelda off lead would catch unwanted attention. If they opted for the west side of the road, where the steep banks bordered the river, they wouldn't be visible from the road and would have less chance of running into other people. The trails were far more technical and thus not heavily used. It was a perfect place to run with Zelda off lead.

Once they dropped down far enough to be out of sight, she unclipped Zelda and let her go. She took off like a rocket and Circe had to race to keep up, or at least keep Zelda in sight. Because of the terrain, she had to concentrate, and she liked it a lot. Kept her mind off other things. It didn't take long before she was into the rhythm of the run and felt great.

Until she saw her.

Sitting on a rock, staring out over the gently flowing river, the young woman had her legs pulled up and her arms wrapped around her knees. When she turned to face her, Circe's heart ached. Blood matted her hair and trailed down her pale cheek. Her shirt was torn, bloody, and dirty. One shoe was missing.

Out of the corner of her eye, Circe caught the snap of Zelda's head right before her body stiffened, and her joyful run morphed into that of a dog working. Her legs dug into the ground and she spun back in Circe's direction. She moved slowly along the trail she'd just come across, and her nose went down as she searched the ground along the river. A moment later, she alerted near the river's edge.

"Good girl," Circe said. "Good girl." This time her voice broke.

The girl on the rock met her gaze, and tears fell from her dark-brown eyes. "Thank you," she whispered before she faded away.

For a few minutes, Circe just knelt next to Zelda, stroking Zelda's head. She'd just wanted to go for a run so she'd feel better. Like so much lately, it hadn't worked out even close to the way she'd hoped. While she didn't have Zelda's reward toy with her, she did have some treats in the pocket of her hydration belt. "Good girl," she said as she gave them to Zelda.

The treats gone, she sighed and pulled her cell phone out of the pocket. First she called Brian, then Diana. Finally she sent Lisa a message to wait for her in the Foley Center Library on the GU campus. As it turned out, she and Zelda were going to be a little late picking her up.

Chapter Twenty-one

Eve never steered him wrong, so he was willing to take her advice now. Ignore the bad behavior and give her a little space. In other words, lull her into a false sense of security. When the time was right, he would make certain she was gone once and for all. Of course he didn't say that to Eve. He was pretty sure that wasn't exactly what she meant.

Sometimes, even as smart as she was, Eve was oblivious. She thought of them as the holy trinity and believed they would be together forever. Oh, they were close and had been there for each other for years. That didn't mean the status quo was the right way or the only way. He definitely saw things differently. The trinity, in his mind, had outlived its usefulness. It might have been important at one point, but not any longer. It was time for her to go, permanently.

Better to keep that to himself. Eve was calm and reasonable ninety percent of the time. Like all of them, she had her moments of temper. They weren't a pretty sight, and he didn't intend to bring one of them on. He still had much work to do but was close to bringing it all together. He didn't want to let a marathon session of calming down Eve sidetrack him.

If he kept to the plan, things would turn glorious. She would be gone permanently and he would be free for the first time ever. Even better, he would have everything he could ever want. It was the promise he'd discovered in the *De Nigromancia*, and he believed in the promise even if no one else did. It had already delivered so much to him. The sheer joy he found in following the instructions gave him as much pleasure as the end result ensured.

As he walked toward the kitchen he stumbled when he stepped on another of her damn high heels. He leaned down, picked it up, and hurled it across the room. One day soon he was going to take every last one of her fucking shoes and burn them all in a giant bonfire out in the backyard. He might even roast hot dogs over the damn things. Not even the healthy chicken ones either. Oh no, he would buy the good-old fashioned mystery-meat variety, put them on the end of a dirty stick, and roast them over her burning shoes. She'd hate that.

In the kitchen he switched on the television. Most of the time he considered it nothing more than background noise, but today it caught his attention. Turning up the volume, he stood motionless and stared until the piece ended.

"God damn it." He threw the remote at the flat-panel mounted on the wall. It bounced off the screen and crashed to the floor, where it broke into several pieces. He kicked the broken plastic across the room. It was fucking unbelievable. He had put her where no one should have found her, yet there they were—police, EMTs, news vans—all of them focusing on his work.

Then he saw her, standing off behind the crime-scene techs and uniformed officers. Her and that pain-in-the-ass dog. How in the hell did she even know to search there? She was like a bad rash that refused to go away. Every time he turned around, there she was with that dog searching out and uncovering his handiwork. Today was the last straw. No more toying with her. She was going away, one way or the other, and as he stood and stared at the news report an idea began to form in his mind.

The initial news report had turned his mood black, but now that he had a solid plan, his mood did a complete turnaround. Apparently she wasn't the only one who had her up and down days. Or moods that could turn on a dime. Maybe she was rubbing off on him after all this time. Didn't matter, because all of a sudden he felt good, and he was smiling as he made himself some lemonade. Despite the setback, the day was turning out to be a fine one after all. In fact, this wasn't a setback at all. No, this was an opportunity tailor-made for his special skill set.

❖

Diana had a bad feeling about this. It was almost as though the killer was watching them fumble around as they tried to find him and enjoying their failures and setbacks. They didn't seem to be getting any closer to the bastard, and he knew it. He was laughing at them, toying with them.

If that wasn't bad enough, all the murders were taking a toll on Circe and Zelda too. It wasn't as obvious in the dog. She was tough and always ready to work, but Diana also sensed a sadness in Zelda that hadn't been there on the first day. Violent death exacted a price from everyone, human and canine alike. She hoped Zelda would soon get a break.

In Circe the toll was much clearer to Diana. Of course, part of that had to be the closeness developing between them. They were in tune, and she'd never experienced that total sense of being dialed in to another person. It excited and frightened her all at the same time.

Nonetheless, the feeling of danger was also growing. This bastard didn't appear to be inclined to stop killing, and each time they discovered another body, the danger seemed to step ever nearer to Circe and Zelda. She had to keep them close and make sure they were safe.

Circe touched Diana on the shoulder. "I need to go pick up Lisa. I'm already almost two hours behind schedule. I let her know we'd be really late, but I don't want her to have to wait any longer."

She started to say okay and changed her mind. She needed eyes on Circe until they tracked this killer down. She wanted to know where she was all the time, if not actually be able to see her. Her reaction wasn't reasonable, since it had taken years to find the last active serial killer in the area. But logic wasn't playing a very strong hand at this particular point in time. She didn't want Circe out of sight. She'd left her earlier today and look what had happened. It was going to be eyes-on from now on, at least until she had a sense of safety once more. Sadly that was missing at the moment.

"I have a better idea," she said as she took Circe's hand. "Paul, can you pick up Lisa from GU?"

"What? Leave the scene?"

He had a right to look surprised. This was an active crime scene, they were the lead detectives, and he should be here—under normal circumstances anyway, which of course these weren't.

She nodded while tipping her head in Circe's direction. "She's been waiting for Circe for two hours."

He opened his mouth and then closed it, understanding clear on his face. He nodded and pulled his car keys out of his pocket. "You run lead here and I'm on my way. Where's she waiting?"

"Foley Center Library," Circe told him. She took his hand and held it at her heart for a long moment. "Thank you."

"I got her." He patted Circe's shoulder.

Diana appreciated his willingness to adapt. She would never ask to him to leave a crime scene if it wasn't important. Accepting her request without lengthy explanation was one thing that made him the best partner possible. "Thanks."

He nodded and jogged to his car. He was driving away when suddenly Circe went pale and started to shake. "What's wrong?"

Her voice was shaking as she said, "They're here."

Diana looked around. All she saw were the same people who'd been working the scene for the last several hours. In fact, the first responders had left, so now the only ones remaining were the crime-scene folks finishing their work and investigators like herself and Paul, before he took off to get Lisa.

"Who's here?"

Circe's words were so quiet it was hard to hear them. "The women. All the women."

"What?" She glanced around again to see who the women might be, and then the lightbulb hit a hundred watts. *The women.*

Circe nodded slowly and turned her gaze to Diana. Her eyes were full of sorrow and something deeper: fear. "All the women he's killed are here."

She was no expert on the paranormal, but that didn't sound good. After their recent conversation on the nature of Circe's gift, it sounded particularly bad. The dead didn't come to her like this. First they'd showed up in Circe's home, and now they'd showed up here. They seemed to be following her, and from everything Circe had explained to her, that wasn't a good omen.

"Do you know why?"

Again she nodded slowly. "They're trying to tell me something, the same thing they said before: "Help her." After Zelda and I came across this woman, I thought maybe that's what they meant when they came to me in my bedroom. I saw this young woman sitting on the rock and figured she was the one they wanted me to find. But now she's here telling me the same thing. Find her. Find her. Diana, I don't know who her is and I'm getting scared." Her voice broke.

To hell with protocol and appearances. Diana pulled her close and held Circe in her arms. "We'll figure it out."

Circe's voice was still shaking as she said, "I know we will, but will we figure it out before it's too late?"

❖

On many levels Paul hated leaving the crime scene and almost didn't. Lead detectives did not walk away. On another level, he was totally okay with bailing on the scene to go pick up Lisa. Seeing her face and having her beside him would go a long way toward giving him a feeling of comfort. Everything about what had been happening made him twitchy, Circe and Zelda finding another body right there at the top of the list.

Combine that with Brenda and her fixation on him, and he was uncomfortable at a very deep level. He wanted to get back to a place of control or, at the very least, the illusion of control. He wasn't dumb; he got that control was pretty much out of everyone's hands. That's not what he was talking about. He wanted to go to work, to go home, to meet his friends and know nothing weird would happen. No crazy ex-girlfriends showing up. No burning cars or broken windows. No dead bodies dropping like fall leaves all over the place. He wasn't really asking for much.

Right now, all he needed to get him one step closer to normalcy was to take Lisa's hand and help her into his car. To see her and know she was fine, and that tomorrow held hope for both of them, was huge. He pressed the accelerator a little harder, his lights flashing as he sped through the streets toward the university.

Parking at the university was challenging on the best of days, and just as he'd come here with lights flashing, he opted to use his official capacity to bypass the process of finding a parking spot. He parked right in front of the huge Foley Center Library and jogged up the steps to the entrance. He wasn't exactly sure how he'd find her in the place once he got inside. But no matter what it took, he'd locate her and then keep her by his side until all the madness stopped.

He checked the obvious places first, the tables on the first and second floors. Nothing. She wasn't there. As much as he hated to do it inside the library, which demanded that everyone be quiet, he pulled out his phone and called her. Still nothing. She didn't pick up, and the call went to voice mail after a few rings. He dialed again and walked through the seating areas on the second floor several times, but the telltale ring of a phone never happened. She wasn't here.

He returned to the first floor and started again. This time the faint melodic ring of a phone made him jog toward the sound. It took him to a table near the windows at the front of the library, which was empty except for a bag. His heart sank. He recognized the bag because Lisa had had it with her when he'd dropped her off this morning. Something was very wrong.

Or maybe he was jumping to conclusions. She could have simply gone to the ladies' room. That sounded reasonable, except as a cop and a former university student, he knew better. People did not get up and leave valuable items unattended at a table in a library. Even at the best schools theft happened, and she wouldn't have left her bag, and especially not her phone, at a table in the middle of the library with no one to watch them.

"Where are you?" he whispered. "Where the hell are you?"

At the nearby information counter he leaned in and said, "Excuse me."

The tall, thin guy manning the station turned and looked at him. "Can I help you?"

He held up his badge for the man to see. "Did you see the woman sitting at that table?" He pointed to the table where Lisa's bag hung on the back of the chair.

He smiled. "Yeah. Figured she'd be back by now."

"When did she leave?" He didn't return the smile.

The guy shrugged and the smile faded. "I don't know. Maybe an hour ago?"

His anger flared, fueled by rising panic. "And you didn't think to call anyone?"

With a raised eyebrow, the guy said, "Seriously? You know how many people come and go from here during a shift? People do weird things all the time. They leave stuff at tables. No biggie. They always come back looking for their crap."

He had a point. Whether Paul liked it or not, what he said was reasonable. Under normal circumstances, he'd let it go. "Who did she leave with?"

Again he shrugged. "Wasn't paying that much attention. Some dude, I guess."

Stay calm, he said silently. Do not reach across the desk and grab him around the neck. "What did some dude look like?"

"Geez. I said I wasn't paying much attention."

"Noted. What did you see?"

He scrunched up his face as if thinking was really hard. Finally his face cleared and he said, "Little guy."

Well, that narrowed it down not at all. "Little how? Short, skinny, athletic? What?"

He pursed his lips, and Paul could tell he was trying to remember. "I guess now that I think about it he was probably medium height, but real skinny, long hair in a ponytail. Not a real muscular guy, if you get me. Kinda femmy, actually. Might have been the ponytail though. Not a ton of guys with hair that long these days."

"But she left with a man, right?"

"I didn't look real close, but from what I saw, yeah, he was a dude all right."

From the sound of it, he wouldn't get much more out of this guy, so he thanked him and walked away. At the table he picked up Lisa's bag and phone. As he was walking out to his car with Lisa's stuff, his cell phone rang. Juggling the bag, he managed to get it out of his pocket without dropping anything. "Yeah," he said.

Will bypassed all pleasantries. "Okay, man, you got more problems than just a psycho ex-girlfriend who's living with another sucker."

The tone in Will's voice put him more on edge than he already was. "I don't think that's possible."

"Well, then you need to think again, partner. I took a look around your girlfriend's house—"

"You did a B&E? Are you fucking nuts, Will? You could lose your license. I don't want you doing shit like that."

"Relax. I'm not gonna lose my license. Not on account of your sorry ass, that is. The way I'd tell it, if by some far-out chance a nosy neighbor stopped me, the door was open, and when no one answered my call, I became concerned about Brenda's welfare. I didn't have a choice but to go in and make sure she was okay. I had to look around the entire house before I could make a call about her safety."

It would work. Will had that genuine way about him that made people believe. That and the fact he really was one of the good guys. "Yeah, okay, they'd buy your lame-ass story. So why am I in trouble? I mean beyond the obvious stalking thing."

"I can't even begin to describe this shit over the phone. You have got to see it to believe it. Hell, I saw it and I'm not sure I believe it. Anyway, I'm sending you pictures and then we'll talk."

Will was good to his word. Less than a minute later, Paul was scrolling through a series of photos taken inside Brenda's house. As he looked at picture after picture, a glacial chill raced through his body.

CHAPTER TWENTY-TWO

C irce was getting nervous because Paul hadn't called yet to let them know he'd picked up Lisa. She should never have left her at the university for so long. It was stupid, and if anything went wrong, she had only herself to blame. She should have skipped the damn run and gone directly to the college instead. So what if she'd had to wait for an hour. Big damn deal.

Her cell rang and she jumped. Relief raced through her as she put her hand in her pocket to grab the phone, but it turned to dismay when the display didn't show Paul's number. Rather than the detective, it was her neighbor Rick.

"What's up, Rick?" She hoped she didn't sound as disappointed as she felt.

His words were fast, his voice almost panicked. "Your house, Circe, it's on fire."

Well, she certainly had to have heard that wrong. She was only half paying attention. Putting the palm of her hand over her free ear, she pressed the phone harder against her other ear. Now she was listening. "Come again."

"Fire! Circe, your house is on fire."

"That can't be." It couldn't. Houses burning down happened to other people, not her. She'd purchased that house all by herself ten years ago, and she loved it. The neighborhood was fantastic, her lot had over an acre of grass for Zelda to run on, and she had privacy most people only dreamed of. No way could her slice of Eden be going up in flames. After everything else that had happened over the last few days, it wasn't fair.

"I'm sorry but it's true. The fire department is here now, but it doesn't look good."

"I'm on my way." She ended the call and grabbed Diana by the sleeve. "I've got to go. My house is on fire."

Diana didn't miss a beat. "I'll go with you."

Circe didn't argue. She just opened the car door for Zelda and then got behind the wheel. She didn't pay a great deal of attention to the speed limit as she raced toward home. From above the hills she could see the rise of black smoke and choked back a sob. Long before she got to her turnoff, she could smell the smoke. The air was full of the acrid scent of burning wood. In these parts that meant a wildfire more often than not. Today it didn't.

Her driveway was full of emergency vehicles, and she had to park out on the street. Tears filled her eyes, partially from the smoke and partially from the crystal-clear evidence smoldering in front of her. She dropped to the grass and no longer tried to hold back her tears. A total loss. Her home was a total loss.

Diana was beside her in moments. She put an arm around her shoulders and hugged her close. "I'm sorry," she said and placed a kiss on the side of her head. "I'm sorry."

In her mind she knew it was just stuff that the flames of the wicked fire destroyed. Everything that mattered, Zelda and Lisa, were safe and sound. It hurt nonetheless to see something she'd loved so much destroyed so callously. Given everything that had happened in the last few days, this was no accident. It wasn't right and it wasn't fair.

They were standing together watching the fire professionals do their work when Diana's cell phone rang. While keeping one arm around Circe, she put it to her ear. Circe could feel the tension in Diana's body as she spoke. Absently she wondered who the bearer of bad news on the other end of the call was. Watching flames shoot skyward made it hard to concentrate on anything beyond the tragedy of her world crumbling in front of her.

Diana shoved the phone back into her pocket and then turned Circe to face her. "I think we have a bigger problem than your house fire."

If it was something bigger than her house burning to the ground, she couldn't imagine what it could be. This was huge, no matter how she looked at it. "Tell me. I don't think anything can shock me at this point."

She was wrong.

❖

Paul made it back to PSB in record time. Hopefully, Diana wouldn't be too far behind him. He wasn't sure how they were going to do this legally, but somehow they had to get into Brenda's house.

Then again, if she was as obsessed with him as it appeared, maybe he didn't need to convince a judge to grant a search warrant. There was no law against friends visiting each other in their homes. He was less concerned about legalities at this point and more concerned about finding the crazy bitch.

He'd like for Diana to go with him, to be his backup. But she was on the other side of town with Circe, and she needed to be. After her call to let him know about the fire at Circe's house, the last thing he expected her to do was leave Circe to come back him up. In fact, the more he thought about it, the more he believed the mess in Diana's garage had Brenda's hand in it. The way she'd shot venom in Diana's direction earlier in his office left no doubt in his mind about how Brenda felt about her. A rival.

No way could he pull off a friendly visit if Diana was standing right behind him. If Brenda was home, she would go ballistic if he showed up with her partner. Will would be his best choice for cover. Brenda knew about his old partner, though she also knew he was Diana's uncle. Hopefully she'd forget that part. The fact that his luck lately sucked didn't matter. It was worth a shot and, the way he saw it, his best shot at getting in her house ASAP.

He sent two texts, one to Will and the second to Diana. It was just as well she stayed with Circe.

Brenda knew something about Lisa, he felt it in his bones, and she was going to tell him or...

No, he wasn't going there. It was going to work out. Brenda had issues, that was a given. Obviously so did the guy she was living with. He and Will just needed to reason with her and this would all be okay. In the back of his mind, though, a bit of ice remained. Despite all the years of training and all the experience of working in his chosen field, one thing remained constant: you can't reason with an unreasonable person. At this point, he was ready to do whatever he needed to get Lisa back safely.

His relief when Will picked up on the first ring was huge. Until he heard his voice, Paul didn't realize how frightened he was that he would have to go this alone. When did he become afraid to face her? Probably at the same time he finally grasped how unbalanced she was.

He and Will decided to park their cars a block away from Brenda's house. She would invite him in, he didn't have any doubt about that, especially since he was coming to her. She would be enthralled to believe he was seeking her out. Even so, it was wiser to go in quietly and unexpectedly. He didn't want to give her time to think about anything or put the guy she was living with on alert. Surprise was a good tactic, given who he was dealing with.

"Boy, I hope you're ready for this," Will said as he stood beside his car patting down the straps of a bullet-proof vest. He was obviously taking no chances. Not only was he wearing the vest, a new one, but he had a gun and a canister of pepper spray in holsters at his waist. Handcuffs glinted at his back. The last time he'd seen Will this geared up, he was still on the job.

Paul would have followed suit and put on his own vest, but he didn't have it with him. He'd driven his personal vehicle and didn't keep a vest in the trunk. After this experience, one of the first things he planned to do was buy one and keep it in his car. He did have his gun, a set of handcuffs, and some zip ties. They would have to be enough. "I'm ready. You think her boyfriend's involved with Lisa's disappearance?"

Will nodded, his face solemn. "From everything I saw in there, I'd say the odds are better than average that the guy is on board for whatever freaky shit your girlfriend is into. This chick is more than obsessed with you, and if she perceived Lisa as a threat, I don't think there's any question she'd do whatever she decided was necessary to get rid of her and away from you. Look what she did to Diana, and we all know there's nothing with any romantic overtones between the two of you." He smacked Paul on the shoulder. "Wait until you see what's inside. Then you'll understand where I'm coming from. The pictures didn't do this place justice. She's wacked, man, and I wouldn't be surprised if her boy toy is too."

He'd taken everything Will had explained after his covert B&E to heart and looked at the pictures he sent over and over. He'd heard Will's description and he'd seen the images, and it still threw him. None of it tracked with the woman he'd lived with for a few months. Even during the short time they'd been together, he'd seen her quirky side, but during those brief months of cohabitation, he didn't notice anything that red-flagged her as an unstable personality. Self-centered and vain, absolutely. Even outrageous and bizarre on occasion. Yet everything Will told him leaned heavily in the direction of clinically insane. Brenda's stalking was creepy and invasive. He hated it, and he'd never deny he'd been calling her crazy since this whole thing began. Still, the behavior he'd witnessed didn't reach the level of true insanity suggested by the pictures, so this he needed to see for himself.

He slapped Will on the back this time. "All right, let's try this nice and friendly. See where it gets us."

"You think you can pull off friendly with this bitch?"

Valid question and he had to think honestly about his answer. "It'll be an effort."

They were walking down the block side by side when his cell phone rang. He pulled it out of his pocket and stared at the display. Diana. "Yeah."

As he listened, he stopped walking and glanced over at Will, who mouthed the word, "What?"

He shook his head slightly and continued to listen. Finally, he asked, "You're kidding, right?"

Ending the call, he slowly put the phone back into his pocket and turned to face Will. "I think we have bigger problems than an ex-girlfriend who might have lost her mind."

Will was shaking his head. "Doubt it, my man." He inclined his head in the direction of Brenda's front porch. "Your biggest problem is right inside that house." Will's hand hadn't moved from his gun since they started walking.

He inwardly cringed at what they were going into, yet after listening to Diana, he didn't know who or what was the biggest threat at the moment. All hell was breaking loose, and it seemed they were right smack in the eye of the storm.

He stared at Brenda's front door and fought the urge to turn around and leave. "Maybe, but this latest wrinkle might be even bigger than what we find on the other side of that door."

"I don't believe it, son."

Paul looked Will in the eyes. "You will. Circe's house isn't the only one on fire. Somebody just tried to burn down Diana's house too."

❖

She'd had her fun and now it was his turn. That was the bargain they'd struck and he planned to hold her to it. Besides, little did she know it was going to be her last fun-and-games adventure. The time he'd been waiting for was now. Eve might not agree, but he didn't really care at this point. It was time. He'd always known that when the day arrived he'd sense it, and in fact, he did. He felt it in every pore of his body.

His prize was already downstairs and waiting for him to return. Really, there was no hurry. He had all day. All night for that matter. When he started out everything was wham bam. Get it done and get it cleaned up before anyone was the wiser. It had worked too, and for years he'd been able to do as he pleased. He'd managed to stay under the radar in every place he lived and worked.

Until he discovered the book and realized how enjoyable and fulfilling it could all be. Being slow and careful, and paying attention to every little detail made it so much more extraordinary. The book validated everything he strove to accomplish. It gave him purpose and a compelling reason to continue his work. Not that he needed much encouragement. He loved what he did. His prize today was truly exceptional, and the danger inherent in having her here made it all the more special. He was so excited as he drove her home that his hands had been shaking.

When he'd come home to find so much of his work destroyed he'd wanted to kill her then and there. Entirely too many years of putting up with her crap had taken its toll. He'd been ready to blast her out of existence at that moment. Eve had stepped in and made him see reason, as she often did. She was right too when she told him to let it go and rebuild. Little did he realize at that moment how special rebuilding would turn out to be. It was more fun than when he began this journey long ago, and the quality of what he harvested was going to be far superior to his first effort. It was guaranteed to enhance the end result.

So, right now he'd forgiven her for the temper tantrum that had caused such damage and destruction to his work. Forgiveness, however, didn't mean she was going to stick around. No, the die was cast on that one. Her usefulness had ended. His patience with her had ended. Regardless of how everything else worked out, she was going away for good, and he intended to be the one to usher her out. He looked forward to it almost as much as he looked forward to working with his basement guest.

"Uh-oh," he said with a smile. "Somebody's awake."

From the basement, sounds of movement and muffled screams drifted up from the open doorway. He wasn't particularly concerned that the sounds would alert neighbors. She was shackled and gagged, after all, and couldn't make enough noise to alert anyone unless they were standing in the doorway. Even then, if they didn't know what they were hearing, the noise would sound more like a pet rustling around than what it really was. He'd keep that little secret to himself.

Just to be on the safe side, he double-checked the front, back, and garage doors to make sure the deadbolts were engaged. It wasn't wise to leave the house unlocked when he was in the basement working. He became so involved with his tasks, he didn't hear what was going on around him. The last thing he needed was for someone to interrupt him while he worked. Sometimes she would leave through one of the doors and forget to lock it, yet another trait of hers that drove him crazy. Soon he wouldn't have to worry about locking up behind her.

He had just taken two steps down toward the basement when the doorbell rang. He frowned. Who could possibly be here? None of them exactly had what anyone would call friends. Especially not the kind of friends who would drop in unannounced. His first thought was neighborhood kids looking for donations to soccer or basketball or band. They were like locusts always looking for money, and he had no trouble blowing them off. He was glad he didn't have kids.

Backtracking to the front door, he peered through the peephole and almost groaned out loud.

Chapter Twenty-three

U nlike Circe's house, which appeared to be a total loss, the fire department had been able to respond quickly and promptly, and did an excellent job at containing the fire before it could erupt into a massive conflagration. The relief Diana felt when the fire chief told her they had the fire under control was greater than she believed possible. It also made her feel even worse for Circe.

Standing in the driveway, she coughed as a gust of air brought the heavy acrid scent of fire wafting from what was once her garage. It would require extensive repairs, but the gods were definitely smiling on her today because the main structure was intact, having suffered just smoke damage. She could work with that.

Only a fool would believe the two fires were coincidences, and she was no fool. As she waited and watched, she also surveyed everything and everyone. How often did the one who set the fire stay around to watch it burn? According to the experts, pretty much all the time. As she scanned the onlookers, she noticed the faces of her neighbors, exactly the people she'd expect to see. No strangers, no one who seemed out of place. Unless one of her long-time neighbors had suddenly morphed into a firebug, and she seriously doubted that was the case. Old Mr. Johnson with his three pugs or perky Lacy Steers with her obsession with yoga? Not likely.

This time might be different and the experts wrong. She'd felt certain Brenda had vandalized her garage earlier, yet now she wasn't so sure. Everything that had happened in the last few days was different, though in the back of her mind two words kept going around and around: common thread. Something about the fires, the murders, the gates, and the vandalism seemed to carry a common thread. Brenda might be pissed enough to trash her garage in a fit of jealousy, but this fire was too far along the violence scale to fit Paul's obsessed ex-girlfriend.

Her hands in her pockets, Diana fingered the small whistle. As the days had rolled by, she'd become more and more convinced that an active serial killer was at work. But was it that simple? Or was there more to this story than a serial killer?

She waited at the house with the fire department until her dad showed up. He could help them with anything they needed in her absence, and she felt compelled to go back up Paul. Her last two calls had gone right to voice mail, as did her calls to Will. Paul hadn't explained in detail what they were up to, but she had a fair idea. After all, she'd been around Will all her life and had been partners with Paul long enough to pretty much read his mind. They were headed over to confront Brenda. Double trouble, the way she looked at, and she was worried they might have stepped in it big time.

"You stay here with my dad," Diana said to Circe, who'd insisted on coming to town with her when she got the call about the fire at her home. Circe's house was a smoldering pile of rubble so there was little need for her to remain there. She'd loaded up Circe and Zelda, and they'd come here with Diana.

Circe was shaking her head as she headed toward the unmarked car Diana had grabbed from the carpool earlier that day. "No way. Come on, Zelda." She opened the back door for Zelda, who jumped in and sat down. Diana didn't think she'd be able to budge her if she tried.

"I'm not kidding, Circe. You and Zelda need to stay here with Dad. Zelda, here girl." She patted the side of her leg, but Zelda just stared out the front window of the car as though Diana hadn't said a word and didn't so much as twitch an ear.

Circe walked to the passenger's side door and opened it. She stared over the hood of the car at Diana. "I'm not kidding either. We go with you. End of discussion."

Diana looked over at her dad, the guy who'd taught her so much. He nodded and said simply, "Let them go. I'll take care of things here."

"Dad, this could go really bad." She didn't think he had a good grasp of the danger she was afraid they were walking into, even though she'd shared with him her thoughts and suspicions. She always welcomed his counsel and counted on him to give solid advice.

His gaze moved between Diana and Circe, and a look she couldn't quite define passed over his face. "Let them go," he said again.

"Come on," Circe said. "Listen to your father and get in the car. We're burning daylight." From the backseat, Zelda barked as if to add her "come on" to the mix. Circe got in the car and slammed the door.

"All right," she said and went around to the driver's side. After she was buckled in and the car was in gear, she turned and looked at Circe. "You have to promise to do exactly what I tell you. I'm not kidding, Circe."

Circe kept her gaze forward. "I hear you, and I will do as you tell me. We will."

Neither of them said a word all the way into town. About a block away from Brenda's house, she noticed the two cars Paul and Will had driven. She pulled in behind Will's black Ford F150 and parked, realizing immediately why they were here when there was plenty of room in the block ahead. If they'd decided they needed to come in unannounced, then she would too.

From the glove box she pulled out her Glock and tucked it in the holster at her waist. She turned in her seat and took Circe's hand. "Please, just wait for me here. I shouldn't be long."

Circe surprised the crap out of her when she simply nodded and squeezed her hand. "Okay. Be careful."

"Count on it." That was a relief. She didn't want to have to worry about Circe too. Zelda could probably take care of business pretty quickly, but Circe wasn't exactly the confrontational type. She felt a whole lot better with them staying in the car a safe distance away from Brenda's house and the trouble she felt certain was just inside the front door. Her own sixth sense was in high gear, almost screaming "beware" at her.

Diana got out and started toward Brenda's house. Twice she glanced back just to make sure Circe and Zelda were still in the car. So far, so good.

The house appeared quiet, and she wanted to look around before she marched up to the door. She really wished it was dark outside instead of broad daylight, but at least bushes, flowering plants, and trees ringed the perimeter of the yard. Lots of nice green cover to hide behind. Thank you, Brenda.

Casually, she walked past the driveway and then ducked in behind the bushes. She made her way to the rear of the house, the greenery effectively camouflaging her. This was turning out to be easier than she'd anticipated. As she moved in slowly toward the house she expected to hear voices. Will and Paul had to be inside, yet she heard nothing. The house was eerily quiet, which made the hairs on the back of her neck stand up. That bad feeling she got when things were wrong at a crime scene came screaming in double time. Her body buzzed as though she'd just downed a pot of coffee in a single gulp. This was not good.

Peering in through a window covered by a partially opened blind, she felt her heart take a leap. Her feelings had never been wrong, and they weren't now. Will lay prone on the floor, one arm flung out to the side and his other underneath his body. It looked like blood pooled by his head. She jumped back and moved to the cover of the shrubs. For just a moment, she closed her eyes and tried to calm the sensations racing through her body. She had a horrible feeling Will wasn't the only one in trouble inside that house. In a voice as quiet as she could keep it, she called for backup.

A smart cop would wait for the backup to arrive. But she wasn't feeling very smart and wasn't about to wait for anyone else to get here. Paul was in there somewhere and maybe Lisa as well. Her psychic sense, or whatever in the hell it was, screamed at her to go, go, go. She couldn't afford to risk the wait. Going now was worth the price.

She made her way to the back door and crouched down. As before, she heard nothing. Reaching out, she took hold of the doorknob and tried to turn it. The door was locked, and it was made of solid wood. She wouldn't be kicking this one down. If she were some TV detective she'd whip out her lock picks and be inside within seconds. Reality sucked. She didn't have lock picks, and even if she did, those things were harder than hell to use.

Frantically, she looked around, finally deciding her best bet for entry wasn't the door. It was the small window to the left of the door. Getting up slowly, she peeked in. The window was off a bathroom, and blessedly, it was empty. With effort, she tore the sleeve off her shirt and then wrapped it around her hand. The fabric kept her hand from being sliced up when she broke the glass of the window and reached through to unlock it. Hoisting herself up to the frame, she wiggled in, dropping to the floor in near silence.

Holding perfectly still, she listened for any sound. As before, nothing. On silent feet she made her way into the front room, where Will was still laid out on the hardwood floor. She put two fingers to his neck, grateful to feel warm skin and a steady pulse. Now all she had to do was find Paul and Brenda. Down the hallway she discovered a single bedroom, a full bath, and a tidy office. The bedroom had a queen-sized bed, fully made up, and it appeared as though anyone rarely used the room. In the closet hung several items of women's clothing, though nothing she ever recalled seeing Brenda wear.

She tried the upstairs next. The first bedroom was a bland room with a full-sized bed and little else. The second room made her pause. A man clearly called this bedroom his, and the closet bore out that assumption. Men's shirts, pants, and boots filled it. Men's cologne and deodorant sat on the chest of drawers. Will was right; a man was indeed living with Brenda. She certainly didn't let any grass grow under her feet, which begged the question: why stalk Paul if she was living with another man?

The final bedroom had to be Brenda's, and she thought she was prepared for what she'd find there. Not for the first time today, she was wrong.

"Mother of God," she whispered as she stood in the open doorway. It was Brenda's room all right. The décor was vintage Brenda, marred only by the hundreds of photographs pinned to every available surface. Most were photographs of Paul. A few were of her and a few more of Lisa. Her feelings toward Diana and Lisa were clear, as evidenced by the bold red-marker slashes across their faces. The sight made her sick to her stomach.

A noise from downstairs made her spin and raise her gun hand. It was the first sound she'd heard since coming inside. Cautiously she made her way downstairs. Peering into the kitchen she almost screamed when she saw Circe tiptoe to the back door and reach to open it.

Softly she hissed, "Circe!"

But she was too late. Circe had already turned the knob and the door flew open. Zelda raced through, and Diana paused for a moment to let her mind register what she saw. Zelda was in full-on search mode, and that's when all hell broke loose.

❖

"Will you please knock it off!" He whirled around and glared at the man handcuffed, gagged, and tied to the support post next to the stairs. He was kicking and screaming against his gag, and frankly, the obnoxious noise was getting on his nerves.

He was trying to set up his little prize for the main event, and everything needed to be in order. How on earth could he concentrate when this ass was making all that noise? Honest to God, what she saw in that piece of shit, he'd never know.

It would be so easy to end it for him right now. Except easy wasn't what he was going for today. He wanted to teach her a lesson before he got her out of his life. The only way to do that was to crush her obsession. And the easiest way to do that? Well, that was a simple one: kill his latest conquest right in front of the eyes of her beloved. God, how she'd whimper and cry. It was so perfect.

He almost laughed. All of this was just as much for his own enjoyment as it was to get back at her. The element of danger involved today was astronomical and the best high he'd ever enjoyed. After today it would be hard to come up with something to match it.

Of course, if everything went as planned, he wouldn't need any of this again. All the pieces would be in place to follow the text of the *De Nigromancia*. Fame, fortune, and power would all be his and his alone. He'd waited a long time, and nothing would stand in his way. Especially not an obnoxious cop.

When he was satisfied that he'd secured his latest conquest to the stainless table, he gave her a pat on the shoulder. "I'll be right back, princess. We need your boyfriend to take it down a notch or twelve so I can concentrate. You and I are going to spend some quality time together, and it's better if we don't have that noise box bothering us."

Before he left the table, he picked up the remote and turned on the music. For today's work he thought something deep, dark, and complicated like Rachmaninov. With the piano strains filling the room, he smiled. Yes, that was the perfect accompaniment for the job. He ran a finger down her cheek. "Now, isn't that nice?"

Laying the remote back on the table, he turned and walked over to his captive. "I said knock it off." He pulled his arm back and then swung as hard as he could. His open hand connected with his cheek, snapping back his head. A bright red outline of his palm and fingers flared up on the side of the man's face. He loved it. Finally the ass was quiet, and for a moment, all he could hear was the wonderful piano concerto blaring from his speakers. Yes, that was much better.

Then another sound made him whip his head up. Was it the other one? If not already dead, he would be soon. No way would he be up and moving. He'd hit him hard enough take down a man twice his size. No, it must have been something outside.

He went back to the table where the woman, now alert, stared at him with eyes wide in terror. He wanted to pause and savor the moment. That look never got old. He counted on the rush it gave him each and every time he had one ready for the main event. He smiled down at her and started to pick up one of the gleaming instruments from his side table.

Another sound pulled his gaze away from her terrified face, and he frowned as he put the instrument down. The old bastard obviously had more in him than he thought. Well, he wouldn't for long. Turning away from the woman, he grabbed a mallet from the workbench near the stainless table and started for the stairs.

When he'd seen these two on his doorstep he'd actually laughed, immediately sensing how much fun they were going to bring to the game. And they had, at first. Now they were both starting to get on his nerves. One couldn't be quiet and the other didn't have the good sense to lie there and die. As usual, he would have to take care of everything himself.

He had one foot on the bottom step when something hit him full on and knocked him backward and very nearly sent the mallet flying. He kept his grip as it dawned on him it was that damned dog. Fury turned his vision red, and he swung the mallet with everything he had.

❖

Circe heard Zelda yelp, and the sound spurred her forward. She knew coming inside was a bad idea. As the minutes had passed while she sat in the car, she'd worried more and more that Diana was in danger. It hadn't been hard to talk herself into following her inside. She might not be a cop, but she wasn't exactly a layperson either. Their search training included what to do in a hostile situation, and this certainly qualified as one of those. With Zelda beside her, they could help, so that's what she'd decided to do.

Like Diana, she'd crawled in through the window and opened the back door for Zelda. The look of dismay on Diana's face when she walked into the kitchen and saw them would have stopped most people. But Circe hadn't had time to do anything other than follow when Zelda's head did the telltale snap as she raced for the basement stairs.

Circe was certain of only one thing: the basement held human remains. Strangely, the dead didn't show themselves to her, so she had nothing to go on other than Zelda's nose. In all their time together, Circe had learned much about Zelda, including the fact that she wasn't wrong when it came to finding the dead. If she was on scent, she would find remains.

Everything went silent after Zelda's yelp came up from the basement, and at the sound of her dog's cry, Circe's heart constricted. If anything happened to Zelda, she didn't know what she'd do. If that woman hurt her dog, well...

She raced to the open basement door, but before she could go down, Diana grabbed her arm and yanked her back. "Are you crazy?" she hissed. "Brenda could be standing down there with a gun ready to blow your head off."

"Zelda," Circe said, and her voice broke. She wanted to sound tough and ready to fight. It didn't work. She was terrified for her best friend and ready to face a gun to protect her.

"I know, I know. It won't help her if you race down there unprepared and get yourself killed."

"I need to get to her."

"And you will, but not until I go first. We don't know who all is down there. It could be Brenda or her boyfriend or both. I'm certain they're dangerous, and you're not tearing down the stairs unprepared. Let me handle this, it's what I do."

Her heart was pounding and adrenaline was flooding her body. She needed to get to Zelda, and at the same time she knew Diana was right. Her grand plan to help had just blown up in her face and might very well have killed Zelda. How would she ever be able to forgive herself?

Diana must have seen those concerns in her face. She quickly kissed her on the cheek and then whispered in her ear. "Go outside and watch for the backup I called. Let them know I'm downstairs and so are the perps."

She wanted to argue her case to rescue Zelda more than anything she'd done in her life. She didn't. Diana was right, and the best thing she could do was go outside, wait for the officers coming to assist, and pray Zelda was going to be all right.

"All right," she whispered back and reached out to give her a hug, even though she knew this was the last time and place to bother with affection. She didn't care, she had to touch her. She needed physical reassurance. "Be careful."

Diana nodded, kissed her quickly one more time, and then disappeared down the stairwell. Circe prayed it wouldn't be the last time she saw her alive.

Chapter Twenty-four

D iana didn't pause to make sure Circe followed her directions because she didn't have time. Zelda's rush down those stairs had eliminated any hope of surprise. Brenda and her boyfriend were sure to be waiting for them with guns locked and loaded. Holding her position until backup arrived would still be the wise course, except she was worried what would happen to Paul here in the house of crazy if she didn't get down there right now. And Zelda, if she was being completely honest. She was as worried about the dog as she suspected Circe was.

Her nerves were tingling as she took the steps carefully, one by one. As she moved down each step, the stairwell opened up and she swept her gaze across the room, capturing everything in an instant. Lisa lying strapped to a stainless table next to a smaller worktable, cutting tools lined up on it with military precision. A drain fitted in the middle of a concrete floor in a full-sized room. Numerous glass jars filled with dark liquid sitting on shelves lining a wall. A sink, a hose, and Zelda, unmoving on the hard floor. Finally, Paul, his arms handcuffed around a support post and a gag in his mouth. Desperately he yanked his head to the left, and for a moment she didn't understand.

And then she understood just before an arm slashed down toward her face, a silver scalpel barely missing her cheek. She whirled in time to see a man, his face distorted with rage, coming at her again.

Her single thought was to stop him. She had no idea if Brenda was here too, and if she was, where? It didn't matter. At the moment, the threat was this man and the fury he directed solely at her. She pulled up her arm, gun in hand. But before she had a chance to shoot, he charged, hitting her with all his weight, and the gun went flying. Diana had made a rookie mistake of misjudging her aggressor.

The scalpel was her foremost concern. He was dangerous with that weapon in his hand, and she had to get it away from him. As he charged at her again, the scalpel front and center, she stepped to the side and hit him in the back of the neck. When this was all over, she was definitely going to thank Paul for insisting on the martial-arts lessons he pushed down her throat on a regular basis. The next Saturday morning she gave up for the lessons, she'd do so smiling.

Whirling, she readied herself for the next assault. The guy was quick on his feet, and just as she'd done, he whirled and launched himself at her again. This time she was ready. The scalpel went flying and they tangled, falling to the ground. The rage in him was evident in the fight. He punched, clawed, bit, and screamed.

As they rolled and fought, each trying to get purchase on the other, he somehow got his hands on the scalpel again. Before she realized what he'd done, he plunged it into her shoulder. She screamed as pain, hot and intense, roared through her body. For a split second, she loosened her grip on him, and he took the opportunity to free himself.

He stood over her panting, the scalpel dripping with her blood. "You stupid bitch," he ground out. "You stupid, interfering bitch. Say good-bye to your boyfriend. You won't be seeing him again."

As he came toward her for the kill, she actually saw his face for the first time. Shock rendered her speechless as the truth hit home and a bullet shot from the stairwell hit Brenda in the shoulder.

❖

Paul rubbed his shoulders, trying to ease the pain created when she'd tied him to the posts. Brenda was screaming incoherently as she was cuffed, spittle flying while she cursed. She looked nothing like the woman Paul had dated and lived with, nothing like the obsessed woman who'd stalked him for months. Dressed in men's clothing, not wearing a trace of makeup, and her hair pulled back in a ponytail, at first glance, she looked like a man. Even her voice sounded different, at least part of the time.

It was like being in some bizarre movie with a plot line that made no sense whatsoever. Except it did in a strange way. The domino pieces were suddenly falling into place. In the time he'd been in this house, and particularly down here watching the odd transitions from woman to man to woman to man, he'd come to understand so much. And it made it him sick.

The second he was freed from his restraints, he raced to Lisa's side. She was sitting on the side of the table that moments before had held her captive. She started to cry as he reached for her.

"You came for me," she cried against his shoulder.

"I'll always come for you," he said against her hair.

He helped her down from the table. She was unsteady on her legs and he didn't blame her. He felt the same way. Getting out of the way of the responding officers, they both sank slowly to the floor, their backs against a concrete wall. Diana, with Circe holding a towel to her wound, sat on the bottom step. At their feet, Zelda rested, having regained consciousness.

He looked around at the horrors of the room and shuddered. He'd come so close to losing Lisa, and it was his fault. He'd let this woman, this insane woman, into his life, and it had almost cost him everything.

"You okay?" Lisa asked him.

Paul put an arm around her shoulder and pulled her close. "I don't honestly know. I've never encountered one of these before."

She leaned her head against his shoulder. "I'm not surprised. They're quite uncommon."

Of course she'd know. This was her area of expertise. "How did I miss the signs?"

"These people are quite adept at appearing normal. Brenda, particularly when she was with you, had to have been a pro at keeping control. She kept the man, whatever his name turns out to be, well under wraps."

"You think it was just the two of them?"

She hugged him tightly. "We'll find out. Someone with expertise in multiple personalities will evaluate her, and we'll know soon enough."

He rubbed his hands over his face as the gravity of what had just happened washed over him. "She...he...almost killed you."

She kissed the side of his head. "But she didn't, and that's what counts."

❖

Circe didn't think she'd ever been this scared before now. She'd gone outside fully intending to wait for law enforcement, but that decision lasted all of about two minutes. She couldn't stand it. Both her woman, and that's how she thought of Diana, and her dog were in there with insane people. Their lives were in danger, and she didn't intend to stand around sucking her thumb.

It finally hit home who the dead were asking her to help: Lisa. They had tried their best to warn her, and until she'd stood outside on Brenda's porch she hadn't been able to see it. While Diana might be in danger too, she had skills and training. Lisa didn't. All she had was a friend who could hear the warnings of those who'd fallen at the hands of the killer who now held her captive. She spun on her heel and retraced her steps.

Back inside, she realized she had to have some type of weapon, and she'd spotted Will's gun. He was still out cold and wasn't going to be able to use it, so she decided it was fair game. She took a few precious seconds to figure out how to take the safety off and then quietly, at first anyway, made her way down the stairs. All she could see, when she got down enough to have an open view of the big room, was Diana and a man fighting on the concrete floor. When he plunged a sharp instrument into Diana's shoulder, her cry of agony nearly undid Circe. First her dog was hurt and now Diana. No way could she stand by and just let it happen.

Her hands were trembling as she brought the gun up, waiting for a clear shot. The man gave it to her as he stood and backed up a few steps. Diana was holding her shoulder, and the look of astonishment on her face surprised Circe. She followed her gaze and saw what had shocked her into inaction.

A man hadn't just stabbed Diana; it was the woman, Brenda. Oh, she was dressed as a man and even looked like one, but it was most certainly her. It didn't make sense, and at the moment, it didn't need to. What mattered was stopping her before she hurt anyone else. As she charged Diana again, with what Circe could see was a scalpel held high, she didn't hesitate. She pulled the trigger.

She was aiming for Brenda's head. Her skills with a handgun being what they were, she hit her in the shoulder. It was enough. The scalpel went down and so did Brenda, screaming in what had to be pain and certainly shock. Circe had to bet she wasn't expecting a dog handler to take her down.

Circe didn't need to do anything else once Brenda was down because suddenly people were everywhere. The backup Diana had called for earlier had just arrived. A little late but welcome just the same. She let one of the officers gently dislodge the gun from her hands. She hoped she never had to hold one again.

She checked to make sure Diana was okay, then saw to Zelda. As she picked up her big head, Zelda's eyes opened. That was enough to make her cry, and she cradled her dog and sobbed. She'd never been so grateful in all her life.

Diana was able to make her way over to the bottom step, where she sat down heavily. Her shoulder was bleeding, and so Circe put Zelda's head down gently and then took off her button-down shirt, which she pressed against the wound in Diana's shoulder.

"You're going to get cold," Diana said as she leaned into Circe.

She glanced down at the tank top she'd worn underneath. "Sweetheart, I have so much adrenaline running right at the moment, it'll be a week before I get cold."

"Thank you," Diana said softly.

She kissed her cheek. "No, thank you."

Diana's laugh was bitter. "For what?"

"Oh, baby, for everything. For not dying. For charging in to save my friend. For being in my life."

"Don't forget, I like your dog."

In spite of everything going on around them, Circe laughed. "Yeah, that too."

EPILOGUE

Being able to see dead people sucked, and that's how it had always felt to Circe. Until now. If her life had been different she probably never would have met Diana. Six months after that day in People's Park, where the bodies of three young women had brought them together, she couldn't imagine a day without her in her life.

She was pretty sure Lisa felt the same way about Paul. All it had taken was a serial killer with multiple personalities to make their lives complete. Who knew?

"Well, what do you think?" Diana draped an arm around her shoulders.

They were standing in Circe's driveway and looking at the beautiful house that had risen from the ashes of the one that had burned down. At first they'd believed Brenda had burned the house because of Paul's interest in Lisa. As it turned out, it hadn't been Brenda but Bryce, her male personality, who'd not only burned the house but had broken the window and cut the gate locks because he was pissed off that Zelda and Circe kept finding his bodies.

Brenda had done her own bit of torching. For her it was Diana's house she'd put a match to, as well as being responsible for the vandalism to her garage. She was furious about Paul's interest in Lisa and also about Diana's close relationship to Paul. It didn't matter that their partnership didn't extend beyond friendship and work. Anyone she perceived as interfering with her obsession with Paul threatened her.

In the end, the doctors found three distinct personalities: Eve, Brenda, and Bryce. It would probably be years before they understood the why behind her fractured psyche. Not that it mattered. As a serial killer, she would spend the rest of her life behind bars. Certainly the bars of a psychiatric facility but bars nonetheless. She wouldn't be surprised if Brenda became a psychiatric favorite, given her obsession with the ancient text she was convinced would eventually give her everything she wanted as long as she completed a series of bloody rituals.

At least they were all free of her threat, and Will, who'd taken a significant blow to the head, had fully recovered. She couldn't hurt any of them again. Paul and Lisa had been able to explore what everyone who knew them declared to be true love. If they weren't married inside of a year, Circe would be shocked. Right now, they were on a plane headed for Vancouver and a long weekend enjoying the beauty of Western Canada. Will was back doing whatever it was that Will did and also checking in every so often to make sure his favorite niece wasn't getting herself into any more trouble.

Today, she and Diana had important things to do. It was letting-go day.

"I think it's beautiful," she said and couldn't help the quaver in her voice. This had been her home, and when it was burned to the ground, the loss had broken her heart. But as it had risen from the ashes and once more grown beautiful, her feelings had changed. So, it appeared, had Zelda's, as she now sat in the car waiting for Circe and Diana. She smiled as she looked over at the beautiful stained-glass front door and freshly painted shutters. It was still a home, just not hers any longer.

"It's looking pretty great. You sure you're okay with this?"

She turned and smiled at Diana. "One hundred percent." She dropped her gaze to the engagement ring on her left hand, and her heart soared. "Come on. Let's go meet the attorney, get the sale papers signed on this place, and go home. We have a wedding to plan."

About the Author

Sheri Lewis Wohl grew up in Northeast Washington State and always thought she'd move away to somewhere exciting. Never happened. Now she happily writes surrounded by unspoiled nature, trying to capture a bit of that beauty in her work. No matter how hard she tries to write *normal*, though, it doesn't work—something of the preternatural variety always sneaks in. When not working or writing stories filled with things that go bump in the night, she trains for triathlons, acts, and is a member of a K9 Search & Rescue team.

Books Available from Bold Strokes Books

A Reunion to Remember by TJ Thomas. Reunited after a decade, Jo Adams and Rhonda Black must navigate a significant age difference, family dynamics, and their own desires and fears to explore an opportunity for love. (978-1-62639-534-3)

Built to Last by Aurora Rey. When Professor Olivia Bennett hires contractor Joss Bauer to restore her dilapidated farmhouse, she learns her heart, as much as her house, is in need of a renovation. (978-1-62639-552-7)

Capsized by Julie Cannon. What happens when a woman turns your life completely upside down? (978-1-62639-479-7)

Girls With Guns by Ali Vali, Carsen Taite, and Michelle Grubb. Three stories by three talented crime writers—Carsen Taite, Ali Vali, and Michelle Grubb—each packing her own special brand of heat. (978-1-62639-585-5)

Heartscapes by MJ Williamz. Will Odette ever recover her memory or is Jesse condemned to remember their love alone? (978-1-62639-532-9)

Murder on the Rocks by Clara Nipper. Detective Jill Rogers lives with two things on her mind: sex and murder. While an ice storm cripples Tulsa, two things stand in Jill's way: her lover and the DA. (978-1-62639-600-5)

Necromantia by Sheri Lewis Wohl. When seeing dead people is more than a movie tagline. (978-1-62639-611-1)

Salvation by I. Beacham. Claire's long-term partner now hates her, for all the wrong reasons, and she sees no future until she meets Regan, who challenges her to face the truth and find love. (978-1-62639-548-0)

Trigger by Jessica Webb. Dr. Kate Morrison races to discover how to defuse human bombs while learning to trust her increasingly strong feelings for the lead investigator, Sergeant Andy Wyles. (978-1-62639-669-2)

24/7 by Yolanda Wallace. When the trip of a lifetime becomes a pitched battle between life and death, will anyone survive? (978-1-62639-6-197)

A Return to Arms by Sheree Greer. When a police shooting makes national headlines, activists Folami and Toya struggle to balance their relationship and political allegiances, a struggle intensified after a fiery young artist enters their lives. (978-1-62639-6-814)

After the Fire by Emily Smith. Paramedic Connor Haus is convinced her time for love has come and gone, but when firefighter Logan Curtis comes into town, she learns it may not be too late after all. (978-1-62639-6-524)

Dian's Ghost by Justine Saracen. The road to genocide is paved with good intentions. (978-1-62639-5-947)

Fortunate Sum by M. Ullrich. Financial advisor Catherine Carter lives a calculated life, but after a collision with spunky Imogene Harris (her latest client) and unsolicited predictions, Catherine finds herself facing an unexpected variable: Love. (978-1-62639-5-305)

Soul to Keep by Rebekah Weatherspoon. What *won't* a vampire do for love... (978-1-62639-6-166)

When I Knew You by KE Payne. Eight letters, three friends, two lovers, one secret. Can the past ever be forgiven? (978-1-62639-5-626)

Wild Shores by Radclyffe. Can two women on opposite sides of an oil spill find a way to save both a wildlife sanctuary and their hearts? (978-1-62639-6-456)

Love on Tap by Karis Walsh. Beer and romance are brewing for Tace Lomond when archaeologist Berit Katsaros comes into her life. (987-1-162639-564-0)

Love on the Red Rocks by Lisa Moreau. An unexpected romance at a lesbian resort forces Malley to face her greatest fears where she must choose between playing it safe or taking a chance at true happiness. (987-1-162639-660-9)

Tracker and the Spy by D. Jackson Leigh. There are lessons for all when Captain Tanisha is assigned untried pyro Kyle and a lovesick dragon horse for a mission to track the leader of a dangerous cult. (987-1-162639-448-3)

Whirlwind Romance by Kris Bryant. Will chasing the girl break Tristan's heart or give her something she's never had before? (987-1-162639-581-7)

Whiskey Sunrise by Missouri Vaun. Culture and religion collide when Lovey Porter, daughter of a local Baptist minister, falls for the handsome thrill-seeking moonshine runner, Royal Duval. (987-1-162639-519-0)

Dyre: By Moon's Light by Rachel E. Bailey. A young werewolf, Des, guards the aging leader of all the Packs: the Dyre. Stable employment—nice work, if you can get it…at least until silver bullets start to fly. (978-1-62639-6-623)

Fragile Wings by Rebecca S. Buck. In Roaring Twenties London, can Evelyn Hopkins find love with Jos Singleton or will the scars of the Great War crush her dreams? (978-1-62639-5-466)

Live and Love Again by Jan Gayle. Jessica Whitney could be Sarah Jarret's second chance at love, but their differences and Sarah's grief continue to come between their budding relationship. (978-1-62639-5-176)

Starstruck by Lesley Davis. Actress Cassidy Hayes and writer Aiden Darrow find out the hard way not all life-threatening drama is confined to the TV screen or the pages of a manuscript. (978-1-62639-5-237)

Stealing Sunshine by Tina Michele. Under the Central Florida sun, two women struggle between fear and love as a dangerous plot of deception and revenge threatens to steal priceless art and lives. (978-1-62639-4-452)

The Fifth Gospel by Michelle Grubb. Hiding a Vatican secret is dangerous—sharing the secret suicidal—can Felicity survive a perilous book tour, and will her PR specialist, Anna, be there when it's all over? (978-1-62639-4-476)

Cold to the Touch by Cari Hunter. A drug addict's murder is the start of a dangerous investigation for Detective Sanne Jensen and Dr. Meg Fielding, as they try to stop a killer with no conscience. (978-1-62639-526-8)

Forsaken by Laydin Michaels. The hunt for a killer teaches one woman that she must overcome her fear in order to love, and another that success is meaningless without happiness. (978-1-62639-481-0)

Infiltration by Jackie D. When a CIA breach is imminent, a Marine instructor must stop the attack while protecting her heart from being disarmed by a recruit. (978-1-62639-521-3)

Midnight at the Orpheus by Alyssa Linn Palmer. Two women desperate to make their way in the world, a man hell-bent on revenge, and a cop risking his career: all in a day's work in Capone's Chicago. (978-1-62639-607-4)

Spirit of the Dance by Mardi Alexander. Major Sorla Reardon's return to her family farm to heal threatens Riley Johnson's safe life when small-town secrets are revealed, and love may not conquer all. (978-1-62639-583-1)

Sweet Hearts by Melissa Brayden, Rachel Spangler, and Karis Walsh. Do you ever wonder *Whatever happened to...*? Find out when you reconnect with your favorite characters from Melissa Brayden's *Heart Block*, Rachel Spangler's *LoveLife*, and Karis Walsh's *Worth the Risk*. (978-1-62639-475-9)

Totally Worth It by Maggie Cummings. Who knew there's an all-lesbian condo community in the NYC suburbs? Join twentysomething BFFs Meg and Lexi at Bay West as they navigate friendships, love, and everything in between. (978-1-62639-512-1)

Illicit Artifacts by Stevie Mikayne. Her foster mother's death cracked open a secret world Jil never wanted to see...and now she has to pick up the stolen pieces. (978-1-62639-472-8)

Pathfinder by Gun Brooke. Heading for their new homeworld, Exodus's chief engineer Adina Vantressa and nurse Briar Lindemay carry game-changing secrets that may well cause them to lose everything when disaster strikes. (978-1-62639-444-5)

Prescription for Love by Radclyffe. Dr. Flannery Rivers finds herself attracted to the new ER chief, city girl Abigail Remy, and the incendiary mix of city and country, fire and ice, tradition and change is combustible. (978-1-62639-570-1)

Ready or Not by Melissa Brayden. Uptight Mallory Spencer finds relinquishing control to bartender Hope Sanders too tall an order in fast-paced New York City. (978-1-62639-443-8)

Summer Passion by MJ Williamz. Women loving women is forbidden in 1946 Hollywood, yet Jean and Maggie strive to keep their love alive and away from prying eyes. (978-1-62639-540-4)

The Princess and the Prix by Nell Stark. "Ugly duckling" Princess Alix of Monaco was resigned to loneliness until she met racecar driver Thalia d'Angelis. (978-1-62639-474-2)

Winter's Harbor by Aurora Rey. Lia Brooks isn't looking for love in Provincetown, but when she discovers chocolate croissants and pastry chef Alex McKinnon, her winter retreat quickly starts heating up. (978-1-62639-498-8)

The Time Before Now by Missouri Vaun. Vivian flees a disastrous affair, embarking on an epic, transformative journey to escape her past, until destiny introduces her to Ida, who helps her rediscover trust, love, and hope. (978-1-62639-446-9)